# $\mathcal{T}$HE NARROW MAN

"The Narrow Man *is a dark thriller with a sinister villain and a promising ending.*"

"In Kip Cassino's troubling thriller *The Narrow Man,* a broken veteran embarks on a killing spree with the hope of reuniting with his doting son."

"The book's prose and dialogue complement each other, alternating between moments of exposition in a smooth way. Some lines are flowery, and their additions are unsettling, functioning to mirror Karl's fractured mind."

"*The Narrow Man* is a dark thriller with a sinister villain and a promising ending."

—**Foreword Reviews**


"Kip Cassino's taut thriller follows a deranged man on a bloody mission, as well as the law enforcement officials on his trail."

"Cassino, a Vietnam vet himself, is a top-notch writer."

"The novel's pace never lets up."

"*The Narrow Man* will be a treat for thriller fans who relish substance with their suspense."

—**Blue Ink Review**


"This thought-provoking thriller focuses on Karl Thibault, a Vietnam War intelligence officer suffering from PTSD."

"The author sets a dizzying narrative pace, taking readers across the country during the pursuit of the murderer."

"An uneven but sobering book that highlights the need for improved care of veterans."

—**Kirkus Reviews**

# THE NARROW MAN

## KIP CASSINO

# THE NARROW MAN

*iUniverse books may be ordered through booksellers or by contacting:*

*iUniverse*
*1663 Liberty Drive*
*Bloomington, IN 47403*
*www.iuniverse.com*
*1-800-Authors (1-800-288-4677)*

*ISBN: 978-1-5320-6801-0 (sc)*
*ISBN: 978-1-5320-6800-3 (e)*

*Library of Congress Control Number: 2019901538*

*Print information available on the last page.*

*iUniverse rev. date: 06/21/2019*

# PREFACE

At its core, this book is about PTSD—post-traumatic stress disorder. That's what we call it now. The condition has been around for millennia and has had many names. In the seventeenth century, Swiss military physicians called it nostalgia. To the Germans, it was heimweh; to the French, maladie du pays. In World War I it was branded sh*ell shock*, and World War II medics coined it the more clinical *battle fatigue*. During the sadness of Southeast Asia, it was sometimes known as *post-Vietnam syndrome*.

Whatever its label, the cause has always been the same. It occurs when a person is presented with the certainty of death. As the barrel of the gun begins to turn, as the nearby explosion starts to flower, as the approaching car fills the windshield, changes occur to the chemistry and structure of a person's brain. The mind prepares for the finality of demise. Time slows down. The focus of attention narrows to exclude all but the unfolding event.

If by some chance death does not come, the brain does not snap back to its normal state. The changes that were triggered are permanent. From that time on, the survivor will be haunted by thoughts, visions, dreams, and memories of the drastic experience. Some are so real they cannot be ignored or denied. Drugs, therapy, and the devotion of loved ones may mediate the symptoms, but they never entirely vanish.

This is a work of fiction. Any similarity between the characters described and actual people, living or dead, is purely coincidental. The events portrayed are imaginary, with one exception. The dreams described are not fictitious. They are real. In fact, they are my own.

# ACKNOWLEDGMENTS

To my wife and life partner, Helen. She made it possible for me to write—and to accomplish so much else that would have passed me by had she not entered my life. My only regret is that I did not meet and love her sooner.

Esther Perkins, my first literary agent, also deserves mention. Had a crushing life experience in 1994 not forced her to end her work, I am sure she would have seen this book published.

Finally, a handful of dedicated and selfless men and women at the Veterans Administration must receive thanks: those who fight daily to help PTSD-afflicted veterans. Often, their victories are small. They cannot guide all the tortured minds they treat to safe harbors, but sometimes they coax a few to reach for sanity and peace.

# PROLOGUE

# Dong Ha, Republic of Vietnam—December 1970

They were three. The unit was larger, but the three were its core, its heart. The others were like pieces of equipment, necessary to its operation but interchangeable. Easton, Thibault, Ky—the three.

They were an odd fraternity in an inexplicable war. Vietnam was not a conflict out of Hemingway or Wouk. It was a tortured mosaic of small groups of men engaged in private battles for a multitude of reasons—*Gravity's Rainbow* married to *Battle Cry*. The men caught up in it fought with rock and roll coursing through their minds instead of patriotic anthems. This was a place where bitter, hopeless firefights took place only yards from major roads as hundreds drove by, where men died because of pointless debate over the meaning of a clause in a "rules of engagement" book, where heroin in slickly manufactured Chinese kits was sold for pennies to GIs driving by in trucks to defend a nameless place—land that might be abandoned and retaken several times in a season by the same puzzled men on both sides.

It was a confused opium dream of war. Its sick sweetness deprived a generation of Americans of their sanity. It was a conflict where the rotation of those in charge guaranteed an annual amnesia, leading to the propagation of the same mistakes over and over again. It was hell on earth.

Easton was the biggest of the trio, a giant mountain of flesh. In happier years he had been first-string offensive line for one of Bear

Bryant's best Alabama football teams. A bad decision in the middle of a drunken weekend had put him into the Marine Corps. A quick mind and almost limitless endurance had brought him to Force Recon—and to Karl Thibault. As the story went, Karl had saved Easton's life a year earlier, calmly disarming a "bouncing Betty" the larger man had tripped in the middle of a raging firefight. Bettys were designed to blast victims into sexless hulks consigned to VA hospitals for the rest of their shattered lives. Easton's gratitude was boundless.

Karl Thibault was the enigma. On the surface he presented a mild, calm young man. In tough combat situations he became a ferocious assailant who acted without fear or remorse. It was as though two personalities inhabited the spare, lean body, each coming forward when it was most needed. The "garrison Karl" would take missions and plan them to the smallest detail, careful to minimize the exposure of his men to danger. He always looked for the extra factor that would maximize gain and erase risk. Another Karl took over in the field. He led by example, taking every risk necessary to inflict the greatest harm to an enemy while completing the mission. Easton was always at his back, protecting him, covering him, even carrying him from danger when it became necessary. They acted almost as one. Karl's men loved him because he brought them back and because he gave them a sense of purpose in this crazy place where they found themselves.

Ky completed the trio. Small dark Ky was no larger than a child but capable of killing so quickly, so silently. Ky was a Chu Hoi, a convert from the other side. The rumor was that he had been a North Vietnamese Army captain and that Thibault and Easton had snatched him from his tent in Quang Ngai province and had then protected him from torture in Da Nang's infamous Green Room. Whether that rumor was true, there was no debating Ky's fierce loyalty to the two Americans or his disdain for anyone else.

The unit had a meaningless, enigmatic name: the Sixteenth Field Communications Detachment (Provisional). Ostensibly, its job was to lay phone lines to remote areas. In reality, as a part of the shadowy Command and Control North (CCN), its mission was deep reconnaissance, the implantation of sensors and radio beacons used to guide air strikes. These missions were not limited to South Vietnam but included Laos, Cambodia, and even North Vietnam itself.

The twenty men who made up the rest of the detachment had a variety of histories. The standing joke was that to get into the Sixteenth you had to be either very good or very bad. Once in, those who learned quickly and listened to Thibault and Easton survived and eventually went home. Those who did not became casualties. The three did not go home. Thibault had been in Vietnam for twenty-three months, Easton two months more. Ky, of course, had been in country much longer.

The unit operated from the sprawling base at Dong Ha. Farther north than any other major US installation, Dong Ha still offered all the comforts of home, in a musty, dust-covered way. There was a dentist, a library, a choice of several bars, even a swimming pool. The airstrip was capable of landing the big C-130s that sometimes took the men of the Sixteenth to their destinations. The men lived in a small collection of wood-framed, metal-roofed huts nearby.

Their area had a peculiar archaeology, like many of the places that defined their bizarre war. It had been the headquarters for a US Marine construction unit several years before. Upon orders to return to the States, the marines—sure that the area would be turned over to the Army of the Republic of Vietnam (ARVN)—had decided to bury their equipment rather than allow it to fall into Vietnamese hands. They knew it would only be sold on the black market or used to construct a big hooch for some crooked ARVN general. After more than a week of continuous rain, the exhaust stack of a buried bulldozer was clearly visible beside the orderly room steps.

Discipline in the Sixteenth was relaxed but not lax. Everyone had to report to reveille, present his weapons, and pack for daily inspection. After all, the unit was subject to immediate call, and no time could be wasted getting ready once a mission came in.

After inspection, a few of the men were consigned to company duty every day: picking up, running errands for Sergeant Easton, and taking care of the odd jobs that permeate and lubricate garrison army life. Unlike most of the units in Dong Ha, the Sixteenth kept no *mamasans* to take care of cleaning up—for security reasons. Even so, the men had little complaint. The duty was light and served to punctuate the boredom of waiting. Those not on duty hung around the barracks, eventually wandering down to the PX or to one of the many unit bars in the area.

Normally, Thibault was called to Quang Tri, headquarters of the embattled Fifth Mech (Fifth Infantry Division), when the order for a new mission came down. There, in deep bunkers paneled to remind visitors of someone's basement rec room gone mad, he would be given the objective and the time required to meet it but never the reason for the job.

Quang Tri was several miles south of Dong Ha, a deceptively pleasant excursion most of the time. The odd, incomplete journey usually occurred just after dusk, and the ambushers had proven too clever to trap. Typically, Thibault would be called in the morning. He would drive over, return in the afternoon, and then plan the mission until early evening. The unit would jump off the next day.

This mission was different. The plans were delivered to the Sixteenth by another officer: Captain George Truly, spit and polish, West Point graduate, destined for bigger things. Since his arrival in the country, Truly had made his plan for an upcoming career move plain to superior and subordinate alike: he meant to be the next commander of the Sixteenth. He saw this assignment as a sure way to garner the decorations necessary for quick promotion in the upcoming peacetime army, and he knew that a combat command would also be a real feather in his cap. Now he strode into the small unit's orderly room, remarking on the people he saw with strength and vigor. His voice had a flat, braying quality, like a horn sounded once too often in a traffic jam. "Lots of lazy troopers in this unit," he announced. "Not much attention to the uniform. Sergeant Easton, I guess you've noticed that. I understand you used to be a marine, Sergeant Easton. Well, mister, you're in the army now. Where's your commander?"

Truly, as usual, was resplendent in his razor-creased issue fatigues, each sleeve rolled to precisely the right distance above his prominent elbows, his jungle boots gleamingly spit-shined beyond any field utility. Easton, on the other hand, still wore the camouflage fatigues he had been issued in the Marine Corps. Many of the troopers in the unit area wore other garb. Thibault, peering from his small office in the back of the hut at the commotion, quickly recognized the cause of all the noise. "Morning, Truly," he said softly, a mild grin forming on his face. "Slumming today, or here on business? Come in and sit down, before you scare these men half to death. Sergeant Easton, get us both a cup of coffee, would you please."

Truly did as he was bid, his eyes still darting nervously about the room. He was a tall, solid man who had not lost any weight from his time in country, and though he was still in his twenties his hair was already beginning to thin. These men made him nervous. There didn't seem to be a real soldier among them. They all lacked discipline and, even worse, they lacked respect! Not just respect for him, but respect for the army in general. He would change things quickly, once he was in charge. These people would learn they were in the army, or they'd be gone. He assumed most of them would be gone. He already had their replacements in mind. He stooped as he stepped through a low doorway into Thibault's tiny office (his plan was to enlarge it considerably, at the expense of that fat ass Easton, who would be gone anyhow) and extended his hand, smiling. "Good to see you again, Karl," he lied.

Karl shook his hand and smiled back. "Good to see you, George. Please, sit down. Out and about early, aren't you?" He looked at his watch. "My God, I don't think the general's briefing is over with yet! Well, what can I do for you?"

His visitor looked around the small room as he reached beneath his shirt. "Are we secure?" he asked in a hushed whisper.

Karl resisted rolling his eyes with some difficulty. "I believe we are, George," he said heavily. "What have you got?"

"Orders, Karl. Your next mission."

Karl reached for the envelope Truly had produced. "Thanks for bringing them by, George, but I could have gotten them myself. Hell, I enjoy that drive to Quang Tri every once in a while. Gives me a chance to think. Now, if that's all—"

Truly thrust the envelope into his hands. "You'd better read this first," he said, still whispering. "There's some new twists to this mission!"

Karl frowned as he scanned the op order. He was a quick reader and noted the "new twists" immediately. The first was the target, an area about halfway to the Laotian town of Tchepone, a place he and his men had just hit less than a month ago. The second was the team, which had been amended to include one extra man: Truly, George, Captain, regular army. He looked up. "George, you've made a mistake," he said flatly.

Truly sucked in his breath and turned a little red, prepared to argue. "What do you mean?" he asked, raising his voice slightly.

Karl looked him in the eyes. "I know you want to come on one of our missions, but you planned a bad one. Going back to where we've just been isn't safer; it's much more dangerous. They'll be looking for us now. Look, George, let me plan one for you."

Truly stood. "You think you're so smart. So smart. You're not even regular army! I took the reports from your last mission and analyzed your every move. I found every error you made. This time we're going to do it right. This time there'll be no place for your grandstand antics!"

Karl stood as well. "Okay, George, okay," he said, trying to calm his visitor. He had known this moment would come and had dreaded it. Nothing in this war was allowed to stay the same. All leadership positions had to be rotated to give more officers the chance for command, no matter what the cost. He knew he was destined to lose the unit, the men he had loved and protected. He now tried to save them from disaster.

"Look," Karl said, "maybe you're right. Things sure did get screwed up out there. Thank God we made it back without losing anybody. Let's you and I go over what went wrong, step by step. Then, you can design a training program to correct the faults. I know you're good at that. Better than I ever was. Let's think about another mission, to the Rockpile, maybe. Or how about Vandergrift? I understand we're going back in there next month. The place could sure stand a look."

Though he kept his voice composed, Karl was frantic. The operation he had just read about would be a disaster under any circumstances. With a raw novice like Truly along, people could be killed. His antagonist stood his ground.

"No dice, Karl," Truly said, shaking his head slowly as a smile formed on his lips. "I got all the way to Corps with this one. It's signed off—official. We go tomorrow. Don't worry, you'll still be in charge. I'm an observer, just going along for the ride." His meaning was clear. Any snafu would be Karl's responsibility.

Realizing he had no chance for compromise, Karl's forced amiability vanished. "Okay, George," he growled. "You asked for it, and you'll get it. Since I'm still in charge, two rules. The first is leave my men alone. I have enough to worry about without you digging in their shit. Second, you do what I say. Got that? My first order is this: go back and get yourself ready. I'll inspect your pack tonight, 1900 hours. Till then, stay out of my face. Clear?"

It was clear enough.

In another setting far from war, George Truly might be a good neighbor. War and its grinding, ever-present tension brought out the worst in him, just as it brought out the best in others. Here, every aspect of humanity was magnified: friendships became deep, lifelong bonds; laughter mutated to hysteria; sadness intensified into grim depression; and annoyance ballooned into deep-seated disdain.

For several minutes after Truly left, Karl sat alone in his tiny room, his head in his hands. He had been here too long, he realized. He was becoming part of the problem instead of the solution. People like George Truly were always around, forever part of the mad equation. He had always shrugged them off before, ignored them, but now he could not. It was finally time for him to go.

First there would be this awful mission—his last, he was pretty sure. Truly would be in charge by the end of the month, if he lived. Karl glanced again at the op order. "Easton!" he bellowed through the thin partition. "Get in here! We have a mission to plan. We'll need eight men."

\* \* \*

# The Next Morning, 0430 Hours

The big chopper—already nicknamed the "jolly green giant" by everyone who flew in it—climbed into the gunmetal sky. Helicopters, especially ungainly monsters like the HHC-1, share none of the brittle grace of other aircraft. Most airplanes, no matter how awkward they seem on the ground, gather a certain beauty about themselves in flight, like pelicans. This is not true of helicopters, which remain as ugly in the air as they ever were at rest, all angles and slab sides, kept aloft only by the raw power of the motors that lift them screaming from the ground. The noise and vibration tell the riders that their situation is precarious, that gravity wants to put this hunk of metal and plastic on the ground again, right now! Yet the choppers go where other aircraft can't, and to a person in need of rescue or pickup, they can seem as beautiful as the angels themselves. Such are the vagaries of war.

Eight men sat in the large main bay of the helicopter, around its edges to rest against the bulkheads. Karl and Truly moved among them, inspecting, whispering, tightening straps, smiling. A few of the men talked among themselves. Two attempted to sleep. It was going to be a long ride to the landing zone.

Finally, after almost two hours of flight, a gesture from the young marine pilot and a flashing red light signaled the time had come to leave the womb of this ungodly metal beast. There would be no landing. Instead, the men would rappel from the chopper, lowering themselves down strong ropes like an elevator moving down a shaft while controlling the speed of their drop by playing the rope between their thighs with thickly gloved hands. They would drop more than one hundred fifty feet into the dark, a feat they all had performed in training and on actual missions hundreds of times. Yet every drop presented a new challenge.

Easton, because of his weight, was always first to land. Ky, for the same reason, was always last. Within five minutes all the men were down without incident, and security was posted. Karl took a compass bearing and nodded to Easton. The mission had begun. "We'll make for the saddle to the immediate north," he said to Truly, who nodded absently. "It's about a day's march. The target area is right below it, another two or three klicks. Any luck, we'll be out of here in four days." Easton shook his head sadly. Ky smiled from ear to ear. They moved out.

The land they trudged through was heavily forested. They were above the high plateau of western Vietnam, on the Laotian side of the Annamese Mountains. The scenery was misty-dream beautiful. It reminded Karl of parts of Pennsylvania or New Jersey, where the wild, aggressive green always seemed to threaten the roads cut through it. Just a pleasant stroll in the woods.

The men walked almost doubled over, splay-legged to improve their balance, since each carried a pack that weighed more than seventy pounds. From a distance, they hardly looked human at all, their enormous loads distorting their silhouettes into those of trolls. Incredibly, they would still walk more than ten miles before evening.

As they pushed and ripped their way through the unforgiving forest, the men were watched by birds and monkeys, by the raucous gecko lizards (whose refrain, "Gekku! Gekku!" caused them to be nicknamed "fuckyou lizards" by the GIs who encountered them), and, from time to time, by people. To the Meo tribesmen who heard and saw them pass, they were another invading force in a small land that had known conquest from every point of the compass for more than a thousand years. So many layers of cruel overlordship covered Laos that its original inhabitants knew themselves as Kha (slaves)—mutually disdained by the Thai who had conquered them from the south and west, the Chinese who had conquered them from the north, and the Viets who had conquered them from the east.

Camp that night was quiet, desultory. The men were too tired for more than a hurried meal and immediate rest. Weapons still had to be maintained, packs readjusted, and sentries posted, all with minimum talk and minimum effort. Everyone knew what had to be done.

Morning came all too quickly and brought with it the ache not yet healed, the chafing sore just beginning, the insect bite, and the instinctive longing to be gone from this awful, wildly overgrown green purgatory. Some of the men smoked, knowing the odor of their cigarettes could be fatal but understanding that their presence was already known to some. If the enemy was nearby the absolution of a last drag would be innocuous. Having smoked, they coughed heartily, for this was a high area and the air was relatively thin. Then, finishing their coffee and breaking camp, they adjusted their heavy packs and moved out again, over the rise and down the saddle toward their objective.

The plan called for them to implant a series of magnetic and acoustic sensors along Route Nine, an old French road that ran from Quang Tri to the town of Tchepone and beyond, eventually reaching the Thai border. The French had christened this road "the street without joy" during their years of combat here. The sensors Thibault's men planned to place would tell command of the presence of North Vietnamese trucks and armored vehicles, allowing an assessment of the number and types of enemy troops in this area to be made. It was known that the North Vietnamese had tanks in the region, but how many? The sensors would tell.

Karl and another team had already implanted sensors here once, a month earlier, but their mission had been discovered. The equipment they left had been seized and destroyed. The last transmission from one of the acoustic sensors carried the conversation of a North Vietnamese work detail, cursing as they dug up, lifted, and transferred each device from its hiding place to a waiting truck. Truly's theory was that no one would expect a mission to the same place for the same reason so soon.

By afternoon of the second day, the team had reached the general area of their objective: a narrow, winding mountain road leading from the village of Aloui. They would wait in a secluded clearing several hundred yards from the road until dark. Then they would plant their equipment and leave quickly for pickup. With any luck, they would be back in Dong Ha in two more days.

A party of three was sent ahead to an area three miles away, where the rest of the team would go after their work was completed. Then, the men had nothing to do but wait. A few played cards or talked softly. Some wrote letters that might never be mailed. They pulled their sentry duty or just sat and thought, trying to remove themselves from the staggering pressure of their stress to another time, a simpler, happier time in another place.

Truly was restive. He had never been a contemplative man, and his training at West Point had convinced him that waiting, just doing nothing, was the mark of a poor operation. How many times in his career had he seen another officer berated by a superior for inactivity? "What'cha gonna do?" the object of scorn would be asked in a loud, sarcastic whisper. "For God's sake, lieutenant, do something, even if it's wrong!" He watched as Karl sat by his pack, almost unmoving, stirring only to post sentries and have brief discussions with Easton and Ky every hour or so. The pressure of inactivity weighed on him intolerably. Eventually, as afternoon moved toward dusk, he reacted to it.

Springing to his feet, he walked briskly to a supine Karl and kicked the mission leader softly on the sole of his boot. "Thibault," he murmured, "I think it's time."

Karl opened his eyes and rose on one elbow. "Wrong," he said simply. "We need another hour, at least. Sit down and relax. Nothing's going to happen. Have a smoke." Reaching into a pocket, he produced a crumpled pack of Salems.

Truly's stare hardened. "What's the matter, Captain?" he asked with a visible sneer. "You got the willies? We can see better now. We'll do a better job of implantation. There's no NVA in the area, or they'd have shot us up by now. They're all in Aloui, having rice. Let's go. We'll be out of here that much sooner." Several of the men, aroused by the sound of Truly's voice, turned to watch the confrontation.

Karl felt anger rise in him. The man was a fool! He felt a new emotion as well: a strong, sensuous desire to end his antagonist's life. It abruptly occurred to him that he wanted to kill George Truly. All he needed was a proper excuse, an event to propel him past the reason that kept his hands from this poor excuse for a soldier. The thought was so immediate that it startled and frightened him. In his confusion, Karl decided to give in, to let Truly have his way, even though the man was wrong. He knew that coming out of concealment at this time of day was dangerous, but he was fairly certain that there were no enemy in the area. He was suddenly aware he was tired, so tired of arguing with people like this who never learned what was right. It was so much easier to give in, to take orders rather than to give them.

"Okay, George," he said slowly as he rose to his feet. "We'll do it your way. I firmly believe you're wrong, but I'll accommodate you this one time." He signaled Easton and Ky. "Get 'em up, Sarge. We're moving out—early." The big marine raised an eyebrow but said nothing as he turned to comply. Ky's face split into a wide, toothy grin. He suspected there would be much killing today.

The men divided themselves into three groups: two groups of three, one led by Karl and the other by Easton, would act as a security screen above and below the road. Truly and another man would implant the sensors. They moved out, carefully and silently, as dusk began to settle on the mountain jungle.

They reached the road in a few minutes, still under the light of a waning sun. The security teams melted unobtrusively into the brush at the roadside just before a hairpin curve, and Truly began unpacking the sensors. There were twelve of them: eight acoustics, two magnetic resonance, and two infrared imaging—designed to pick up and measure heat sources. Each had to be lovingly buried, as a turtle takes care of its eggs, and then surrounded with "surprise firing devices" to extract a final toll upon discovery. The traps were pocketbook-sized, trip-wire-activated Claymore mines. They were designed to drive hundreds of bolt-size, red-hot metal particles through anyone unlucky enough to stumble over them. The trouble began as the fifth sensor was put in place.

Ky heard the noise first and signaled across the road. A vehicle was coming, a truck of some kind. As he acknowledged Ky's signal, Karl looked to the curve and noticed Truly's pack and cap, placed neatly and in full view of the road. "Truly," he called, breaking his own rule of silence. "Get your pack out of sight. There's someone coming."

Truly apparently did not hear, even though the sound of the approaching truck was already loud enough for all to notice. In desperation, Karl slapped the pack of the man nearest him, a veteran of six previous missions, a young man now very old.

"Corporal Henley," he said quickly. "Run over and get that pack out of sight before that truck gets here. Then tell Truly to finish up. Right now. We're getting out of here as soon as the truck goes by." He knew there was no logical reason for haste. If they were not seen, they should be able to proceed as planned. That wouldn't happen. The mission felt bad. Something was very wrong. Maybe Truly's presence had upset the precarious balance of luck that these covert missions depended upon. Maybe he had just had too much of this shit. It didn't matter. He was ending this mission. He was certain he had to get his men out of this area as quickly as he could.

Henley scurried across the road, leaving his pack behind him, keeping low to the ground. The truck was close now. They could hear it grinding its gears as it labored up the hill. Any second now it would be in view.

Truly worked slowly, methodically, oblivious to all but the holes he dug and the sensors he put in them. This was not really officer's work, he told himself. It was Thibault's way of making him small in the eyes of the troops. That was okay. They would soon be his. Next time out, someone else would dig the holes. He would see to that.

A sudden noise and the unexpected impact of his pack landing near his hand upset Truly's reverie. "What the fuck?" he started to say as Henley landed on his back. "Down," the young corporal breathed. "Truck coming. Stay down."

Face pressed to the earth, unable to move, Truly coughed in surprise. "Get off me, you asshole," he bawled.

"Shut up. Do you want to get us fucking killed?" was his only answer.

The truck was old, a Chinese copy of a Russian copy of a World War II vintage Ford. It carried a dozen NVA soldiers, back from a detail foraging for food. Roots and tubers were the rule for them these days, little enough to mix with the rice so dearly carried down this, a major subbranch of the Ho Chi Minh trail.

Three men sat in the truck's cab, and one of them noticed Truly's cap, still sitting by the side of the road. The truck slid and creaked to a stop about twenty feet from where Truly and his two unwilling companions lay hidden. With much high-pitched singsong shouting, the soldiers clambered from the truck's bay. Under the direction of an increasingly agitated sergeant, they began sullenly poking among the bushes that lined the mountain road. It was plain that these rear area troops were not looking for trouble. They were tired and wanted nothing more than to be back at their base camp for rice and sleep. Realizing that the emplacement team was bound to be discovered, Karl signaled an assault with a shrill whistle.

Describing a firefight is like trying to describe a train wreck one event at a time. Many things happen almost at once, and all of them are horribly violent. Ky lobbed a grenade into the truck's cab and then died as a fragment from the explosion caught him squarely in the face. The muffled pop of a second explosion shook the just-shattered truck as gas lines ignited, briefly bathing the hulk in flame. Still barely alive, the truck's driver began to shriek in pain, but no one noticed. Everyone was screaming now.

At the same time, Easton's team stood from their positions at the side of the road, spraying the surprised NVA with fire from their M-16s. Later, Karl remembered Easton's last moments as he died from the return fire—how he held a Claymore mine to his vast chest and set it off with his own ruined hands. The mine killed most of the enemy. Its rear blowback shredded Easton's midsection, killing him as well. An instant later, Karl stood and fired his own weapon from the opposite side of the road. Within a matter of seconds, all of the NVA from the truck were dying or dead.

Quickly, the men threw the bodies of friend and foe alike into the back of the sluggishly smoldering wrecked truck and then levered and pushed the hulk over the side of the road into a gully far below. With any luck, the search party that was bound to be sent out soon would initially assume that there had been some kind of accident, giving Karl's surviving men more time to run.

And run they must. Soon, an entire army would be looking for them. These hills were the main staging area for three crack North Vietnamese divisions: the 320th, the 308th, and the 304th infantries. No guerilla bands, these units boasted tanks, artillery, and very bad tempers. The missing truck would be found. A quick examination would lead to the inescapable conclusion. The hunt for Karl's team would begin, probably by the coming morning.

He had about that long to get his men to a place where the chopper could pick them up. First, he would have to go to the planned base camp to pick up the men he had sent ahead. Then, everyone would run all night.

Karl shook his head, trying to clear his mind of the anguish he felt over the sudden, inexplicable death of the two men he loved most in the world. He called out, no need for soft voices now. "Form up!" he said, "We've got to get our butts out of here. Sergeant Morris, do we have any more casualties?" How much more to add to the butcher's bill? Ky and Easton, the men who had held him together all these horrible, endless months, were dead. That was enough.

There was one more casualty. Henley, who had been lying across Truly's back when the firefight began, had been killed by a dying soldier's reflex firing an AK-47. His body had protected Truly from any harm. The shaken officer had now thrown the body from him and sat shuddering and sobbing by the side of the road. He stank of Henley's blood and his own excrement.

"Your life came expensive, George," Karl said softly. He felt rage and then a curious anticipation, as though his mind was waiting for something to happen. The thought that had frightened him before resurfaced: *Now is the time to kill Truly*, it murmured to him.

"Henley was a fine man," Karl continued haltingly. He tried hard to fight the dark embrace of the ideas that now coursed through his mind. "He would have gone on to be somebody, if he'd been allowed to live. You owe him. Now get up and let's get going."

Truly nodded but did not move. He continued to sob. All at once, as Karl stood over him, a dark, sensuous passion enveloped him, clouding his thinking, welling up from deep inside him. He knew as he gave himself up to this overpowering need, this delicious blackness, that what he was going to do was wrong. That thought was too weak and was swept from his consciousness as a leaf is swept from a tree in late autumn. "Morris," he called, his voice thick with emotion. "Take the men and start for the camp. I'll follow in a minute."

Morris and the rest of the team moved quickly around the curve of the road and then down into the brush. Almost at once, Karl and Truly were alone. Truly continued to weep. "What are you going to do?" he finally gasped, looking up.

"Do?" Karl whispered. "Do? Why, George, I'm going to take you to meet some friends of mine, people you should get to know. It will be a good career move. You'll be decorated for sure." He felt powerful now, light and strong. The thoughts that pulsed through his brain invigorated him like a drug. He could almost feel the raw energy emanating from him.

Truly was confused. Karl wasn't making any sense, and he had a wild look in his eyes. What was he talking about?

Karl giggled. "Yes, George," he said softly, "you've got to get to know Sergeant Easton better! Ky too, my little friend Ky. There's a lot he can teach you. Not to mention our mutual friend, Corporal Henley!"

"Karl, what the fuck are you talking about? Those men are dead!" Truly tried to rise, only to be shoved to the ground.

Grinning savagely, Karl shot Truly in the groin as the syrupy, sensual need to murder overpowered him. "You're right, George. They're dead. Your fault. So you don't deserve to live either," he snarled, finishing off his howling victim with a single shot to the man's head. Then, after dragging the body into the brush to Henley's feet, he scampered after the rest of his team.

He felt light and giddy, as if a pressure that had weighed upon him for a long time had been lifted. A song came to mind, a song he had often heard around the compound in Dong Ha. He felt the urge to sing. A nameless tune, all bass guitar and wailing sax, coursed through his mind. He hummed it as he ran breathlessly down the hill.

# Chapter 1

## Tucson, Arizona—August 15, 1986

The woman struggling at the bar was beautiful. Months later, he would remember that first impression. She was small and darkly brunette, with a short, almost boyish haircut. Her complexion was lucent, porcelain. In a place where everyone sported deep tans, it set her apart from anyone Chris had ever known. As she frowned and whispered through clenched teeth, her assailant succeeded in capturing both her arms by the wrists.

"Dammit, Harry," she spat. "Let me go. You're causing a scene. It's over for us. It's been over a long time. I want to leave, now!"

When the fight erupted, Chris Carpenter had been sitting at Salucci's enormous bar, nursing a Coors. Since its opening in May, Salucci's had become a popular place. Big and pretentious, it glistened with the patina of manufactured, prebuilt, faux antiquity common to many clubs on Tucson's Broadway Boulevard. Two thirds of the buildings here were less than a decade old, almost as though the harsh desert wind blew the new in with the tumbleweeds. The people in these clubs were new themselves, young and tan with the insolence of early success and money to spend. They were in real estate, investments, computers, development. Their attitude said, "Look at me! I live in a place you can only visit." The names and faces of these people changed as well and often, far more often than the buildings.

Sipping his beer, Chris had been absently scanning the people reflected in the mirror before him. In its own way, the careful informality unfolding behind his seat was as stylized as a seventeenth-century minuet. Soon, he would join in it himself. Chris liked people and seldom had trouble finding company. His hair, a dark honey shade neither blonde nor brown, lay thickly across a broad forehead, just above ice blue eyes and handsome regular features. Big but not heavy, at six feet two and 190 pounds, Chris's large hands and thick fingers belied a gentleness at odds, some would say, with his profession. Chris was a cop, with fourteen years of service in Tucson's finest.

The sharp noise of breaking glass interrupted his casual inspection of the bar. Chris turned abruptly as a man seated two stools from him wrestled to control the flailing arms of the strikingly attractive woman. It was an uneven contest. Even seated, he towered over her.

The man pivoted slightly as he fought, revealing a round, fleshy face and a quizzical, sardonic expression. "Come on, now," he drawled without apparent anger. "Just simmer down. You know you really don't want to leave. You quit fussing and I'll get you that drink I promised." The woman continued to struggle as the man, still smiling, drew her closer in the parody of an embrace until their heads almost touched.

"There now, Marianne," he muttered. "It's better if you don't fight. No one's watching, anyhow. Now, there's no reason to be so mean. Just sit and have one drink with me, that's all. We'll talk about old times. Is that asking too much?" Pulling her even closer, he licked her ear. In answer, she renewed her efforts, weaving her body from side to side in a vain attempt to break his hold on her wrists.

Chris decided to intervene before the situation became more serious. Leaving his stool, he walked up to the quarreling couple.

"You folks having some trouble?" he asked mildly.

"Nothing we can't handle, cowboy," the man sneered, hardly looking in Chris's direction. "Now why don't you just mind your own business, okay?"

Chris slowly shook his head. "I don't think so. I think your argument is getting out of hand." Reaching to his back pocket, he pulled out and flipped open his wallet, revealing his badge. "I'm a police officer, off duty, and looking for a little relaxation, just like the rest of the people here. Now, there's no need for trouble. Let the lady free, and we'll forget this ever happened." He paused. "Unless, of course, she wants to press charges."

The man's arms fell to his sides. He smiled nervously. "There," he sighed. "See? No trouble. And you're okay too, aren't you, Marianne?" He turned to put his arm around her, but she deftly slipped beyond his reach. She looked up, and Chris felt the warmth of a blush cross his face.

"Yes, I'm okay," she said, rubbing her wrists. She wore a simple turtleneck sweater and slacks, showing off a good figure. Frowning deeply, she stared at her recent assailant. She spoke clearly and slowly, as if addressing a child. "Harry just misunderstood our relationship. I'm sure he understands now that it's finished between us. I don't intend to get within an arm's length of him again, so there won't be any more trouble."

The woman turned to face Chris again. She shrugged, as if to shake recent events from her. "I have to go," she said evenly. "I was about to leave when all this got started. Thanks for your help." With that, she turned on her heel—ducking an abortive grab for her shoulder—and disappeared into the growing crowd.

"I'm sorry about this," the man said after a few seconds of uncomfortable silence, shaking his head. "I don't know what got into me. Look, let me buy you a beer." As he waved for the bartender, he extended a hand laden with heavy gold rings. "My name's Harry Grissom. I'm in land development. You?"

"Chris Carpenter," replied Chris, trying to avoid a frown as he shook Harry's hand. Grissom's hand was cold, his grip weak. Chris felt the urge to wipe his right hand on his trousers and wondered if Grissom would notice.

Grissom turned back to the bar, grimly inspecting his drink, which he finished in one gulp. Wiping his mouth with the back of his hand as he signaled for another, he looked at Chris.

"Don't let her fool you with that Girl Scout pose of hers," he said. "Marianne's no Mother Teresa."

Chris didn't answer. Grissom smiled. "Bet you'd like some of that, wouldn't you?" he asked, his voice thick with emotion.

Chris turned away. It was a stupid thing for the man to say. He decided to finish his beer and leave.

"Well, I've had her. Lots of times," Grissom continued, turning to gaze intently at his own reflection in the bar's mirror. "When Marianne gets hot, she'll beg for it. You just got to wait." He smiled broadly, as if enjoying a joke.

Chris grimaced. He really didn't like this guy. "Look, Grissom, I don't want to hear about your sex life," he said. "This isn't a high school locker room—"

"Yeah? Well, who asked you?" Grissom interrupted. He was beginning to feel his liquor. He turned to explain to his new companion just who he was, how much money he had, how many women he could get with just a phone call. The impulse was useless. Chris had already left.

* * *

The house was dark and quiet. David stayed in his room with the door shut and locked. Mom would be home soon, he hoped. Meanwhile, to his ten-year-old mind, the more closed doors there were between him and the world outside, the safer he became. Sometimes he crept to the den and, after making sure all the doors were shut and locked, he played video games for hours or watched TV with owl-eyed intensity. For though he prayed for his mother's instant return, reason told him she would be gone long after fatigue forced him to sleep. Tonight he would stay in his room.

A slimly serious boy, David Thibault's large hazel eyes and pale, freckled complexion pointed to his northern European heritage. He favored his mother physically, but his mind and thoughts belonged to his father, whom he loved and missed with a fervor that would have greatly disturbed Marianne, had she been able to measure it. He had just decided to spend the next hour resorting his large collection of baseball cards when he was startled by the ringing phone.

Cautiously, he opened his bedroom door and padded to the kitchen, where he carefully lifted the receiver to his ear.

"Hello?" he said, almost whispering.

The answering voice was rich and warm, exactly as the boy had hoped. "David? It's your dad. How are you, son?"

"Oh, hi, Dad!" the boy said with a great sigh of relief. "I'm home alone. Where are you? Still at the hospital? Are you coming home? I really, really miss you." David still whispered with an urgency that transcended whatever fear he might have felt before. This was Dad! Maybe with good news. Maybe somehow the bad times were going to be over now. Maybe he really could come home.

David could barely remember the times before his dad had gone away. The way his mom had cried for days on end. The people with the cameras and the microphones leaning over the wall of their small town house's courtyard, trying to get him to speak. The time he saw Dad on TV, walking from a police car into a building, hands behind his back. Since then, there had only been the calls when Mom was away. Still, that was pretty often. They got to talk a lot.

His wishes were almost answered. "Yes, Tiger, I am coming home! I'm already closer than anybody knows. What do you think about that?"

"Dad! That's great! When will you be here? Can I tell Mom?"

"No, David. It has to be our secret, at least for now. Soon I'm going to come and get you and give you the biggest hug I've got. Then you'll never have to be alone again. I promise."

"Oh, Dad. When? When will you come?"

"Soon, Tiger, real soon, but you must keep it a secret. Even from your mom. It will be a big surprise! You can't tell her yet, or you'll spoil it. Just like our other talks. You've kept them secret, haven't you?" While Marianne was aware of the "official" calls her ex-husband made to their son, the number and content of the unofficial calls would have shocked her.

"Yes, Dad. I've never told. I just don't understand why you wanted to know about those others? About Mr. Grissom and Mr. Haldron?"

His father chuckled. "Well, David, I need to talk to them, to make sure they're treating your mother the right way. I still love your mom. You know that, don't you? By the way, are there any new friends? Anyone else I should know about?"

"I don't think so, Dad. Just a second and I'll check."

Carefully placing the telephone on the counter, David walked through his mother's bedroom to her bedside table. He opened and quickly scanned the pages in her address book, looking for any new entries. As he suspected, there were none. He quickly made his way back to the kitchen. "No, Dad," he reported. "Nobody new. Mr. Haldron was the last one, and he hasn't been here in a long time."

His father sighed deeply. "Okay, son. Good job. Keep a lookout, now. It's important, like secret agent work. Like I used to do in the war."

"I keep all of it secret, Dad. Just like your best agents. I try real hard."

"I know you do, son. I'm proud of you. Now, I've got to go. Tell you what—start thinking about what you want to bring along when I come to get you. We can't take a lot, remember. We'll get brand new stuff when we get where we're going."

"Where's that, Dad?" David was really excited now. His dreams were going to come true, even though it had taken so, so long.

"We'll talk about when I see you, Tiger. Now, give me kisses."

The sound of an airy kiss embraced his ear. "That's my boy. I love you, son. See you. Soon." With a click, the line went dead.

Quickly, David retreated to his room. Now, instead of sorting baseball cards, he got out his crayons and drawing paper. He fell asleep later in the middle of drawing the fantasy place he and his dad would be going soon.

* * *

Chris shouldered his way through the crowd around the bar at the Golden Parrot, looking for the face he thought he'd seen. There she was! Moving as quickly as he could without bowling people over, he edged his way forward. "Ginny," he called. "Hey, Ginny!"

Ginny Semper heard the voice and turned to search the throng around her for its source. A tall, attractive woman in her late twenties, she smiled broadly when she saw Chris shouldering his way toward her.

Ginny and Chris had been friends, and sometimes lovers, for the past seven years. They'd met after a very bad traffic accident, when Chris was still in uniform and Ginny—then as now—worked as a paramedic for the Tucson Fire Department. There had been times when each had wished the relationship would become more permanent, but the two had never crossed the invisible barrier that separates friends from life mates.

"Wow! I was afraid you wouldn't see me," Chris said as he finally made his way to Ginny's side. "If I'd lost you in this crowd, I'd never have found you again."

"I'm glad you did, Chris," Ginny said, and she pecked his cheek. "I was wondering when I'd see you again. I missed you."

"I've missed you too," Chris replied, smiling. "It's been too long. Are you with anybody?"

"No, I'm alone. You?"

"All by myself," Chris said, looking around the crowded bar. "Buy you a beer?"

"Sure," she said as she looked around the crowded bar. "First let's find a place to sit."

As if their thoughts had been read, a couple in a booth to their left rose to leave. Ginny hurried over to secure the seats, while Chris pushed his way to the bar and ordered two Coronas, with lime slices topping their long necks.

"Whew," he said as he reached the booth. "This place is packed tonight." He handed Ginny her beer. He looked at her, feeling a sense of comfortable well-being. "You're good for me," he told her.

Ginny felt the same way about Chris. She wondered why they'd never gotten really serious. Maybe now was the time.

"Let me tell you about this bar fight I broke up tonight," Chris said with a grin.

*  *  *

# August 16

The phone rang. And rang. And rang. After what seemed like the fiftieth ring, Harry Grissom sullenly rose from silk sheets to silence it. Rolling over to grab the offending plastic frog, he glanced at the time and winced. Only ten o'clock. *Who the hell would call this early?* Nobody who knew him, that was certain. The number was unlisted, so it had to be some kind of telemarketer.

Damn! He grabbed the receiver fiercely, ready to bellow at the cretin on the other end for daring to try to sell him magazines, or light bulbs, or anything at this time of day. Before he could speak, his thoughts were assaulted by a combination of raw sound and speech. "Heeey! Is this Harry Grissom?" blared the trained voice, overlaid to a jingle of some kind. It sounded vaguely familiar, like something Harry had heard on his radio.

"Well ... yeah," he answered dully.

"Well, Harry," continued the mile-a-minute voice, "this could be your lucky day! Are you a KQIT listener, Harry? Are you?"

"Well ... ah," Harry really couldn't remember whether he was or not.

"Hey! Don't answer! We know you are! Tell me this, Harry Grissom—how would you like to win a weekend in Vegas, in beautiful Las Vegas, all expenses paid? Would you like that, Harry?"

"Sure. Sure I would." Grissom smiled. Now he knew. This was one of those bullshit radio promos. He wondered how his name had been chosen.

"All you have to do, Harry, is this: I'm going to ask you a rock and roll question. It's one that all KQITers have got to know! If you give the right answer in ten seconds, you're our lucky winner! Are you ready?" Before Grissom could answer, the question began.

"What Beatles song," the announcer began, "hit the charts at number one and stayed at numero uno the longest? You've got ten seconds, Harry. Starting now!" In the background, he heard the sound of a clock ticking.

*Shit,* Grissom thought. He had no idea what the answer was.

Now it was too late. "Time's up! What's your answer?"

"I don't know. 'Twist and Shout'?"

Immediately, the sound of coronets and a roaring crowd offended his ear.

"That's right! That's right, Harry Grissom! You're our new KQIT winner! A weekend for you and ... are you married, Harry?"

"Ah ... no, I'm not."

"A weekend for you and your lady, all expenses paid! Look for our letter in the mail, Harry! Got anything to say, you lucky guy?"

Harry smiled. "Love that KQIT!" he declared.

"Good for you, my man," said the announcer's voice. "Have a great time, but don't spend too much! Bye now!" Abruptly, the phone went dead.

Grissom's mind raced. A weekend in Vegas! He'd been planning to go anyway. Free was even better. Now, who to go with? He mentally inventoried his current list of partners. Joyce? Maybe, but this was too special. Maybe, just maybe ... He reached for the phone and called a local architectural firm.

"Geller Associates," came the prompt reply.

"I need to speak to Marianne Thibault," Grissom said in a low, dry voice.

"Just a minute, sir. I'll see if Ms. Thibault is in. Who should I say is calling?"

"Tell her it's her favorite client."

After a few moments of elevator music, Harry heard the bell-like voice. "Hello, who is this?"

"Marianne, don't hang up—"

"Who ... Harry, is that you?" The voice became high and sharp. "You know I don't like calls this time of day, even when we were friends. If you're calling to apologize about the other night, don't bother. Just keep your hands to yourself and away from me, from now on."

"Now, Marianne, don't get sore. This is special. I've won a contest. I wanted to share the prize. You're the first one I thought of."

The voice warmed, if only slightly. "That's nice, Harry. What's the prize?"

"A weekend in Vegas. Look, I know you're not with anybody now. How about it? You used to be real special to me. I thought you felt the same way. We could have a big time."

The silence lasted several seconds and ended with a sigh. "Harry, no. You're not good for me; you never were. Sex isn't all there is, and that's all you could give me. I told you it was over three years ago, and I meant it. So, thanks but no thanks. Have a good time, though." She hung up.

Enraged, Grissom threw the phone across the room. *Bitch!* She hadn't always been that cold. When he'd first met her at the Hilton East four years back, she'd been ready! Sometimes, all it took was a single caress, a single kiss, to get her hot to go—anywhere. His apartment, his car, a hotel room, wherever was closest and at least semiprivate. She was passionate, insatiable, and without shame.

Then, as quickly as it had begun, she had lost interest. She stopped calling him and eventually stopped taking his calls. When he finally confronted her for a reason, her blunt response had surprised him.

"You've got no emotion, no tenderness, Harry," she had said. "For you, it's just fucking. That was all right for a while. I needed it. You are very good, but I need a lot more than technique from a man now. I need companionship. I need to talk. I need to know that I mean something more than a good lay. Go find someone who just wants what you give, Harry. It's not me, not anymore."

With that, she had turned and left. He had seen her since, lots of times. She had always been pleasant but distant. He'd left messages on her answering machine but had never gotten a reply. He'd sent flowers and gifts, but they'd been refused or returned unopened.

Aw, well. There was Betty. She was always ready. Maybe, when he told her about Vegas, she would want to see him right now. Smiling again, he picked up the phone and started punching numbers.

# CHAPTER 2

## Federal Facility for the Criminally Insane—Benniston, West Virginia

### Two Months Earlier

Bobby Dolents surveyed the wreckage of his last gambit, calculating his next options. He estimated that his king would face checkmate in no more than five moves. Looking across the chessboard, through the barred cell front, he tried to read his opponent's face.

Karl Thibault met his gaze with a tight smile, took a long draw on his cigarette, and returned his attention to the board. Once again, Dolents wondered just how crazy inmates like Thibault really were. In his ten years at Benniston he had dealt with some real crazies. Men who raved for days on end, who had to be force fed, who lashed out at any attendant foolish enough to come within range of hands or feet or teeth. As dangerous as these men were, they were also predictable. With enough force, enough drugs, and enough barriers, they could be contained and, eventually, tamed.

Bobby, at six feet four and 260 pounds of solid muscle, could deal with them. He was bigger and tougher, and over the years he had gained enough experience to foresee most of their moves. And he was smart, more intelligent by far than most of the men he had to subdue. He was careful to maintain every edge, to leave no momentary advantage that could be seized by the crazed or the desperate.

Thibault represented a special case. A man of ordinary build and middle height, he had offered no resistance to authority since his incarceration, following his conviction for murder. On the contrary, he had—from the first day—followed all instructions to the letter. More than that, Thibault had done his best to improve his personal situation by freely volunteering to help Bobby and the rest of the Benniston staff. At first, he was only allowed to clean up the messes that were a daily occurrence in this combination of asylum and prison. As time went by and federal budgets continued to shrink, he was given more responsibility. By now, five years after his first night in Benniston, he was a de facto medical aide and was even allowed to dispense drugs to some of the other patients on his cell block. He cultivated Bobby's approval and later his friendship, becoming the first interesting chess opponent the huge attendant had faced in years.

Thibault had gained a few privileges for his effort, but they were minor. He was allowed to call home from time to time to talk to his son (most well-behaved inmates could gain approval for such calls, though not with such frequency or privacy). He was allowed reading material—mostly magazine and book club subscriptions—and access to the computer at the nurse's station, which he used to write short stories for a variety of magazines. (Thibault had enjoyed mild success in selling several science fiction and mystery stories over the past two years.) In general, everyone agreed that this model inmate gave far more than he took.

Yet this prisoner, for all his good works, still set off the guard's alarms. On nights like tonight, Dolents thought he sensed real danger behind the mild blue eyes of his chess opponent. Not the rage of the confined maniac, but something far more controlled, more cultivated, like a snake waiting for the proper time to strike. "Probably just my own imagination," he decided, shrugging his massive shoulders and shaking his head. He turned his attention to the chessboard once again, carefully considering his next move. Although his impending loss was assured, he saw no reason to make the victory an easy one.

Karl drew again on his cigarette, aware of his opponent's scrutiny. Though he appeared outwardly calm, his mind seethed with emotion. This was the night he had chosen to escape. Theoretically, his level of medication should have made such thoughts impossible. In fact, Thibault had not taken his proper dosage of meds for several months. Once he had established the trust of the staff, once he had gotten access to the computer on the ward, it was simple to learn to edit the results of his monthly blood chemistry samples.

Now Karl was ready. He had a plan and a mission. He would punish those who had used his wife, his Marianne. After that, he would rescue his son and start a new life. The first step was the elimination of Bobby. He sighed inwardly. Killing him was wrong, he knew. The attendant had been kind to him, after a fashion, and had always allowed him to keep the few tattered remnants of dignity he had brought with him into this steel and concrete piece of hell. He spoke to the man he had just condemned. "I guess you've handled your share of dangerous people, haven't you, Mr. Dolents?" He asked, leaning back in his chair so that his feet actually protruded through the bars of his cell front. As he had surmised, the hulking attendant leaned further across the table, closer to Thibault's face, as he made his reply.

"I've seen my share, Karl, that's for sure. Some of your neighbors would kill us both in a minute without a second thought, if they got the chance."

"So tell me, Mr. Dolents, what makes a man truly dangerous? Is it size and strength, or cleverness? Or something else?"

Bobby shook his head, smiling. "Some of all those things, I guess. Though the biggest ones are seldom quick or clever. I think it's something more. The really scary guys share two qualities: they concentrate completely, and they have no sense of wrong at all. Those guys feel no remorse, no pity. Killing another man is no different than swatting a fly to them."

"I think you're right, but there's even more," Karl said calmly. He could almost see the words as they left his brain and effortlessly flew from his lips. His excitement was growing. He felt the power within himself throb through his body like a flood of molten steel. "A really dangerous man does whatever he must to kill."

"What do you mean?" Bobby was genuinely puzzled. Much to

Karl's satisfaction, he leaned forward even further, well over the forgotten chessboard.

"Here's an example: in the army we were all taught to gouge an opponent's eyes out. Sometimes it could be necessary, to win in hand-to-hand combat. How many could actually do it? Very few. Just the idea of such a thing is too violent, too frightening for most of us."

As he finished his sentence Karl kicked viciously upward, causing the small chess table to pivot where it attached to the cell bars. As Karl had predicted, the edge of the table hit Bobby squarely under his jaw, sending him senseless to the floor in front of the cell. Karl reached through the bars, dragging the unconscious attendant closer, reaching for the keys to his freedom.

As he worked, he continued to explain. "You see, Bobby, the really bad ones can call on power! We can will ourselves to levels of strength and speed the rest of you can't hope to match." He grabbed Bobby's head by the hair and drew him to the cell door. Then, reaching through the bars with both hands, he gave the unconscious attendant's neck a vicious twist, breaking it instantly. The new corpse slumped again to the floor, as Karl rotated the body to grab the keys to his cell from its belt.

In another minute, Karl was free. Free! He had to restrain himself from rushing headlong through the ward, alerting other staff and security. Carefully, he surveyed the cell area, looking for obvious signs of the struggle. The small table and the chess board were quickly put away, and the dead attendant was deposited on a nearby gurney and covered with a sheet, serving a useful purpose even in death. The symmetry appealed to Karl. He smiled broadly and began to hum softly to himself as he continued his preparations for escape. He still had three major barriers to overcome: three security doors that separated his ward from the outside world. Each was manned by two well-trained guards, men who had known Bobby for years. No one else would be allowed through those doors. "I guess I'll just have to become Bobby," Karl whispered.

He pulled the huge attendant's ward jacket over his own clothes, stuffing it with bedding and pillows from the supply cabinet to create the illusion of bulk. He also donned the dead man's boots, after first stuffing them with rags to increase his height. Going into his cell, he retrieved some of his own excrement from the toilet, smearing it on the corpse. The stench was strong, giving excellent reason for the surgical mask he now put on. Bobby's baseball cap completed the disguise. With any luck, the guards would fail to notice the charade, when confronted by what appeared to be an attendant they knew pushing the stinking corpse to the infirmary.

His final step was the most crucial. Wheeling the gurney to the attendant's station, he called the first guard. "Joe, this is Bobby," he rasped, breathing heavily through the mask. He knew that Joe could see as well as hear him, through a closed circuit TV monitor. He hoped the blurred picture would give added weight to his impersonation.

"That you, Dolents?" the guard replied. "What ya got the mask on for? Who's that on the gurney?"

Karl kept his head down. "Karl Thibault. Must have been a heart attack. I just found him in his cell. Dead as a doornail and stinks like hell. Let me through so I can get him to the infirmary. Then I'm going to burn my clothes."

"Okay, I'm opening the doors. But don't slow down on your way through. Gawd! I can smell him from here!"

Karl hurried through the narrow portal down another hall to the next security door, bent low over the gurney. "Joe, do me a favor. Call the guys down the line and have them open up for me," he choked as he spoke. "I want to get this over with as soon as possible."

The guard waved, holding his nose. "I'll do it. You owe me a beer later for this, Bobby. Procedure says you've got to stop at every door."

Karl waved in acknowledgment as he hurried down the hall. "Fuck procedure," he muttered, loud enough for Joe to hear.

He passed unchallenged through the next security door but found the final barrier still closed. Impatiently, with a growing tingling in the pit of his stomach, he turned to the monitor and complained. "Who's on in there? It's Bobby, goddammit. Didn't you hear from Joe?"

The answer was bad news. "Dolents, this is Supervisor Erlich. What do you think you're pulling? You've already got Joe in trouble with this silly-assed stunt of yours. You know the procedure. I'm coming out to inspect the body. Then you and me are going to have a little chat."

Karl couldn't feel fear, not now. Instead he felt the irritation he had always known when a plan didn't quite work. He decided to bluff. "Come on out if you want to, inspector. But you better bring a mask yourself. This guy smells of everything he ate for the last day and a half. The more time you take, the more I gotta breathe it. Shit, I think I'm going to be sick right now." With that, he bent to the far side of the gurney, making loud retching sounds.

The effect was immediate. "Jesus, Bobby. Stop that. Okay, get going. This place is enough of a mess already. Are you all right? Do you need help?"

Inwardly, Karl breathed a sigh of relief. It was going to be all right. "Nah, I'm okay," he answered with a heavy nod. "The smell is just too much tonight. Maybe something I ate. Sooner I'm done, the better, that's all."

As the heavy doors slid open and he pushed the gurney through, Karl smiled under his mask. It was working! Most of his plans had worked, for as long as he could remember. He only failed when he rushed and overlooked an obvious detail. This plan had taken months to conceive. There were no details missed.

Rounding a final corner, he pushed the gurney past the darkened infirmary, bringing it to rest in a secluded corner. Turning to a convenient supply closet, Karl quickly changed his clothes, pulling on the baggy mint green sweats worn by the medical orderlies. Then, he methodically sprayed the corpse that had served him so well with disinfectant to mask its odor for a time. "Goodbye, Bobby," he whispered as he grabbed the attendant's car keys and turned to go. "Your chess was awful."

Walking through the darkened infirmary, he stopped to collect a supply of drugs and hypodermic needles, ignoring the alarms that began ringing as soon as he smashed the first cabinet door.

He would be gone in seconds, and the drugs were necessary to his plan—a plan he now knew could not fail. As the lights in the corridor brightened and the pounding of approaching booted feet grew louder, he carefully closed the outer door, barring it from the outside with a convenient mop handle. A memory from one of his Officer Candidate School classes popped into his head: "A good officer makes full use of the materials available to him in the field." He smiled. Full use indeed.

He climbed down the outside stairway and took in his first breath of freedom in half a decade. Free! Loping to Bobby Dolents's two-year-old Ford (which was easy to find because they'd had a long talk about which car to buy and Bobby had shown him all the brochures), Karl quickly backed from the parking space without lights and cruised from the facility, relearning his driving skills as he accelerated down the darkened road.

Within thirty minutes, he had accosted a salesman in a motel ten miles away and changed cars. The salesman would not alert authorities. The stench from his motel room, eventually revealing its grisly secret, would not begin for another day or so.

He headed west for the Ohio border, driving with more confidence now. His mind whirled with the joy of his new freedom. Wordless music bubbled from his memory. A wailing saxophone clashed with the jarring thrum of a bass guitar, filling his consciousness. He hummed along, delighted with his inner music.

\* \* \*

Because of the three-hour time difference, it was still very early when Marianne's phone rang. She answered it groggily, still half asleep. "Hello," she whispered.

The voice on the line sounded strident, worried. "Mrs. Thibault? Mrs. Marianne Thibault?"

"Yes, what is it? Is there some kind of trouble?"

"Mrs. Thibault, my name is Thomas Waters. I am an agent with the Federal Bureau of Investigation. I'm calling to alert you. Your ex-husband has escaped from Benniston. Several hours ago. He killed an attendant and took his car. It doesn't look like we're going to get him, at least not tonight."

Marianne felt faint. Her gasp was sharply audible over the phone. "My God," she cried. "Karl escaped? You've got to catch him. He can't be left free!"

The voice was grim. "I know, ma'am, I know. We're doing everything we can. But I wanted to call you. We have so little to work with. We think you may be in danger—"

She interrupted him, her voice much stronger now. "No, Mr. Waters. That's one concern you must not have. Karl would never harm me. Look at your records. Talk to his doctors. I'm the one person he will never kill. Anyone else—"

"Do you think he'll try to come home?"

"No. Karl knows there is nothing for him here. For all that's wrong with him, he's very smart, you know. I think he'll go somewhere else, somewhere he hopes you'll never look. But, Mr. Waters?"

"Yes?"

"You must catch him. He's much too sick to be free. He won't stop killing, if he thinks he needs to. He can't."

"I know, Mrs. Thibault. I know. Well, I am sorry to have disturbed you. We will keep your house under surveillance until Karl is found. I'll coordinate it with the local police right away."

"Thank you, Mr. Waters. That will make me feel better, even though I think you'll be wasting your time. Thank you for the call. I hope you find him quickly."

"Yes, ma'am. Well, good morning, then."

"Thanks again."

Long after the phone call ended, Marianne stood by the nightstand, still numb with shock and disbelief. "Oh, Karl," she sighed to herself. "Can't you leave us alone? Can't you let us have our lives?"

The dark silence of the house gave back no answer.

\* \* \*

The story in the next day's *Washington Post*, page A3, read as follows:

> Killer Escapes from Fed Asylum
> Benniston, WV (AP) Authorities widened their search today for escaped murderer Karl Thibault. Thibault, confined to the Federal Facility for the Criminally Insane here following the brutal slaying of his estranged wife's lover, had been a model prisoner for the past five years. Two days ago he overpowered and killed an attendant and escaped the facility disguised as a staff member.
> According to Sheriff Erwin Gloucher, Thibault may have left the local area entirely. "We found his car ten miles from Benniston," Gloucher said. "If he was on foot, we'd have caught him by now. There ain't that many places to hide." Thibault has stolen another car and may be hundreds of miles away by now, Gloucher said.

Then this story ran in the *St. Louis Post Dispatch* one week later, page A4:

> Man Found Dead in Springfield Motel
> Springfield, MO (Copley) Police and sheriff's deputies continue to search for clues to the murder of Herbert Mossbach, a police spokesman announced today. Mr. Mossbach, an industrial salesman from Vandalia, Mich., was found strangled yesterday in his room at the Valley Inn in Springfield. He had been dead for at least two days, the coroner said. According to police, robbery was the apparent motive for the crime. Mossbach's car is missing, as are his wallet and credit cards. Mossbach is survived by his wife and three children.

# CHAPTER 3

## Maslo, Nevada—August 10

Judy looked up from finishing the dishes as the glare of headlights flashed across the diner's window. It was late, far too late for customers. Sometimes people stopped at the diner for directions or to look for a place to spend the night—sometimes, but seldom this late.

Removing her apron, Judy walked carefully to the screen door. The dust settled in the gravel parking lot, and she could see the car now. It was a big Ford, a salesman's car. Why stop here? The lights were out, the "closed" sign prominent in the front window. Now the driver's side door opened and a man emerged, stretching and yawning. Looking in Judy's direction, he saw the dim light from within the diner and started trudging toward her. His slow footsteps in the gravel made angry, crunching sounds. She watched as he drew nearer, taking shape in the dim light.

He was of medium height, fortyish, with a neat moustache and pleasant, even features. His suit was baggy and wrinkled from hours of driving, and he looked very tired. "Hi," he said with a small wave of his hand as he saw her behind the screen. "Excuse me. I saw the sign—"

She cut him off. "We're closed, mister. It's late."

He nodded. "I know. I'm sorry if I startled you." His voice was low and fluidly easy. "I saw the sign, the apartment for rent. I know it's late, but …"

Judy's thoughts soared. Maybe there was a God in heaven after all! A real renter! She had all but given up. In fact, she had planned to take the sign down tomorrow. A renter would mean she could finance Nori, her daughter, through one more semester at UNLV. Could it happen? She forced herself back to calm and caution.

"There is an apartment for rent all right, mister."

The man smiled and breathed a sigh of relief. "Talley. Kenneth Talley. I'm a regional rep for an industrial bearings firm. Just got the job. I have four states to cover, and I've spent the last two weeks mostly lost." Grinning, he shook his head. "Your town, eh—what's its name again?"

"Maslo. You passed the reason for the name, coming into town. You must have seen the ruins. There used to be a big hospital here, a funny farm for rich people from LA. It sat here about thirty years. Most of the town grew up around it. About ten years ago there was some kind of scandal and then a fire. Still, the name stuck. Some of the people did too."

"Yeah. Maslo. Anyhow, Maslo is just about centered on most of my accounts. So I thought, *Why not rent something here?* and then I saw your sign. I know it's late, and I'll come back tomorrow if you'd rather, but I'd really like to see the place."

"Gee, I don't know, Mr. Talley. Look at the time."

"Look, Mrs.—what did you say your name was?" The smile was broader now.

She hadn't said, but that was all right. "Judy Carnover," she answered simply.

"Well, Mrs. Carnover, if I like the place, I'll take it tonight. Believe me, I need somewhere to rest in a hurry. I can pay you right now."

She shook her head. "I couldn't let you in until the check cleared."

He held up his hand in peace. "I know that, Mrs. Carnover, but surely you'd take cash." Pulling a wallet from his jacket, he revealed a neat stack of twenty- and fifty-dollar bills. "There should be plenty here for the first and last month's deposit. What do you say?"

What could she say, indeed! Judy's mind raced. The place would go for $275. With an extra $550 in cash, she could wire Nori enough money to cover registration tomorrow, just in time.

Nodding her head, she carefully unlatched the diner's screen door. "Okay, Mr. Talley."

"Call me Ken."

"Okay then, Ken. The place is here, in the back. Not much of a view, but then there's not much to see, except the desert." She led him behind the diner to what appeared to be a large barn or garage.

"I like the desert. Always have," the man said. Now they were climbing a wide wooden stairway built into the barn's wall. She looked back. "Not afraid of heights are you, Ken?"

"No, ma'am." He chuckled. "Just big holes."

She laughed back. "Well, here we are. Before we go in, here's the rules. Payment first of the month, no excuses. The place is furnished, but if you put your own stuff in we'll help you move ours out. You can use the garage downstairs. I'll give you a key for that too. Rent includes water; you pay your own electric. I'll call in the morning and set it up. I keep a key. If I come in and find the place trashed, you're out. No arguments. You can eat at the diner at a discount. Any questions?"

"No, ma'am. It all sounds fair to me."

She smiled again as she worked the lock to open the door. Maybe this would work. As the door swung open, she ushered him in and turned on the light. The subdued glow from a table lamp revealed a large room, simply furnished with a couch and two easy chairs. The wood floor was partially hidden by a worn area rug. A small breakfast table and three chairs fronted what was obviously the kitchen, near a window that looked out over the mesa behind. A dark hallway led to the bath and bedrooms.

"It's not the Ritz by any means, but it's clean. Bedrooms are down the hall. Take a look for yourself. The bedding's been changed weekly, so it's not dusty. If you put it out, I'll run it with my wash. Bathroom's on the right."

Judy watched and then listened as the salesman disappeared from sight, the sound of his footsteps tracing his progress down the hall. For ageless seconds there was no sound at all, and then she heard the hurry of his returning to the living room. He emerged from the hall with a broad smile on his face.

"It's just what I need," he announced. "I'll take it. If you'll get a receipt, I'll pay you right now."

Judy nodded dumbly, overcome with relief she tried unsuccessfully to mask. "I'll bring it by with the lease tomorrow, ah, Ken. I know you'll like it here."

He shook her hand firmly as he handed her the cash. "I know I will, Mrs. Carnover. This place is exactly what I wanted."

For several minutes after his new landlady left, Karl Thibault stood motionless in the center of his newly rented living room. He was tired, having put more than six hundred hard miles on his car since morning, but his elation overcame all fatigue.

Ken Talley. Not much of a name, but close enough to his own that he would quickly learn to react to it—another detail he had given much thought. Details could sometimes make the difference between a failed plan and one that worked. He surveyed his new home with grim satisfaction. Now he had a base of operations. Now the most important part of his plan could begin.

He sprang down the steps, sprinted to his car, and then drove it to the base of the garage apartment's stairway. Moving more slowly, he carried his suitcase and shaving kit up the steps and into his rooms. Suddenly weary again, he quickly stripped to his underwear, brushed his teeth, and settled into the stiff white sheets of one of the single beds in the room across the hall from the small bathroom. A shower could wait until morning, he decided. Almost as soon as his head hit the slightly gritty feather pillow, he slept.

Sometime during the night, he dreamed. In many ways, Karl's dreams had redefined his life. For these were not the random images of a brain reordering its memories, preparing for a new day. Instead, Karl's dreams were visions of the grotesque sickness he harbored.

He had first become aware of the dreams seven years ago, two years before he committed the crime that sent him to Benniston (although Marianne later testified that his sleep had been disturbed for as long as she had known him). At first there was only one, which repeated itself several times a week. After a while there were more, and they crowded into his mind every night.

Finally, even consciousness could not keep them at bay. The sight of a certain type of tree, military trucks going the other way, sunlight through a cloud, or any of a thousand things could send him spinning from concrete reality into a world of violence, fear, and confusion. He tried his best to keep track of the real world through this mist of chaos. At business meetings, he would give presentations while, in his mind, he cowered in what had to be a landing zone, waiting for the chopper that would never come, while unseen enemies prepared to rush him from the edges of a place he could never quite see. Reality was still there, but it was distant, as though he was viewing it through the wrong end of a telescope. His words rang hollow and senseless in his own ears. Only a tremendous force of will prevented him from crying out and running away forever.

A few times, some trigger careened him into this awful place while he was driving. Once, he had to endure the ignominy of an afternoon of blood, urine, and other tests, conducted by a highway patrol officer who was sure he was either drunk or on drugs. Badly frightened, he sought help from the Veterans Administration.

The VA shrugged collectively, offering therapy he didn't understand and drugs that he took mechanically. Almost every time he visited the local VA clinic to renew a prescription, the doctor he saw had changed, requiring Karl to recite his case history over and over until it became divorced from him, like a half-remembered religious litany mumbled in church. Tegretol, then Desipramine, then other medications whose names he couldn't remember—all prescribed by squads of physicians who barely glanced at the notes of their predecessors. Eventually, the worst of his daytime horrors, his "intrusive thoughts" or flashbacks, were controlled by the drugs. The dreams were never curbed. Every night they eroded his will to fight them and every night his strength to resist was less until he finally gave in to the black release of madness that encompassed him still.

The dreams came in no particular order, and he didn't always have each one. Since his incarceration, he had almost begun to look forward to them. After all, they were the only part of his life that had not changed. Here was the first one, coalescing from the gray behind his eyes. Men from his unit in Vietnam—Easton, Henley, little Ky, and the others—sat before a pier. They were about to board a boat and cross the lake behind them, he was always sure, although no boat could be seen. The sky was a sullen expanse of gray: monsoon season. The men didn't move, didn't speak. Their ghastly wounds, still present from the last time he'd actually seen them, didn't bleed. They merely looked at him, timelessly. He often thought he could sense small movements, as if they beckoned him nearer. On other occasions, he was sure they were angry or happy.

Sometimes, he was able to move close enough to examine their faces intimately, but tonight he could not. He wished they would move or speak, even to curse or accuse him. In his soul, he knew they never would, not until death put him with them on that pier. Then they would all cross the awful lake together.

A second dream overlaid the first. He was above a clearing in a heavy forest, as though sitting on the branch of a tree. Below and in front of him, a friend stood smiling broadly, dressed in his best khakis—probably about to go on leave. The friend's identity changed from night to night. Sometimes, it wasn't a single person at all but a montage of people Karl had liked or respected. As he watched, tonight and every night, small bright yellow figures, no taller than dolls, crept from behind rocks and bushes to surround the man, who ignored them completely. Karl called out warnings that weren't heard. He tried to move from his perch but found himself paralyzed. He continued to watch helplessly while the industrious little men constructed ingenious ladders and ropes from vines and sticks and began climbing the man's legs. At last, Karl's friend noticed the creatures, but as always it was much too late. They had engulfed him to his waist, and now they pulled him to the ground and swarmed over him as he screamed and swatted at them ineffectually. Finally, the little men left to creep back to their hiding places behind the rocks and the trees, leaving only gleaming bones where Karl's friend had stood.

Suddenly he was in that same glade, completely alone. There was no noise at all. That was a bad sign since it meant something large had scared the geckos away. With his back to the tree, Karl scanned the brush and the forest he could see. Behind a large tree in front of him, the barely visible silhouette of a man became apparent. He was almost completely hidden, but the edges of his cheek and shoulder were clearly visible. He was smoking one of those awful locally made copies of Galois cigarettes. Karl thought sometimes he could smell the greasy, smoky odor. He knew the man was a North Vietnamese soldier. He would move from hiding any moment, Karl was sure, along with the other enemy troops hidden nearby. They would take Karl prisoner and torture him horribly before killing him. This second of silence was utterly terrifying.

As he turned to run, Karl found himself in a helicopter. To his front, several men dropped through a large hatch to rappel to the ground. All the men, including Karl, were heavily armed and carried bulky packs, indicating a long mission. The ground below wasn't visible, but the sky was a sullen gray with tendrils of orange red, as though a fire were nearby. In the corner of the chopper's bay, a large good-natured officer who looked to Karl a lot like John Goodman cheerfully urged the men on.

"Come on, men," the jolly major rumbled, "Got to move! Got to jump!" He turned to Karl with a wide smile on his friendly face and a gleam in his honest blue eyes. "Your turn, little buddy!" he said. "Come on now, got to jump!"

Karl was confused. "I don't know the mission, major," he said. "Where are we going?"

"On your mission, of course! The big one! The biggest mission you've ever had," the major replied with a deep chuckle. "Off you go, now! Everybody's out but you!"

To his own surprise, Karl started to cry. "Please don't make me go," he pleaded. "I'm so scared. I was always so scared, but I couldn't say it. I couldn't tell anybody …"

The laughing major stopped smiling and grabbed Karl's shoulders with his great big hands. Karl suddenly felt very cold.

"You people never understand," he said calmly as he forced Karl to the hatch. "You think these wars just go on and on by themselves." By now, Karl was at the hatch, grabbing and adjusting his line. "Nobody realizes," the major continued. "These things gotta be fed!"

Karl looked down, as he always did, and his eyes followed the lines of the men who had left before him—down, down, but not to the ground. Instead, the end of each line dangled before the open jaws of a huge beast whose eyes reflected the mad red glare from the sky above. An enormous tongue lolled against fangs the size of boulders, and the monster's fetid breath made Karl reel with nausea.

The smiling major was behind him now. "Goodbye, little buddy," he whispered with a buff chuckle as he threw Karl into the waiting maw of the beast.

Karl awoke, as he always did, bathed in sweat. He felt fatigued, unrested, and giddy. It was almost as though he were still dreaming. In fact, since his escape, the boundaries between his dreams and reality had blurred considerably. Karl didn't mind. In other dreams, he could act out his plans perfectly.

He rose from his bed and walked to the bathroom, where he drew a glass of water from the sink. His throat felt raw and sore. That was hardly surprising since he had been screaming in his sleep.

After shaving and dressing, Karl walked to the phone, a dusty cream unit sitting on a low end table in the apartment's living room. Taking a card of thumbtacks from his briefcase, he quickly mounted detailed road maps of Nevada and Arizona to the nearest wall. He would bring up the equipment and his few belongings tomorrow, he decided. Then, as soon as the phone line was connected, he would begin. He would lure his prey to the killing ground of his choice. His military training on ambush technique had been specific: "Choose a kill zone where both retreat and relief are difficult." His first victim would find both escape and rescue impossible.

Karl smiled.

# CHAPTER 4

## Las Vegas, Nevada—September 15

The cab hadn't stopped yet, but Harry Grissom had already jumped from his seat, throwing his overnight bag to the curb in front of the hotel's doorman. "For crissake, Betty," he whined, "get your ass in gear. Just because it's free doesn't mean we have to waste it. C'mon, will ya?" He grabbed his companion's hand and arm, almost dragging her from the cab's back seat.

Betty frowned, a small line furrowing the almost perfect symmetry of her attractive, regular features. Harry could be such a putz! He probably wanted to lay her right now, before they even went out. That was okay, but she wanted a shower first. The plane ride had made her sticky. Then, a thought—maybe there was room in the shower.

Releasing Betty's arm, Harry hurriedly paid the cabby and turned to the doorman. "I got three bags," he announced. Without paying further attention to his luggage, he paused to survey his home for the weekend, his all-expenses-paid weekend. He immediately decided he was not going to like the Miramar Hotel. Oh, it looked nice enough—not dirty or anything. It wasn't on the Strip though, and it didn't look like it had a bar at all. Hell, it was just a glorified motel!

He strode to the registration desk, determined to make sure these people realized just who he was. His eyes narrowed as he stood before the clerk, a small young man who paid no attention to him as he filled out some kind of printed form. Harry frowned and cleared his throat, loudly.

The young man peered up through thick glasses. "Yes, sir!" he said quickly. "Can I help you?"

"I'm Harry Grissom. Party of two. The KQIT contest."

"Yes, Mr. Grissom. We've been expecting you. The station has already made all the arrangements. You're getting our largest suite." Looking at Betty as she came through the door, the clerk meekly added, "You know, Mr. Grissom, we normally use your suite for the bridal parties we get."

Harry's laugh was a harsh short bark. "Just make sure it's clean, stud. Otherwise, you and I are gonna have words. You guys have a bar in this joint?"

"No, sir, but I have coupons good at—"

A wave of Harry's hand cut him off. "I got coupons of my own. Hell, gimme the keys. I got to get going." Grabbing the keys from the clerk's hand with unnecessary force, Harry trudged after the porter, a grim expression on his face.

Betty followed, puzzled as always by Harry's quickness to anger. She was an effortlessly beautiful woman, small and blonde with an easy, languid grace that always attracted stares from the men around her. Betty was not intellectual, as she had barely finished high school, but her intelligence would have astounded Harry if he had ever noticed it. She seldom showed the men she chose how smart she was, having learned some years ago that many found it unnerving, even aggravating. Instead she gloried in their worship of her physical shell and kept her thoughts to herself. The men she liked were strong and had plenty of money. They often missed the small verbal barbs she threw their way, and these became her private amusements. They used her as a symbol of their potency, their success. She used their money and enjoyed them physically. In her mind, it was an even bargain.

Harry waited impatiently as the porter fumbled with the key to the suite's double doors. As they opened, he pushed past the man and looked with amazement at the suite he had won. The carpet was deep white shag, the walls a florid hot pink. In the center of the room, a waterfall fountain emptied into a large heart-shaped pool. There were mirrors on the ceiling and on every wall. A mirrored door stood ajar, revealing an enormous heart-shaped bed in the adjoining room.

Harry's mood brightened. In a place like this with a girl like Betty, he might never hit the tables—at least not for a while. He turned to her as she came up behind him, grinning widely. "Betty," he said, "we are going to have one hell of a weekend. Thank you, KQIT, wherever you are."

He hurriedly tipped the porter, with only a cursory glance at the bills he handed out, and then pushed the man out the door before he locked and bolted it. He felt his need for Betty grow from a single thought to a consuming passion, like shells exploding in his head and loins. "Come here," he whispered, already beginning to unbutton his shirt.

Betty glided to his side, sensing his need and warming to it. "Harry," she said to his ear as his lips assaulted her neck, "let's do it in that tub. Now." She reached back to unbutton her dress.

A loud knock on the door startled them both. "Who the hell is it?" Harry bellowed. "Go away!"

"Room service," came the muffled reply. "Your complimentary champagne."

"Okay, okay, wheel it in." Harry rezipped his trousers as he shuffled to the door. Champagne would be good.

The man behind the champagne cart was not their porter. He was older, of medium height, and sported a neat moustache. His hands were shiny, as though covered in saran wrap, and his uniform was ill fitting, cut for someone taller. As he wheeled the cart to the center of the room, he smiled. "May I uncork the bottle, sir?" he asked.

"Yeah, yeah. Go ahead. Snap it up. We're busy."

"Naturally, sir." With a flourish, the new porter sliced away the metallic wrapping, pulled away the wire, and quickly popped the cork into his waiting towel. In the process he had shaken the bottle vigorously, and now the champagne sprayed Harry's face, momentarily blinding him.

Instinctively he raised his hands to his eyes, trying to rub the stinging liquid away. Before he could speak to curse the porter, he felt a savage blow to his head, then darkness …

\* \* \*

Harry regained consciousness to find himself lying spread eagle on the heart-shaped bed, his wrists and ankles firmly tied to its posts. He and Betty were alone in the garish room; she was slumped in a chair like a rag doll tossed aside. His head throbbed with pain from the blow he had suffered. He moaned incoherently.

The porter who had assaulted him came into the room, alerted by the sounds. He had taken off his jacket and now stood straighter, somehow taller. It was obvious now that he wore some kind of thin surgical gloves. Harry thought he had seen the man somewhere before, but it was hard to remember. He began to weep with frustration and pain. "Let me go. Untie me," he said weakly. "I'll pay you. I've got money."

The man smiled broadly and then shook his head. "Ah, Mr. Grissom! I'm afraid I can't let you go. I've been planning our meeting far too long to end it now. You and I have much to discuss, and the whole weekend to do it. We have mutual friends."

Harry tossed on the bed, trying mightily to free himself. It was no use. The bonds were tight, the knots strong and unassailable. He called to Betty, still slumped in the chair. "Help me, Betty! Run for the cops! Get up, you lazy bitch!"

The man shook his head, still smiling. "She can't help you, Harry. She can't hear you either. A massive overdose of morphine has taken her where you'll never touch her again. She felt no pain, if you care."

"You killed her? You son of a bitch! You killed Betty! Who the fuck are you? Why are you doing this?" Harry was certain now that he'd seen this man before, somewhere. Where? Where had it been? He desperately searched the corners of his memory.

The man came closer to the bed. "Of course. I have the advantage. You and I are going to get to know each other so well, Harry, that it's only right that you know who I am. My name is Karl Thibault." Then, changing his voice to another pitch, "but I'm also your favorite radio station, KQIT!"

"Thibault? Marianne's ex? You're supposed to be locked up somewhere."

Karl's smile widened. "Obviously not, Harry. And maybe you recall why I was incarcerated in the first place. I do not like other men to touch my wife."

"Look, you bastard, I didn't do anything she didn't ask for. Hell, she begged me to lay her. Your fight is with Marianne, not me." Harry tried to smile. "Listen, let me up. Bring me a phone. I'll get her up here, and then you can do what you want with her. Just let me go, for crissake!"

His captor slowly shook his head. "Harry, Harry. It was you who soiled her, and it is you who will pay. Not without instruction, however. Pay attention. You'll learn something today that you can take with you wherever you go." He walked to the edge of the garish bed and then reached behind his back to produce a large kitchen knife.

"Did Marianne tell you I'm a veteran, Harry? Maybe not. You two probably didn't talk much. I spent a lot of time in Southeast Asia, defending democracy. I learned—"

"God, don't kill me! Please don't hurt me!" Harry mewed and wept as the knife and its purpose assailed his frantic mind.

Now sitting on the bed, Karl slapped him casually, almost playfully. "Quiet, Harry," he said. "You're disturbing my chain of thought. I'll gag you if I have to, but then your responses won't be the same. I haven't hurt you yet, have I? Maybe I'm going to cut you free. Maybe I just want to scare you."

"Betty! You killed Betty."

"Did I? Maybe I just wanted you to think that. Maybe she's just drugged. Be quiet, Harry. The hotel is used to loud noises coming from this suite. Your only hope is that I decide to let you go. Promise me now. Go ahead."

"Okay, okay. I promise." Harry was confused. The man's words were comforting in a small way. Still, Betty hadn't moved. Harry was sure she was really dead.

Karl resumed. "As I was saying, I learned a lot in Vietnam. For a while, I worked in intelligence with the ARVN—their army. They had a unique way of interrogating prisoners." As he spoke, Karl caressed the knife he held with his right hand, his free hand. Harry watched him intently, like a rat hypnotized by a cobra.

"We used the standard methods: drugs, sensory and sleep deprivation, endless questioning. The ARVN had other, more direct techniques. When we were done with a prisoner, when we had gotten from him all we could, they would sometimes ask to interrogate him themselves. Often, I was invited to watch. Never to participate, Harry, only to watch."

Harry mewed in fear. He emptied his bladder, unable to stop himself.

"Calm now, Harry. No one has hurt you. The Vietnamese had a place in Da Nang, an interrogation chamber they called the green room because the walls were painted a vivid electric green. I'll always remember that color. The subject was naked, tied to a chair, sitting on a small gray stage in the center of the room. The rest of us sat in chairs around him, as though we were watching a play. We smoked, we drank coffee, we took notes, we asked questions from time to time. The sessions often lasted all day.

"The interrogator and his assistant stood beside the subject on the small stage. He would ask questions, just like the ones I'm going to ask you. Will you answer my questions, Harry? Will you always tell me the truth?"

Harry was weeping now, frantic with fear. "Oh, yes. God, yes," he bawled. "You crazy motherfucker! Just let me go. Let me go now!"

"Harry, we haven't even started yet. Not really. Now, when did you first debase my wife?"

Harry tried to answer calmly. "I don't know, about four years ago. There was a party at the Hilton East. Marianne was there, by herself. We started dancing. We both had a lot to drink. I left to take her to my place." Harry smiled, the strength of the memory momentarily overshadowing his violent fear. "We didn't even make it out of the parking lot before she unzipped my pants—"

Karl interrupted. "When, Harry? The exact date, please. It's important."

"I don't know. It was September. Sometime in September. I can't remember more than that."

"Sometimes, in the green room, the subject couldn't remember," Karl continued. "Then the interrogator—he was usually a major—would ask the ARVN in charge for permission to refresh his memory. He always got permission, Harry." Karl leaned over the bed, stroking Harry's abdomen with his large knife.

"Americans make a mistake. We make it all the time," Karl said in a low voice. "We believe other people think like us. They don't, Harry. Here's an example: we think all thoughts, all emotions are controlled by the brain, by the mind. The Viets, they don't agree. They believe a lot of thought comes from the gut!" With a single savage thrust, Karl cut Harry's abdomen open with the razor-sharp kitchen knife. It was a clean cut from one side of the stomach to the other.

Harry felt no pain, just a tingling and then a rushing, cold, numb feeling—as though his insides had gone to sleep. The sight of the awful wound alone was enough. "Oh God! Look what you did! You're killing me! Oh shit, I'm dying!" He screamed, knotting his muscles in a futile effort to break his bonds.

Calmly, quietly, Karl produced a towel and padded Harry's forehead. "Quiet, now, Harry. Quiet. You're not dead yet. People survive worse wounds every day. You can still live, if you don't move around and make things worse. Now, I ask you again. What was the date?"

Harry's eyes rolled in their sockets. A date. A fucking date! What did it matter? He couldn't possibly check! "The tenth," he cried. "It was on September tenth!"

"Very good, Harry. Now, another question. When was the first time you soiled her in her own home, the home of my son? When was it, Harry?"

His answer was immediate. Harry could see his way out now. The man was crazy, but maybe he would be spared if he gave a date, any date. "It was in January. January fifth." Although he couldn't remember when it was, he remembered what happened vividly.

He had taken her to dinner. As they left, she had whispered in his ear, "I want you all night tonight, Harry. I don't want to leave. I want you in me till morning. We'll do it in my bed this time." A searing pain interrupted his thoughts. His body bucked on the bed, trying to arch in agony.

Karl bent over his wound and began pulling Harry's intestines from his body. He looked Harry in the eyes and made a soft "tsk, tsk" sound. "Bad answer, Harry," he said flatly. "The ARVN had the same trouble. The subject would make up dates and facts, anything to try to survive. It won't work. Think about this: every inch of gut I draw from you makes your life a little shorter. I haven't done much, not yet. Still, it hurts like hell, doesn't it? Maybe all this handling will cause a knot, an obstruction. Peritonitis, Harry. A bad way to die. Remember the old nursery rhyme? 'All the king's horses and all the king's men, couldn't put Humpty together again.' Keep lying to me, Harry, and they won't be able to put you back together either. Now, what was the date? The real date. I know you can do it."

Harry tried to reach for the fact he needed, to part the dull red haze that had become his reality. It was hard. The pain was now an intense, living thing, consuming him like some hungry beast. He knew he had voided himself but didn't care. He knew he was dying and wept in his anguish. He realized now that he would never leave this room alive.

\* \* \*

Karl emerged from the honeymoon suite's shower, toweled himself off vigorously, and put on the clothes he had carefully hidden prior to Harry and Betty's arrival. Placing his scrupulously cleaned knife and his tape recorder in a gym bag, he left the suite, studiously avoiding the ghastly bedroom. Harry had expired after only two hours of questioning. In the end, his heart had given out. Before he died, Harry had told Karl many things. "He spilled his guts," Karl mused.

It would be a five-hour drive back to Maslo. As he walked out a side exit to his car, the music of a nameless concert erupted in Karl's mind. Strident horns and cymbals clashed with wailing woodwinds. Karl grinned widely as he hummed along, thrilled at the rush of sound only he could hear and understand.

# CHAPTER 5

## Tucson, Arizona—September 24

Chris was working the day watch, catching up on the mountain of forms and reports that chokes the arteries of all police work, when his lieutenant called him in.

"Got a request from Vegas PD," he began, beckoning Chris to a seat as he closed his office door. "They had a triple murder in a hotel up there about a week ago. Turns out two of the victims were from here."

"Drugs?" Chris asked with a shrug. Many murders of people from Tucson were drug-related these days. The border around Nogales had become a sieve for methamphetamine, cocaine, and marijuana traffic.

The lieutenant shook his head and sighed. "Could be. A hotel porter and the woman died from morphine overdose—intravenous. She and her boyfriend were from here. They're asking for background on both of them. The man had one of those little black books."

Chris arched his eyebrows. A lover! Probably some jealous husband or boyfriend had done the couple in. Maybe the porter had stumbled into it by accident. "How did lover boy buy it?" he asked.

"Ugly. He was slit open like a Christmas turkey. Coroner's report says he died of heart failure, though. Must have taken a long time."

"What's the assignment?"

The lieutenant winked, tossing Chris a small black address book. "The lab's been all over this thing. The only prints belong to the victim. His name was Grissom. Harry Grissom."

"Huh. I met the guy. At Salucci's, about a month back. A real hair-bag."

"Don't speak ill of the dead, Sergeant. I'm giving you a dream assignment, compliments of Mr. Grissom. Interview the people in the book. See if you can find any leads. Get a profile of this guy's lifestyle. Who knows? You might even get lucky."

Chris smiled ruefully. Work like this was seldom a social boon. It meant hours on the phone and lots of interviews at odd hours with people who didn't want to say much. "Is the dead girl in here?" he asked.

"Sure is. Betty Clooney. Grissom apparently rated his partners. Ol' Betty got four stars. Only one other name in the whole book got those marks. Maybe that's a place to start."

Returning to his desk, Chris thumbed through the small worn address book. As he had suspected, no male names were included. The listings all had crudely drawn stars beside them, anywhere from one to four—but only two names had four, just as the lieutenant had said. The dead "Clooney, Betty" was one. "Thibault, Marianne" was the other.

* * *

Marianne received the call at work late that afternoon. It had been a routine day, spent for the most part reviewing plans for the atrium of Geller Engineering's major project—Cobblestone Mall. As the firm's single landscape architect, Marianne understood the importance of her work. Big projects were hard to come by in Tucson, overbuilt as it had become during years of a "boom" economy. The loss of this job, or its diminution through subcontracting, could mean the end of a firm that had been in business for more than three decades.

She could normally depend on Vi, the matronly receptionist, to carefully screen her calls. So when her intercom buzzed, she knew it was probably important.

"It's a Mr. Carpenter on line two," Vi announced. "He says he's with the city."

"Thanks, Vi," she replied automatically. Her mind raced for a connection and found none. He could be one of those functionaries checking for restricted plant life, she decided. Tucson had banned the use of several kinds of trees and many varieties of grass from new construction several years before. There were two major reasons for these regulations: first, to avoid the use of vegetation that required excessive water, and second, and even more important, a good fraction of Tucson's population was extremely allergic to many grasses and plants. It was ironic that, as they moved west to escape their allergies, many residents had willfully imported the cause of their suffering in the form of lawns and trees.

She picked up the phone. "Hello?"

"Is this Marianne Thibault?"

"Yes. How may I help you?"

"Ms. Thibault, my name is Chris Carpenter. I'm with the Tucson Police Department. I believe we met last month, at Salucci's."

"Really, Mr. Carpenter. I don't have time for social calls now. I'm very busy."

"I'm sorry, ma'am, but this is not a personal call. It's concerning Harry Grissom."

"I can't help you," Marianne said. "Harry and I don't see each other anymore."

"I'm afraid Harry won't be seeing anyone anymore, Ms. Thibault. He was found murdered last week in Las Vegas. He was with another woman, a Betty Clooney. Did you know her as well?"

For a long while, the line was silent. Finally, Marianne spoke. "You'll have to excuse me, Mr. Carpenter. This comes as something of a shock."

"It made the papers and the nightly news."

"I don't keep up with the news the way I should. I'm far too busy in my work. Yes, I knew Betty, but only slightly. We met at several, um, several functions we both attended. As I say, I haven't been close to Harry for almost three years. What an awful thing. What do you need from me?"

"I'm trying to form a profile of Harry's lifestyle, so I'm interviewing people who knew him. Your name's come up. I'd like to talk to you. It shouldn't take more than an hour."

She thought for a minute, frowning. "All right," she said slowly, "but not here. Not at work. Can you come to my home? Tonight around eight?"

"It's a deal," he answered, "if you'll make some coffee."

"I'll make some for you, Mr. Carpenter, but I won't need any. Believe me, talking about Harry gets me wide awake."

* * *

Chris drove to Marianne's town house that night, through narrow lanes that reminded him of pictures he'd seen of Arab villages. It took him several minutes of wrong turns and backtracking before he finally found the small lane fronting the Thibault home. As he turned his car into the nearby parking area, he noticed a friend sitting in an anonymous Chevy nearby. "Hi, Juan," he said, waving as he slammed his door. "What brings you to suburbia?"

Juan Escobar waved back. "Surveillance. Gal in 1423. Seems her ex is a psycho, escaped from a funny farm back east. Federal boys asked for the help. No action, but I'm catching up on my reading. By the way, I saw Ginny the other night. She says to say hi."

Chris nodded, realizing that 1423 was the Thibault unit. *Coincidence?* he wondered. He'd been in police work long enough to know that some people attracted trouble, especially pretty women. Maybe Marianne Thibault was such a magnet. "Well, I'm here to see the lady. Other business, though. Log me in."

"You'll be the first this week. Her and the boy really keep to themselves. I don't think the kid ever goes out."

Nodding again, Chris turned to the wooden gate inset with "1423" on tile plates. He rang the bell. For a long minute there was no reaction to the sound, though he could hear its ring. Then the town house's door slowly opened, and Marianne appeared. She recognized Chris immediately.

"Hello. I remember you," Marianne said. "You saved me from

Harry at Salucci's. What was it, a month ago? Did you know him?" As she spoke she unlocked the outer gate and ushered him through her front door into a well-furnished living room. The walls were painted an unexpected deep cherry, accenting the greens of the chairs and a thick berber carpet. The couch was a strong plaid, incorporating the red of the walls as well as the greens of the other furniture. Brass lamps, gleaming light wood end tables, a fireplace, and a sweep of bookcases that lined the interior wall from floor to ceiling completed the room. It was impressive.

He sat on the large couch before a glass and brass coffee table stacked with oversized art books as he answered her question. "No, I'd never met him before. It's odd how small the world seems, sometimes. You did know him, didn't you, Ms. Thibault?"

She sighed, every bit as beautiful as his memory had recalled. Casually dressed in a deep blue floor-length caftan that hinted at the fullness of her figure when she moved, she seemed an odd partner for the crude, florid man he had briefly encountered last month.

"Yes, Mr. Carpenter—"

"Call me Chris."

"Okay, Chris, and I'm Marianne. Yes, I knew him. As well as anyone, I guess. I'll tell you about it. First let me get you that coffee I promised and put my son to bed. Would you mind meeting him? I told him you were coming, and he's very excited. He's never met a real police detective before."

Chris smiled. "Sure, bring the kid out. I hope he won't be disappointed."

Marianne rushed from the room, returning in less than a minute with a boy who was obviously her child. Thin but standing ramrod straight, his pale complexion and large eyes mirrored hers—though his were a delicate hazel to her warm brown. "David, meet Mr. Carpenter. He's a real detective from the police department."

With almost exaggerated formality, the boy extended his hand. "I'm glad to meet you," he said in a clear, high voice. Then, cocking his head slightly to one side, he asked, "Can I see your badge?"

"Sure, David." Chris reached to his back pocket, pulled out his wallet, and flipped it open so that the large gold and silver emblem was displayed.

"Wow! It says you're a sergeant."

"That's right. Police detectives don't wear uniforms. At least, not very much."

"My dad was in the army. He wore a uniform all the time, but he got sick. Do you have to carry a gun?"

"Yes, I do, but I'm not going to show it to you. Guns are much too dangerous to play with. The only time I take it from its holster is when I really have to."

"That's okay," the boy said seriously. "My dad always said the same thing. He hates guns."

Marianne intervened. "David, it's your bedtime now," she said softly. "You can read for a while. I'll come in and turn off the lights later."

"Okay, Mom," David answered, retreating to the hallway. "Nice to meet you, Sergeant Carpenter."

Marianne returned in a few minutes, carrying a coffee tray. Chris looked up from the book he'd been leafing through, an illustrated biography of Gaugin.

"His paintings are like dreams," she said, handing him a brimming cup.

"Have you seen any of this work?" Chris asked, stirring the single teaspoon of sugar he allowed himself into his coffee.

"Yes. Once. There's a museum in Philadelphia where a lot of French Impressionist art is shown."

She sat near him on the couch and gently took the book from his hands. "Let's talk about why you're here," she said.

He took his notepad and pencil from his pocket. "You're right. We might as well get started. When did you first meet Harry Grissom?"

Marianne threw her head back, as though seeing the scene again. "It was four years ago, almost exactly. There was a party at the Wilshire East. You know, that horribly ugly pink hotel over on Broadway. I had gone with a girlfriend. Harry was there. I was feeling kind of blue, kind of wild. I had a lot to drink, much more than I normally allow myself.

We started dancing, and he really turned me on. We left together and went to his place. I know this makes me look cheap, but I needed a man like him that night, someone who would use up my body. I'd been alone for almost a year. Harry was a very good lover, in a detached, mechanical way. He knew all the buttons to push."

"And after that?"

"I went with Harry for about six months. I guess my work must have suffered. The whole time is kind of a blur. He brought out all of my instincts for pleasure. After a while, he could get me going with just a touch, just a word. Almost like hypnosis. We partied all of the time, tried things I'd never done before—things I've never wanted to do again since. Do I need to explain them to you? Do you need the details?"

Chris shook his head. "No. Not if it makes you uncomfortable."

Marianne shrugged. "I made up my mind a long time ago never to be ashamed of anything I did that didn't harm anyone else."

"You know how we found your name."

"No."

"Harry kept a little book. Your name's in it, along with about thirty other women."

Marianne laughed. It was a pretty, bell-like sound. "That would be just like him. He was horny all the time, and he liked his variety."

"Did you know that he rated every woman in his little book? He used a one- to four-star system."

"No, I didn't know, but I'm not surprised. It's juvenile, isn't it? Harry wasn't really grown up in a lot of ways."

"What do you mean?"

"Well, he had a very bad temper, and he could lose it in a hurry. He could fall in love in an afternoon and change his mind the next morning. He'd sulk for days over an imagined slight, but a gift could make him as happy as a child. That was Harry." She laughed again.

"You sound like you really liked him."

"It was hard not to, once you accepted his emotional immaturity. He was probably the best lover I've ever had."

"Back to those stars. Only two women in his little book got four:

you and Betty Clooney. She was killed with him, as you know. Why just the two of you?"

Marianne took a deep breath and then looked Chris in the eyes. "Harry could be demanding," she said. "Not all of his partners would try everything he asked of them."

"You and Betty would."

Marianne nodded slowly. "That's where I met her. I never knew her, except from Harry's little get-togethers. I was always with Harry. She had different partners. A guy named Paul, once. I don't remember the other names." She thought back to those jumbled, delirious nights. At first, when Harry had told her about them, she was certain she would never take part.

He had agreed. "Sure, angel, sure," he would croon. "You're enough for me, all by yourself." Over time, as he coaxed her to new levels of sensual awareness, new heights of pleasure, she became more compliant. At last, she had consented. It was uncomfortable at first, being watched by others as she and Harry stroked and loved and sucked each other. Surprisingly soon, her discomfort was replaced by a new level of release. She began to proudly revel in their gaze and warm to the new dimension of being handled and penetrated by many hands, many bodies at once. There seemed to be no end to the experience short of total, mind-blanking exhaustion.

"So what made you stop? Why did you leave him?"

"I guess I grew out of my need for raw sex without any love, without any meaning beyond immediate pleasure. Harry couldn't understand the need for tenderness, for communication. Besides, I couldn't keep up with him forever. I have a career I'm proud of and a little boy who depends on me. He found other partners with less responsibility and more time."

"Like Betty, for example."

"That's right. Like Betty."

"When did you see Harry last?"

"As a matter of fact, it was the night I first saw you. We hadn't had anything going for a long time before that. It's interesting though—he called me after he'd won a contest. He asked me to go with him to

Vegas. You know, I almost went. It's hard to say no to a man who can give you that much pleasure."

Chris looked up from his notes. "Contest? What contest?"

Marianne looked puzzled. "Didn't you know? That's why he went to Las Vegas in the first place. He'd won some kind of a contest, something from a radio station. The prize was a weekend for two in Las Vegas, all expenses paid."

"You figure he asked Betty when you turned him down?"

"I guess so. Betty and Harry had a lot in common."

"Marianne, do you know anybody who'd like to do Harry harm?"

She smiled. "Dozens, but none who'd want to kill him. Husbands and boyfriends, mostly. Anyone whose wife is in that little book we've talked about. He could have made someone very angry. I've told you about his temper. Harry really was like a child. He couldn't stay mad very long. I really don't know of anyone who took him seriously. Can I get you some more coffee?"

Chris shook his head. "No. No thanks. You've been more helpful than I'd hoped. More candid too."

Marianne rose from the couch. "You'd have found out about it eventually. I'm not ashamed of what I did, but I don't need it in the papers either. I hope I can depend on your discretion."

"You have my word," Chris said. He got up as well.

"Are you leaving?" she asked.

"Yeah, I have a lot more work to do tonight. Before I go, I have one more question to ask you."

She stopped halfway to the door and turned to him. "Is this still police business?"

He shook his head. "No, this is just from me. I've wanted to meet you since that night I saw you in Salucci's. I'd like to take you to dinner. Will you go?"

She looked down. "No, Chris. I'm sorry, but not now. I'd wonder if you really wanted to go out or if you were just reacting to what I've told you."

"Marianne, believe me, I want to get to know you. This other stuff, you and Harry, that's not even in my mind."

She looked up at him as she opened the door. "Isn't it, Chris? Well, then, ask me again in a little while. I may say yes."

His hand brushed hers as he turned to go. "It's a promise," he whispered.

# CHAPTER 6

## Maslo, Nevada—October 16

Judy Carnover watched with satisfaction as her new tenant finished his lunch. The food at the diner was plain but good and attracted many local residents. *If the town were only bigger, I could make a real living from this,* she thought.

Unfortunately, Maslo was small and getting smaller. Without the psychiatric hospital that had been the core of its economy, the town was slowly dissolving—fading into the desert as residents left or died, unreplaced. Hunting and fishing parties, headed for the wild country to the north, brought a trickle of commerce every year. Judy's was the only diner still operating, and only her own prodigious work kept that small business in existence. She stood in the kitchen, head down as she thought. The cost of everything kept going up. If it weren't for renting that apartment, she might have had to close up this month.

No one would have called Judy beautiful. At forty-two, she had acquired the indelible stamp of all those who live in the dry, hot places of the world. Her skin was deep brown, having lost youth's freckles and softness. A spider web of wrinkles encompassed her eyes and generous mouth, surrounding a small pug nose. Those lines portrayed a long history of laughter because Judy smiled much more often than she frowned. Her slim waist was also a memory, partly due to a difficult pregnancy, partly due to the surgery that had removed both ovaries. ("Cancer," they had said. "You've got no choice. It has to be now." So she had finally let them end her ability to conceive but

47

only to save her life. Since the operation, she had felt strangely hollow, incomplete.)

For all of that, no one would have thought of her as plain. Judy's love of life shone through her like a beacon, making the smile she often flashed wonderful. She wore her simple grace and honesty like an ermine robe. Men's eyes still followed her with interest.

She had come to Maslo fifteen years ago with Jerry, the original owner of the diner. They had met in Reno, she at the end of a bitter marriage, he reaching for companionship as aging bachelors often do. In Jerry she found a sharing partner, work she could be proud of, and a good home for Nori, her daughter, the only positive result of what had been an ugly, damaging relationship.

At that time Maslo was a prosperous town, feeding from the wages of the professionals who ran the institute and from the casual tips of the wealthy and famous who came to be cured. The maladies of these "guests" ran through the usual admixture of addictions and emotional excesses that plague those with too much money, power, and time. The future seemed assured. Jerry had plans for adding a motel and starting a limo service ("Gotta get them to and from that funny farm," he'd said in his flat, slow drawl. How she had loved him!).

The people of Maslo had been among the last to learn of the scandal that ushered the institute's demise. They were still debating among themselves what the news reports meant when the angry shadows of fire and smoke announced its final collapse. The few resources in the town weren't up to the task of containing such a blaze, and by the time additional equipment arrived from Alamo very little remained.

The town's population shrank by half within a month, as nurses, medical technicians, and orderlies (as well as the few doctors who had remained) streamed west to a beckoning coast. After that, Maslo continued to die by inches—a family here, a storefront there. Now there was almost nothing left. Soon, there would be too little to justify the small post office crowded into the corner of the sole remaining store down the street. Already, some of the empty houses had been invaded and vandalized by drifters and kids passing through.

So Ken Talley was a real anomaly: a new resident in a dying town.

"Don't look a gift horse in the mouth," Judy reminded herself. "Without him, Nori wouldn't be in school." She watched as he rose from his table. He seemed to cherish the simple fare she served, like a man who had been locked away. Had he been in prison?

He was certainly pale enough, but he didn't act like a con. He showed none of their suspicious, casually vicious traits. No, she decided. He was simply a desk jockey who'd lost his job, trying to start over as a salesman.

He seemed to have plenty of money and always paid in cash, even though his wallet bulged with credit cards. He was almost agonizingly polite and still called her ma'am, long after others would have stopped. He was as neat as a pin and so quiet that she seldom knew when he returned from a trip, except by his presence in the diner for meals. She found herself attracted to him, interested in the mystery he kept locked just behind his eyes.

He walked slowly toward her now, reaching into his pocket for the money to pay for his supper. He looked at her directly as he handed her his check. "Thanks," he said with a shy smile. "The food here is the best I've eaten in years." She could tell by his tone that he wasn't lying or flattering.

Returning his gaze, Judy smiled back. "I don't know where you've been keeping yourself then, Ken. The food here is as plain as Kansas."

"Maybe so, but you don't cook the flavor out of it, and the portions are big. Maybe too big, Judy. You'd make more if you'd cut them down a little."

She shook her head, her smile broadening. "Why, Ken! Are you angling to be my management consultant? I couldn't stint on the portions. Too many people around here depend on this place for most of their food. Besides, the diner doesn't have to bring in the bucks, not when I've got renters paying me through the nose."

She thought that would end the conversation and was surprised when it didn't. "I've been meaning to talk to you about that too, Judy," Ken continued. "I'm well aware of the bargain I'm getting, with you helping out with the linens and the discounts I get here. I'm really thankful."

Judy frowned. Where was this leading? She had planned to ask Ken for an extra seventy-five dollars a month, starting next month. Maybe now was as good a time as any. "Okay, Ken. I agree. Would it be more fair if I upped the rent, say to three hundred fifty a month?"

To her surprise, Ken nodded affirmation. "It's fine with me," he said simply.

She decided to play along. "Then it's a deal," she said, extending her hand. "You know I can use the extra money. I'll get a revised lease to you tomorrow. Let's go across the street after I've cleaned up here. I'll buy you a drink." The Sagebrush Saloon, another holdover from the town's happier days, was the only watering hole left in Maslo.

Ken shook his head. "I'd like to celebrate a little more than that, Judy, if you don't mind. I have to go to Caliente on business tomorrow. Come with me and I'll buy us some dinner."

Now Judy understood. Well, give him credit for a unique approach. She felt mildly aroused by his interest. There hadn't been a man in her life for some time. Salesmen often had a girl in every city but not all the time. Maybe he was lonely too.

"Okay," she said slowly. "As long as you don't have to leave before lunch is over. I don't trust Archie to cover more than one meal." Archie, her part-time counter help and fry cook, was retired from the institute, where he had been in charge of the kitchen. He was energetic, but like many old men he got cranky easily. He was always asking for more work and would love this opportunity to run things on his own. She guessed she could fix whatever he messed up when she got back.

Her tenant beamed. "Then it's a date. I'll pick you up around two."

She nodded her head in agreement and meant to say more, but just then two customers called for her attention. Lots of people asked for adjustments to their bills these days, as times got leaner. She approved the reductions without even thinking. When she looked his way again Ken had already left.

Karl smiled to himself as he climbed the steps to Ken Talley's apartment. Another detail, another part of his plan, sliding into place. By making the woman his ally he would erect another barrier between his mission and those who were trying to find him, he knew, even now.

Besides, she appealed to him. She was not beautiful like his Marianne—his soiled, unattainable Marianne. That didn't matter. Since the Grissom man's interrogation (Karl would never think of it as a murder), he had felt changes in himself. He recognized the faint stirrings of need, buried so long by his hate and his single-minded passion for revenge. He wondered if he could be with a woman again. Toward the end of his time with Marianne, it had become impossible. Then, when she had told another man his horrible secret, the truth she never should have spoken ...

He shook his head violently, willing the thought to retreat to the cobwebbed edges of his mind, where it must stay until the time was right. His hands shook visibly as he opened the door to his apartment. He knew his dreams would be very bad tonight.

* * *

# Springfield, Missouri

Like most FBI agents, Thomas Waters was a superb investigator. His mind could calmly and methodically sift through thousands of unrelated details from the chaos of a crime scene, often identifying the one or two important pieces of information that eventually could become useful evidence. This intuition—along with resolute determination and endless patience—made him an implacable adversary, which is why the bureau assigned him to the more difficult fugitive cases.

It was a leap of faith to ascribe the death of a salesman in a Pennsboro, West Virginia, motel to Karl, but not a great one. According to the coroner, the man had been killed within a few hours of Karl's escape. The salesman's car was missing, and his credit cards and cash were gone. Karl would have needed them. Bobby Dolents's car had been found hidden in heavy brush less than a mile away. Yes, it had been Karl. Strangulation was not his known MO, but he had only two other murders in his file until now.

Operating on that assumption, Waters cast his net, looking for credit card use, other crimes, something to establish a direction of escape. Once he knew where Karl was going, he would follow and trap him.

Another murder took him south to rural Georgia, but it was a bad lead. The killer was a farmer who had found his wife with another man—a local matter. He waited again.

The salesman's car turned up in southwestern Indiana, driven by a farmhand who had bought it from a man in a bar—a man looking for money to get out of town. The description was sketchy (the farmhand had been very drunk), but it could have been Karl.

Where had he gone from there? How had he traveled? North by bus to Terre Haute, south to Louisville, or east to Cincinnati? *Many predators double back*, Waters thought idly. He continued to wait, examining in tireless detail the hundreds of thefts and murders reported to him every day, the gruesome diary of a nation's inhumanity.

The murder of another salesman in Springfield, Missouri, attracted his attention, simply because it was very much like the one in Pennsboro. Of course there was no absolute evidence—no prints, no eyewitness descriptions. Waters stood in the dead man's motel room days later, with sullenly puzzled local police at his side, and recognized the feel of this crime at once. Now he perceived a direction as well: Marianne Thibault had been wrong. Karl was going home. He called the closest bureau office immediately and requested tickets for Tucson, Arizona.

* * *

# Tucson, Arizona

David turned off the television, tired of the endless repetition of his video games. He had mastered them all so that any real challenge was gone. He tried to create competition with himself by recording his scores and trying to exceed them, but it wasn't enough. Maybe Mom would rent him a new game this weekend. He decided to ask her in the morning while she drove him to school.

She had promised to be home early tonight. She said it was a business thing, a dinner with important clients. He knew she would get home as soon as she could. This wasn't like those times she had gone out with Mr. Grissom (who David liked, kind of) or Mr. Haldron (who he didn't like at all).

He had decided to make himself a banana milkshake, determined not to make a mess, when the phone rang. Its first sound shocked him, like an alarm going off. He jumped away from the refrigerator, his eyes wide. Looking from the kitchen through the silent house, he walked slowly to the phone and pulled it from its cradle.

"Hello?" he whispered.

"Hi, son. It's Dad!"

The boy's heart sang. Finally! It had been so long. He had thought maybe something bad had happened. But now everything was going to be all right.

"Dad," he said earnestly, "where are you? When are you coming? I've been waiting and waiting. When can I tell Mom? Where—"

"Hold on, Tiger! Hold on! So many questions. I knew you must be anxious, so I had to call. It won't be much longer now, maybe another month."

David gasped audibly. "Another month? That's so long! Can't I see you, Dad? Can't you come now?"

Karl sighed. "Nobody wants to see you more than I do, David. Still, we're going to have to wait, just a little more. I'm on a special mission, you see, and I can't come to get you till it's over. You understand, don't you?"

The boy reluctantly agreed. "It's okay, Dad. I understand, but it's not fair." He stifled a sob. "You've already been away so long. And you were real sick—in the hospital all that time! Why can't they find somebody else? I miss you, Dad." He swallowed heavily, trying to stop his tears.

Karl was near tears as well. "Oh, David," he sighed. "You know I don't want to stay away. No one can do this job except me—that's the problem. Now, we've both got to be soldiers. Okay?"

"Okay, Dad. Can you at least tell me where we're going to go?"

"Sure, Tiger. You deserve to know. Remember, now, this is still secret agent stuff. You can't tell anybody else, not yet. Not even your mom."

The boy answered gravely, his small voice low. "I know, Dad. I promise I won't tell. I've never told."

His father's voice grew warm. "I know, David. You're the best secret agent I've ever had, son. So tell me, have you ever heard of Brazil?"

David had. He visualized the globe in his room, thinking about the big triangular country that covered most of South America.

"Wow, Dad! That's a long way from here! Do they speak English? Where will I go to school? Do they have scouts there? How about video games?" The questions poured out.

Karl chuckled, a warm, low sound. "Whoa, tiger. Too many questions for tonight. Yes, it is a long way off, but that's okay. No, they don't speak English there; they speak a language called Portuguese. It's like Spanish. I'm sure they've got scouts, and you'll go to the neatest school you've ever been to. Now, I've got to go—"

"Oh, Dad. One more thing. I forgot to tell you. A man came to our house the other night. To see mom."

"A man? Do you know his name?"

"His name was Carpenter. You know what? He was a real police detective. He even showed me his badge."

On the other end of the line, Karl frowned. Probably investigating the Grissom thing, but he couldn't be sure. "Listen to me, David," he said.

"Okay, Dad."

"If the policeman comes back, you must pay attention to what he asks your mom. Make some notes. Try to remember all of it. Then, the next time I call, you must report to me, just like a real secret agent."

"Okay, Dad, but why?"

"Because this may have to do with my mission, that's why. Can you do it, son?"

There was no doubt in the boy's mind. "Of course. I'd do anything for you. I love you, Dad."

"I love you too, son, with all of my heart. Now I have to go.

Remember what I said. Take good notes. Learn all you can about Brazil!"

"I will, Dad. I can't wait. Here's your kisses!" He kissed the phone that brought his father's voice to him, then hung it up, and ran to the living room. His mother found him later sleeping on the couch, tucked between volumes B and P from their encyclopedia set and a large world atlas.

# CHAPTER 7

## Tucson, Arizona—October 18

Perry Haldron sat in the private office that was also his den, deep in thought. He could remain silent and unmoving for hours at a time while he turned the events of the day over in his mind—replaying them until their outcomes suited him. His son and his wife knew better than to disturb him. Though Perry gave many the impression that he was jovial man, they knew that his mood could change in an instant and that his dark side was utterly black. Of course, he would always apologize later. Even so, the stings of his shocking slaps and the echoes of his harsh words, bitterly remembered over the years, had built a high wall between his family and him. It was a wall he had enjoyed building.

As a partner and vice president for Janes and Delott, one of the Southwest's leading construction and architectural firms, Perry's problems should have been few. Though times were lean, a big company like J & D could always rely on its share of state and county contracts to keep the wolves from the door.

It was the big, private contracts that made the accountants happy, though. And such projects were still available, even in these tough times. Perry had built his career on his ability to find and close the big jobs. Now the magic seemed to have left him.

Oh, he had been close, several times. Unlike before, in his recent efforts, some unexpected problem, some tiny flaw, had continued to thwart him.

Most recently, he had lost Cobble Creek Mall by a hair's breadth, bested by Geller Associates of all outfits! Who could have expected a piss-ant company like that to come out of the woodwork? It was true—their design had been brilliant. He got a copy as soon as it was presented and had worked through the night in a desperate effort to save the contract.

Futile! There was no way to rework the J & D design, which was similar to many others the giant firm had presented over the last decade. A tried-and-true formula! Who could know that the developers—out of sheer conceit, nothing more—would push convention aside in favor of unproven innovation from an unknown firm.

Someday, someday soon perhaps, they would be sorry. For now, it was Perry Haldron's neck on the line. He had bet his reputation on this one, and he had come up short. Try as he might, he could not turn these events from negative to positive. Even in the biased theater of his own mind, their sting remained sharp, no matter how he tried to reshape them. He could imagine the whispers as he walked to his office and the hidden smiles of the young Turks who wanted his job, his office, his power. He would show them, though. Something was bound to come up. He had beaten better than them and would again.

His thick, spatulate fingers drummed the jade blotter that covered his massive mahogany desk. Perry was a square, thickly built man, low browed and heavily muscled. He still resembled the halfback he had been twenty-five years ago, and aside from some thickening around the waist, his physique had lost little of its youthful tone. He looked powerful, as though he could move obstacles from his path. He could, and he did.

The phone on his desk rang several times before he noticed it. It was his private line, inaccessible to the rest of the house. Who could be calling? He carefully raised the receiver to his ear.

"Hello?"

"Excuse me," came the clipped reply. "Am I speaking to Mr. Perry Haldron?"

"Why, yes. Who—"

"Mr. Haldron, good evening. I'm calling you from KQIT, your station for music from the sixties, the seventies, the eighties, and today."

Perry became angry. A promotion! How had they gotten his number? Someone would be in trouble for this. He started to speak, but the cultured voice continued before his words were formed.

"Mr. Haldron, we at KQIT are grateful for your part in making our station a part of your workplace. Because you were instrumental in making us the background music in your offices, your name was submitted for our drawing. Congratulations, sir! You've won!"

"Won? Won what? What are you—" Perry couldn't remember any of this.

The calm voice continued as though he had not spoken at all. "Your prize is an all-expenses-paid weekend in Lake Tahoe for you and your wife. With our sincere compliments, sir. Details are on their way to you by mail."

"Hmm. Weekend, you say. What's the catch?"

"Why, nothing, sir, aside from enjoying yourself. Of course, someone from our staff will contact you for a brief interview while you're there. PR—I'm sure you understand."

Perry's confusion gave way to elation. Finally, some good luck! "Certainly!" he boomed, smiling broadly. "And I'm happy to accept, Mr.—ah, your name, sir?"

"Theobald, Mr. Haldron. Malcolm Theobald. Happy to speak to you and to bring you this good news. If it's not premature, how soon do you think you'll take advantage of this prize? We'd like to get things rolling, you see."

They would indeed, Perry thought. These promotions aged quickly. "Within the next three weeks, I'm sure," he answered.

"Well, as I've said, all arrangements will be made. You'll get full instructions by mail. Thank you, Mr. Haldron, and have a good time. Good night."

"Good night." Perry hung up the phone and then leaned back in his overstuffed executive chair, deep in thought once again. A weekend to look forward to—but who to take with him? Surely not his wife. The idea was ludicrous. He and Carol had not been intimate, or even friendly for that matter, for years. Oh, she was attractive enough, in a pale, gray sort of way—certainly acceptable for the functions they had to attend as a couple. She lacked the fiber, the strength he looked for in his intimate partners, however.

Perry demanded absolute compliance from the women he took, but he enjoyed it best when he knew there was still resistance behind it. Since his rise to power at J & D, the company had become the field for most of his conquests. There was always a girl in the typing pool or the drafting department who was either hungry with ambition or afraid of losing the job she had. It had become increasingly easy to spot such a woman. Once he'd identified a candidate, all it took was a discreet lunch and a few suggestions before the contest of wills began. It was a contest he always won.

True, a few had walked away. Not many, though. Most consented to his desires. Some even seemed to truly enjoy themselves, although that never really mattered. In the end, of course, he moved on to a new partner. Even so, some lingered for a long time.

Marcie, his current mistress, had been with him for almost three months. He had found her in legal, about to be fired for substandard typing skills. Her strong features, fiery red hair, and supple young body had appealed to him immediately. Better yet, she understood him perfectly! There was no questioning or feigned shock or surprise when he outlined their arrangement. He knew she probably hated him. She knew her job would end the day he no longer wanted her. Tucson had few jobs for a young single mother with little job training and certainly none that paid as well as Janes and Delott.

They met twice a week. She would rent the motel room and leave a key in his desk. That afternoon, he would leave his meetings and spend the hours till early evening with her. His routine was almost always the same. She would remove his clothes, kneel at his feet, take him in her mouth, then bathe him, remove her own clothes, and await his further commands. These varied, according to his mood.

Through it all, she stared into his eyes, showing the spirit that still excited him. Without a word, her steady gaze proved she had not yet given up, not yet given in to his will. She was simply complying to save her life.

He made up his mind. He would take Marcie on this free holiday. She had never been forced to bear his attentions for so long a time.

Perhaps this would finally break her. He savored the idea as he silently considered how he would tell her when they met the next time. He smiled again. Not a bad ending to the day after all.

* * *

# October 19

When Chris got to work he found a man waiting by his desk, neatly dressed in shades of gray and black with an unobtrusive overcoat draped beside his chair—in a place where few people wore coats and ties at all—and his quiet patience said federal government. The man's eyes inventoried Chris with silent efficiency as he rose, extending his hand. "Sergeant Carpenter, I've been waiting to see you. Special Agent Thomas Waters, FBI."

They shook hands briefly, and then both sat down. "Agent Waters, what can I do for you?" Chris asked. "I'm working purely local stuff right now."

"Your lieutenant tells me you did the local work on the Grissom-Clooney murder. I'd like to talk to you about that."

"On what basis?" All levels of law enforcement have their own jurisdictions, their own turf. Most police departments are sensitive to invasion of their backyards by the feds.

Waters sighed inwardly. He had hoped he could get information without much explanation, but he could see that Carpenter was much too bright to give in so easily. "As part of your follow-up, you interviewed one of Grissom's former girlfriends—a Marianne Thibault."

Chris nodded. "Yeah, but she couldn't help much. She hadn't seen him in a couple of years."

"I know. I've read your reports. Your work is excellent, by the way. It's thorough and well written."

"Thanks. I still don't see any federal connection."

"Okay, try this. Thibault's husband, Karl, was sent up for murdering her boyfriend with a big kitchen knife. Did you read that file?"

Chris had. It had been big news, as well: "Tortured Nam Vet

Cracks, Murders Wife's Lover." The media had had a field day. The story was simple enough. Marianne had been cheating on her husband with a pilot from Davis-Monthan, the nearby air force base. On the night of the crime, the pilot had driven Marianne home. Karl followed him back to his base quarters and attacked him with a large kitchen knife, stabbing him more than thirty times.

At the trial, Karl's life had been saved by the evidence that he suffered from profound and deepening mental illness stemming from his combat experience in Southeast Asia. Also, he had been drinking heavily while on considerable medication. That plus the jury's reluctance to condemn a man for killing an adulterer had resulted in an insanity verdict. Karl had been consigned to a maximum-security federal institution in West Virginia. Inwardly, Chris shuddered. Benniston was rumored to be like being buried alive.

"If you've read the file," Waters continued, "you know that Karl's escaped."

Chris nodded, scowling. "Yeah, I know. The wife says he won't come home, and we've been surveilling the house for over a month now. No result."

"I think she's wrong," the FBI agent said. He spoke softly, almost as if he were talking to himself. "I've traced him through the murders he's committed on his way here, the ones he's done to get the money and the cars he's needed. I think he's in this area. I can feel it! I think he killed Grissom for the same reason he killed Captain McDonall in 1981: because the man touched his wife. I think he'll kill anyone he finds out has been with her. She's the key to catching him."

Chris shook his head. "You're off base, Waters. First of all, how would Karl even know about Grissom? His wife—his ex-wife now—hasn't dated the guy in years. Read the report. Second, how would Karl know where to find Grissom? Remember, the guy was killed in Vegas, not here. Look, it's a simple case, really. Grissom and his girlfriend go to Vegas. Grissom tries to score some drugs, gets involved with some heavy people. They get mad; he gets iced. It happens around here."

Waters continued to argue. "Look at the similarities—Grissom was killed with a kitchen knife. The coroner identified the serrations beyond doubt."

Chris nodded grimly. "Yeah. Do you know how many people around here buy it the same way every year? These knives are common. They're used all the time."

"Okay, Sergeant, explain this to me: explain the way Grissom was killed."

Chris was silent for several seconds. "I'll admit, that's got us wondering," he said slowly. "We figure Grissom was tortured, maybe for information about his bank cards. Both his accounts were drawn down a little later."

"We both know how people here make somebody talk," Waters said. "They use cigarettes to burn their victims. Nobody pulls a man's guts out like measuring tape."

Chris had to agree. "Okay, you're right. What's the point?"

Waters looked at him sadly. "You're about five years too young to know what the point is," he said. "There was a place where they treated people like that. I was there. So was Karl. I'd forgotten about it. I guess he hasn't."

"You mean Vietnam."

"That's right, Sergeant. Believe me—I'm not grasping at straws. Everything I see points to Karl. Here. And if he is here, you've got trouble. By my count, he's killed six people already, and he won't stop by himself. He's smart, too smart to make very many mistakes."

Chris found himself beginning to agree with the man. "All right, Agent Waters—"

"Call me Tom."

"Tom, what do we do? Where do we start? Tucson isn't exactly the Naked City, but there's an awful lot of places to hide."

"We have to start with the wife. I believe that Karl will be drawn to her."

"He hasn't been. At least not yet. We've watched that place day and night."

"I know. I've seen the reports. He must have some kind of plan, but I'm sure that he'll eventually go to her."

"Do you think she knows what he's doing?"

"I think we have to talk to her—soon."

"Okay. I'll set it up. When's good for you?"

"Tomorrow. Today I'm down at the courthouse all day, going through the transcripts of the trial. I'm hoping some thread of his motive is sitting there. He was on the stand for almost three days."

Both men rose, and Chris extended his hand again. "Tom, I hope you're wrong, but I'll do my best to help. See you tomorrow."

As Waters turned to leave, the phone rang. "It's for you," Chris called, handing him the receiver.

Chris watched the conversation with interest. Waters said very little and took many notes. Finally, the agent rose from his seat.

"Book the flight," he said. "I'll be at the airport within the hour." He hung up and turned to Chris. "Our meeting will have to wait," he said in a low voice. "I have to get to Minnesota as soon as possible. Two murders have just been discovered there. Both salesmen in motels. Both strangled and robbed. Karl Thibault's fingerprints were found in one of the rooms."

"I guess that shoots a big hole in your theory," Chris said with a sigh of relief. "I was beginning to believe it myself. Looks like you were wrong."

Waters nodded as he hurried from the room. He walked from the building to his nondescript Plymouth, wincing at the bright sunlight. "I still think he's coming here, but I hope I'm wrong, Chris." He thought as he slid behind the wheel, *If I'm not, a lot more people are going to die.*

\* \* \*

# In the Air between Seattle and Los Angeles

Karl settled back in his seat, nursing a martini. This "business trip" had been mildly disappointing, but these things averaged out over time.

Since he had started his fund-raising activities three weeks ago, his plan had worked flawlessly.

Actually, the idea had hit him during the Grissom interrogation. Harry, in a moment of great pain about an hour before he died, had blurted out the PIN to his bank card, hoping that the information would somehow save his life.

Later, as he drove from Las Vegas, Karl had stopped at a string of ATMs and had successfully drawn down those accounts by several hundred dollars. It occurred to him that this could be a way to raise money for his escape to Brazil with David.

Karl knew he couldn't work the area near his hiding place, not with police already questioning Marianne. No, he would have to be far cleverer than that. So he picked locations distant from Nevada.

The first time, for instance, he chose Charlotte, North Carolina. He booked a flight out of Las Vegas, paying in cash that he'd gotten from Grissom and what was left from the two men he'd killed earlier. Landing at his destination, he dispatched his first victim in a men's room, simply for money and credit cards. He immediately used the cards he'd taken to book a flight late that night to Chicago, through Washington. Then, renting a car, he drove to his first motel.

He picked a man who was traveling alone and stupid from drinking at the motel bar. He used the choke hold he'd been taught so well all those years before. Then, abandoning his rental car for that of his victim, he drove on to another location.

He had been nervous the first time, but as he refined his technique, his confidence grew. These men were so vulnerable, and they carried such large sums of money! Karl limited himself to two motels per trip (in his mind, he thought of them as "raids"). He was always careful to book several return flights to different places using a variety of credit cards. He was able to sell most of the extra tickets to people in the waiting areas. That would confuse investigators. Finally, one of the tickets was always paid for in cash, and that destination was always a bus trip from Las Vegas.

After South Carolina, he had chosen Minnesota. Now, he was returning from the Seattle-Tacoma area. This time, much more sure of himself, he had tried keeping his victims alive long enough to get the numbers that allowed access to their bank cards (he had been successful once in the two attempts). By his calculations, after expenses, he had netted close to $40,000 already—almost half of what he thought he needed for his eventual escape. He sipped his drink. With any luck, he'd be through by January.

# CHAPTER 8

# Lake Tahoe, California—November 3

Marcie Sherman stood in the lobby of the Lakecrest Hotel, nervously glancing from their luggage to the counter where Perry was checking them in. She was a tall, healthy, young woman, whose good posture and firm features spoke well of her small-town Midwest background. Her freckles added dimension to the flush of a slight tan, accentuating deep blue eyes and coppery red hair. Her wide, handsome mouth showed no smile today, just a flat line of tension.

She had dreaded this weekend. Perry had broken the news to her two weeks ago during one of their afternoons together. His beating had been particularly brutal, beginning with her naked buttocks and working up her back, ending with two vicious slaps to her breasts. Finally, he had left her to sob on the crumpled disarray of the motel bed while he disappeared to wash and dress. She had relaxed, knowing that her ordeal was over.

Suddenly, he had been by her side again, looming over her and whispering in her ear. "Good news, Marcie," he had breathed. "We're going to spend a whole weekend together. On the fourth, in Tahoe. It's all been arranged. Get a babysitter for your brat. I'll pay. Think of it, Marcie. Two days, without a break. I can't wait. Can you?"

She had cringed. She couldn't help it. Later, she wondered if he had seen the fear in her eyes. If he had, she knew she would have to give up, to finally run from this monster's grasp. *Not just yet! God, please, not just yet!* In two or three more months she'd have saved enough money for the computer graphics school she was set on attending. Then she could leave. Until then, for little Andy's sake, she'd have to take the abuse he heaped on her every week and make him think she could stand it.

God, what a mess! At first it had seemed like an adventure, like something out of a romance novel. She'd been bored. After high school, courses at the Davenport Community College had seemed like just more of the same—the same friends, the same boys. Nothing ever changed.

Charlie Burris was different. He was from out of town, drove a dented pickup truck, wore those tight, faded jeans and flannel shirts. He always had beer, smoked cigarettes without filters, and had a smile that melted her heart. Before she knew what was happening to her, they were driving out of town together in that old truck, south on Illinois 67, headed for Saint Louis. Her savings had paid for the gas.

It had been fun, living in cheap motels, partying, making love all the time. After a while their hectic pace had slowed. By then, St. Louis had given way to Tulsa and Tulsa to Abilene. Charlie and Marcie had worked from time to time but only to pay for food, beer, cigarettes, and enough gas to move on to the next town.

Marcie had decided to get a real job, but Charlie had scoffed. "Hell, babe, there's about a million miles of country we ain't seen yet," he'd said, laughing and scratching his head. In the end he'd gone along with her. He'd even gotten a job himself, a real job as a mechanic at a transmission repair place.

They had rented a small apartment after about a month, and things had seemed okay. She got work as a warehouse clerk, wishing she'd paid more attention in typing class. On the weekends, they'd look at used furniture, buying the first few pieces of the home they were beginning.

Marcie wasn't surprised when the pregnancy came. Charlie had always refused to use a condom, and she'd never kept up with her pills after they left Davenport. Besides, she could sense her need for a child, to complete the family she now wanted to build.

She thought Charlie was happy too. He had grinned and laughed and slapped his thighs, and he'd made love to her that night just like the first time. After that, he seemed so gentle, so concerned about her comfort.

Within less than month her plans began to unravel. Charlie started coming home late and keeping his paychecks. Finally, he was home before her, finishing his third beer as she walked in. "Fuck it, honey. I quit the damn job," he'd said simply. They hadn't treated him right, he explained. Always giving him the dirty work. Always blaming him when things went wrong. What was so bad about having a few beers on a break anyhow? he'd asked as he opened another.

He promised he'd get another job and had gone looking every day—or so he'd said. There was no unemployment (he'd been fired for cause), and her pay alone couldn't handle the rent. Not with his beer and cigarettes as well. In the end, they'd snuck out of town, leaving most of the furniture and all of the unpaid bills. She was five months pregnant. He'd gotten a call from a friend in Tucson, offering a place for them to stay.

By the time Andrew Burris was born, Charlie had long since moved on—to Bakersfield, she heard later. He just couldn't wait, he'd said. She could catch up in a few months. Marcie dismissed that forlorn hope. Charlie hadn't been alone when he had driven out of town. She knew there was nothing more for her to seek with him.

She gave Andy his father's last name even though there had been no marriage or even the thought of one. Somewhere along the line, in Tulsa she thought, he had bought her a ring—a simple band of gold she still wore. From the first, she could see Charlie in the boy and could imagine that same crooked smile on the tiny face.

Six weeks after she left the hospital with Andy, she started looking for a job. She tried waitressing but couldn't stand the casual rudeness of the customers, the low pay, the bad hours, and the poor management. In desperation, she lied about her typing skills and landed the job at J & D. She had hoped she could pick up the speed and accuracy she lacked. It hadn't worked. She had already been counseled twice and knew that her termination notice was imminent when Perry Haldron had invited her to lunch.

She had known the purpose of his attentions from the start. His adventures made up a good part of the coffee-break gossip she had heard. She had met his last mistress a few times, before the haunted young woman quit so abruptly. Their lunch had taken place at a secluded restaurant about two miles from work. He had been carefully polite and didn't get to his proposals until after the meal. "I need a friend," he had said with a sigh. "A soul mate. The pressures on me are tremendous, and no one understands. Not even my dear wife."

She had almost laughed. "Mr. Haldron," she had said with the biggest smile she could muster, "there's no need to beat around the bush. I'm in trouble. J & D is going to fire me, and they've got good reason. I need the paycheck. I'd lay with the devil himself if it would save my job. You just show me how you want it, mister, and you'll have it just that way. Starting right now, if you need to." Calling on courage she hadn't thought she had, she had reached under the table and stroked his thigh.

Her ordeal began two days later. He had explained his needs in detail, as well as the punishment he would mete out for every error or oversight. As time went by, his abuse increased in both severity and frequency. She managed to withstand it, totaling every week's addition to her savings account in her head, over and over, as she cringed and moaned beneath his heavy fists. When he entered her, it was always from the rear so that he could slap and beat her while they coupled. She was never prepared since her pleasure didn't matter to him. It was abuse—nothing more.

At least he was punctual. He always left the motel before seven, so she knew exactly how long she had to put up with his use of her. That was what made this weekend so horrible! There would be no end, no stopping. She wasn't sure she could stand it. Maybe if she pretended to be ill, maybe then ...

Perry gently pulled at her elbow, disturbing her thoughts. "My goodness, Marcie," he purred, "you certainly were lost in another world. Come on, dear. Our rooms are ready now."

She nodded dumbly. Shoulders slumped, she wandered after him to the electric cart that would take them to their cabin. The Lakecrest consisted of a central building and restaurant surrounded by more than fifty individual units set on a winding series of paved trails that ended at the lakefront. The view was breathtaking, and even though this hotel was older than many in Tahoe, it still maintained a steady level of business.

In no time at all, the little cart stopped beside the small house that would be her prison for the next two days. She wondered if the beautiful scenery would make her torture any less difficult to bear. Their luggage was quickly unloaded, the tip paid, and Perry and Marcie were alone.

Perry quickly locked and bolted the door and closed the curtains. He walked slowly toward her, hands on his hips. "No reason to waste any time, is there? Come to me. I'm ready."

Marcie quickly dropped to her hands and knees, as she had been taught, and crawled toward him. Reaching his feet, she kissed each shoe, careful to use as much saliva as possible in order to leave clear evidence of her attention. Then, rising to her knees, she began to slowly unbuckle his belt. He stood in silence, watching her closely.

The phone rang, startling them both. "Damn!" cried Perry, reaching down to slap her sharply across the face as he turned to pick it up. "Hello!" he shouted hoarsely.

"Mr. Haldron? So glad you've arrived. It's me, Malcolm Theobald. KQIT? I must have missed you at the lodge. Sorry to disturb, but I must know when we can meet for the interview. Surely you recall."

Perry struggled to control himself. This simpering wimp was interfering with his most important personal moments! Still, if he was put off, the little shit would probably call back again and again. Might as well get it over with. He forced calm joviality into his voice. "Yes, Theobald. Of course. Glad to take the time. Say, this place is beautiful, isn't it? Tell me, can you come over here? I'm not planning to leave my cabin for a while, not till dinner, at least."

The clipped voice responded at once. "Of course. Glad to come up! I'll bring some champagne on the house, a token of our thanks! Shall we say, ah, half an hour?"

Half an hour would be fine. By then, Marcie would have had time to complete the project she had only just started. He hung up the phone and turned to her. "We'll be having a guest, my dear. Keep quiet and be polite. In the meantime, I believe there was something you were working on. Better start again. With the shoes, please."

\* \* \*

# Seattle, Washington

Thomas Waters rose from his desk, rubbing fatigue from his eyes. The local police had been helpful, and their work at the crime scenes had been more thorough than he had expected—a welcome surprise. There was no question that the murders of two salesmen here and two more in Minnesota were the work of the same criminal. Two more in North Carolina were probably his, as well. Karl Thibault had done them all, Waters had no doubt.

The man's motive was obvious: money. He had probably realized the potential when he killed to change cars in Pennsboro, right after his escape. His victims were alone and wouldn't be missed for long periods of time. Many carried large amounts of cash, and all had several credit and bank cards. Left in their motel rooms, they wouldn't be discovered for at least a day, maybe longer. By then, using their cars, he would be many miles away. Booking his flights with their credit cards, he could be in another part of the country in a matter of hours. He could strike anywhere at will. Karl's base had to be found—the place he went back to after every crime. It was a search for a malignant needle in a continent-wide haystack.

Waters started with two guesses: first, that Karl hid somewhere near his wife's home, and second, that he used the credit cards of his victims to travel. Clever though he was, Karl might not be aware of the advances that had happened in computer technology during the last five years. Faster processing and relational databases made complicated searches for information relatively easy, if big enough machines could be accessed.

Waters got the access by begging, borrowing, or outright stealing it from other departments and agencies. He traced all tickets booked from airports adjacent to the crime areas in North Carolina, Minnesota, and Washington within three days of the murders, paying specific attention to any booked with the dead salesmen's credit cards. A total of twenty were found: Karl had covered his tracks by booking to several places. Ticket agents, flight service crews, and other passengers were located and interviewed. Seventeen passengers who used the tickets were found. All told the same story: a man had sold them tickets they needed for an impossibly low price, right at the gate. In all cases, Karl fit the description of the man.

Karl had been smart, Waters realized. He had not used the credit cards of his victims to book his own flights but only to camouflage his movements, to waste the time of the pursuers he had known he must have by now.

Okay, back to square one. Waters made another assumption: Karl could have no plastic of his own. He would have to use cash to purchase his tickets. So his massive computer power found all tickets purchased with cash at the airports already identified on the days when the other tickets were given away. Of the thousands of people identified, most could be eliminated immediately. Over six hundred more were interviewed by phone or in person. In the end, only twenty could not be found. Of these, five had landed in the Midwest or Southwest; when plotted on a map, they created a lozenge that extended west from Dallas to San Diego and north from El Paso to Denver. Karl's hiding place was somewhere in that space, Waters was sure.

The designated area was huge, filled with small towns and obscure motels where the psychopath might hide. Assuming that Karl might further obscure his base, the special agent sent the killer's description to all train stations, airline ticket offices, bus depots, and rental car agencies within the borders of the area he had established. Desk agents were given Karl's picture and told to watch for tickets purchased with cash. Now Waters could only wait. He hoped no one else would have to die to make the territory he searched smaller. He knew Karl would be caught, but when? And at what price?

# CHAPTER 9

# Lake Tahoe, California—November 3

Karl walked toward the Haldron cabin, careful to keep to the shaded side of the trail. He hated to be seen by passersby. He couldn't kill them all, and those hunting him would be thorough.

Within a few minutes, he was at the unit's door and tapped carefully. The man who answered didn't fit Karl's idea of Marianne's taste in partners, but then, neither had the other fellow. Darkly tanned and heavily muscled, he was built like a side of beef. He smiled as he extended a large square hand, but Haldron's eyes were not happy at all. Karl chuckled inwardly. He would enjoy his time with this one. He shook the hand. "Mr. Haldron? Malcolm Theobald. Happy to meet you, sir. I trust the cabin is adequate?"

Perry nodded brusquely. "Yes, it's very nice, Mr. Theobald. Very nice. Though I'd have liked something on the Nevada side." He moved aside with obvious reluctance, allowing his unwanted guest to enter his room.

Karl laughed. "Gift horses, Mr. Haldron. Mustn't look them in the mouth, you know. Now, just a few questions and I'll be out of your hair. I've brought a recorder along, as you can see." He reached into the gym bag he carried, removed the small black box, and placed it on a low table between two chairs. "First, let's sample the champagne I promised, to put us in a festive mood."

Addressing the bag again, he pulled out plastic cups and a bottle. Looking for a place to put them down, he noticed Marcie for the first time. She sat silently on a couch at the other end of the room, gazing fixedly out a large window. Reacting to his attention, she jerked her head to face him. *She's scared*, Karl thought. *Not of me. She's frightened of Haldron.*

Realizing she'd been seen, Perry spoke, his low voice bubbling from an amiable chuckle. "Ah, Mr. Theobald, let me introduce Marcie, my, ah, companion this weekend. Marcie, Mr. Theobald. His radio station made our little vacation possible."

Marcie rose stiffly from her chair and walked carefully toward Karl, her eyes nervously darting from him to Haldron and back again. Karl recognized her movements. He had seen the same reaction at Benniston when inmates had been beaten too often. *He hurts her*, Karl decided. His anger toward this man increased. He knew a thick, sensual feeling would soon engulf him, as it always did when he killed. He prepared himself to give in to it, to flow with it. *Soon, soon.* Calming himself with great effort, he turned his attention to the champagne, hoping Haldron had not seen the tremor in his hands.

"Ah, Marcie. So nice to meet you. What a lovely young lady. Well, Mr. Haldron, let me pour us all a drink." Quickly, almost feverishly, he stripped the foil from the bottle and popped its cork into a towel. Then, with his back to Haldron, he poured three cups, turned, and handed one to each of his hosts. "A toast," he declared, smiling wildly as he raised his cup. "A toast to an exciting future!"

They all drank. Marcie drained her cup in a single swallow, while Perry sipped, taking his time. Karl, his face flushed with mounting excitement he could barely contain, gulped his down as well. "Now, Mr. Haldron," he said, laughing and shaking his head as he bounded across the room back to the low table. "Let me turn on this tape recorder, so we can begin."

"Yes, indeed, Mr. Theobald." Perry walked to a low chair by the table, having finished his champagne. Theobald was acting strangely. So excited! Perhaps he wasn't used to giving these interviews. *Or maybe I intimidate him*, Perry mused. He often had that effect on people. *That must be it*, he decided, smugly chuckling to himself as he relaxed in the chair. He noticed that Marcie had retreated to the other end of the room, just as she had been warned to do.

Theobald was before him, pacing in a small arc in front of his chair. "Now, Mr. Haldron. May I call you Perry?"

Perry nodded brusquely. He felt a deep lethargy permeating him, a profound fatigue he had never felt before. Theobald stopped his nervous pacing and leaned close to Perry's face. "Comfy? You never know with these drugs. I've seen them work, but I was never allowed to use them. I'll bet you're pretty tired right now, aren't you, Perry? Hard to move those arms of yours? Well, just relax and enjoy it. Things will get much more lively after a while. By the way, the stuff is called Haldol. I put quite a dose in your drink." He giggled. "Now, just to make sure, I'm going to give you and your lovely lady a shot of Seconal. It should put you out. I hope so. It always worked at Benniston." He reached in his bag and produced a hypodermic needle.

Perry realized something was wrong, very wrong. He tried to speak, but the voice he heard was a meaningless, blurred mumble. He tried to move, but his limbs felt encased in lead. Oddly, he felt no fear or discomfort. His only desire was to stay where he was, motionless, for the rest of time. He watched as the man he knew as Theobald approached him with the needle and roughly pulled up his sleeve, noticed the tiny sting as the injection invaded his forearm, felt a brief wave of nausea and overwhelming lethargy, and then tumbled into unconsciousness.

* * *

When Perry awoke, the first sensations he noticed were a terrible, splitting headache and a foul taste in his mouth. Attempting to put his hand to his aching head, he found his arms securely tied to a chair. He felt his legs secured as well. As his consciousness increased, he realized that he was naked and that the bottom cushion of the chair had been removed, causing his buttocks to sag through the slats. He shook his head violently and then howled in anger. Pushing against the floor, he tried mightily to free himself.

Theobald stepped into his field of vision. The man had removed his jacket and tie and put on rubber gloves—the kind housewives wear to do dishes—and a cheesecloth apron. As he moved closer to Perry, he smiled.

"Ah, Mr. Haldron. Awake at last. You were out a long time. I was getting worried that I'd given you too much. That would have made me very sad. I've worked so hard to arrange our meeting, and I've waited a long time."

Perry bellowed in rage. "Who are you, you son of a bitch? Let me free right now! You may think you'll get away with this, but let me tell you, let me tell you right now——"

His captor hit him across the mouth as hard as he could. The force of the blow loosened several teeth and stunned Perry momentarily. He shook his head, moaning.

"There now," Karl hissed. "Does that put things in perspective?" He laughed. "You asshole. Do you think you can cow me with your threats? You should be begging, not yelling. Begging for your life."

Perry looked at him, confused. It had been a long time since a situation had been so thoroughly out of his control. His mouth hurt. He was trapped by this maniac. "Who are you?" he asked in a low voice. "What do you want?"

"Sensible questions, finally. Let me introduce myself. My name is Karl Thibault, Mr. Haldron. I'm the husband of the woman you've been abusing. As for what I want, that should be obvious. Did you think you could get away with defiling my wife?"

The gravity of the situation dawned on Perry. Marianne's husband! He was a psychopath, had been locked up for years for McDonall's murder. How had he gotten out? "Listen," he said thickly. "You've got it wrong. I helped Marianne. Nothing more. If it hadn't been for me, she'd have lost her job at J & D. They wanted to fire her, you know, after the trial. I stopped them. You should thank me."

Karl laughed again, turned, and left the room. When he returned, he carried an odd assortment of equipment. Perry couldn't see it clearly in the gloom, but it seemed to consist of a car battery, some wire, and some kind of control box.

Karl sat down on the bed facing Perry and began to set up his equipment. "You know, Perry, I almost believe you," he said, humming and chuckling as he carefully laid the wires under Perry's chair. They ended in alligator clips. "It would be a shame to punish you for being a good Samaritan." He stood up and frowned. "I'm just not sure. I'd hate to be wrong. I've waited so long for this, you see.

"So we're going to try a test. I'm going to ask you a question. If I'm not satisfied with your answer, I'll ask it again. In fact, I'll ask as many times as I think I have to."

Perry allowed himself to laugh. "Ask away. I'll always give you the same answer. You'll see." *What are those wires for?* he wondered.

Still humming to himself, Karl reached under Perry's chair. "Will you? I don't know. That hasn't been my experience. In Vietnam, where I first saw this used, the answers varied widely! The little major I worked with said he learned this from the French. The parts are available at any hardware store." Suddenly, he reached under the chair and pulled Perry's scrotal sack from between his legs. Quickly, professionally, he applied the alligator clips to Perry's genitals, causing the frightened man to howl in pain.

Standing once again, Karl slapped Perry across the face with his left hand. In his right, he held a bulky black switch box. It reminded Perry of the controls he'd had for his electric trains when he was a boy. "Shut up!" Karl snapped. "Now, listen to me. You and I are going to play a little game. I'm going to ask you a question. If I don't believe your answer, you'll get some of this."

He pulled the switch.

Perry stiffened in his chair. The constriction of his muscles strained the bonds that held him. The pain was more than he had ever felt, more than he could stand. He sucked air sharply and then gave it up in a keening, bawling shriek that terminated as he explosively vomited all the food in his stomach, spraying the floor in front of him.

Karl turned the power off. He had seen this method used in the field but only against those who had been aware of its purpose. Haldron had been genuinely surprised, he was sure. Leaving the man to moan and gurgle, his head lolling on his fouled chest, Karl turned to the attention of a new sound coming from the king-sized bed. Marcie was stirring.

He walked to her side. Her arms, legs, and hands were bound securely, and she was tied to the bed. "What are you doing?" she whispered faintly. "What's happening to Perry?" She struggled to turn face up with only partial success.

Karl stroked her auburn hair. "Turnabout is fair play," he said softly. "Perry's getting back what he likes to give out. Pay attention. Listen. He's about to be punished for everything he's done to you." Humming a nameless tune, he went to the bathroom, dampened a towel, and then sprang back to his victim's side.

Perry was recovering from the shock of the immense pain he'd just felt, moaning and weeping to himself. "I'm sorry," he murmured as he wept. "I'll pay anything. I'll never do this again. Please."

Karl stroked his head softly and padded his forehead and chin with the damp towel. "I know," he sighed. "I know you won't. It will be all right." He stepped back and picked up the transformer switch again.

"Now, Perry," he said softly, almost sadly, "tell me. Tell me all of it. When did you first defile my wife, my Marianne?"

Perry tried to collect his thoughts. The pain had been awful. He had thought he was dying. This man was a lunatic. If he found out the truth about Marianne there was no telling what he might do. How could the man know anything? He had been in prison somewhere back east. Perry would bluff. He had always been able to bluff. "Look," he said, "it was never that way. Sure, we were close, but it was—"

A searing bolt of pure pain choked off his words. He was being ripped apart. He heard himself yelling, a low roar that climbed to high falsetto keening as the pain continued and then ended as he retched bitter bile. Finally, the agony ceased just before he lost all consciousness. Too weak to move, he slumped in his chair, weeping.

Karl threw a glassful of water in his face, reviving him. "Perry," he whispered, "it's too late to bluff. See how much that hurt you? Now, tell me the truth. I don't want to fry your balls to nothing, but I will. We only used this method when we didn't have a lot of time. The other side used it too. Secrets are such perishable things. You think you have to hold onto them, protect them. You don't. In the end, everything comes out, and you've ruined yourself for nothing. For nothing, Perry. Now, tell me the truth. Tell me about Marianne."

It was easy. Her memory was still vivid. He had noticed her even before the murder. But she was a competent draftsperson. Her job was in no jeopardy. No one knew of her affair with McDonall.

After the murder, during the publicity of the trial, the board had decided to sack her at once. He had intervened. Janes, chairman and son of the founder, had sneered openly. "Come on, Perry," he had said. "We've put up with your little conquests for years, but this goes too far. The woman is pretty, but the newspapers are killing us. Let it rest, will you?"

Perry had laughed. "Mr. Janes, with all respect, there's no such thing as bad publicity," he had said. "Besides, letting her go now with no other cause will get the women's libbers all over us. These gals make more decisions every day, gentlemen. I have to deal with them. Let's do a little spin control. Why not announce that we're keeping her on despite the bad situation! We'll look like heroes." In the end, they had agreed.

After that, he had been cautious. He hadn't moved right away. He had waited until he knew she was aware of why she hadn't been fired, of who her benefactor was. He knew he could depend on the company grapevine. Old man Janes was cranky and voluble.

It had taken almost a year. He was patient. Finally, he had stopped her at the company picnic, standing behind her in line for food. "I understand I have you to thank for my job, Mr. Haldron," she had said, her eyes lowered.

"Me and your excellent work, of course," he had replied glibly.

"Well, I want to thank you," she had continued, still not meeting his gaze.

He had seen his opportunity. "Of course," he had whispered, "there are still those who want you gone." His hand had brushed across her thigh, as if by accident.

She had stiffened. A bleak smile had crossed her lips. "Of course," she had answered simply. Then, after a second's hesitation, she had subtly backed against him.

"Naturally, I'll continue to do what I can," he had growled. His excitement had grown. This was going well, better than he had allowed himself to expect.

Half turning, shielding her hand from view with her paper plate, she had suddenly, brazenly stroked him through his trousers.

"I'll see you tonight. At my place," she had said. "My son is sleeping over with one of his friends."

He had gone, expecting a better-than-usual experience. She had not disappointed him.

She had known, of course, about some of his needs, some of the rules. Coffee-break gossip had taken care of that. Unlike the others, she had taken the initiative from the first, giving him pleasure he had never received from his cowed, frightened mistresses in the past. When she took him in her mouth, she paid great attention to every part of his penis, and she took every inch of him without gagging or choking. Later, when he mounted her, he was surprised to find her well lubricated, and her cries were those of pleasure, not of discomfort. Even when he beat her, she smiled as she moved willfully under his thrusts and begged him to hit her more, to split her in two. As he rose from her, having spent himself, she ducked under his blows to take him in her mouth again, stroking his balls and bringing him to a third, unexpected climax.

During the months that followed, he found himself becoming entranced with Marianne, feeling emotions he'd never had before. He still hit her, but she enjoyed it, or seemed to. She wept, but she smiled through her tears and begged him not to stop. He began losing track of the rigorous discipline he had always maintained with other women, giving himself up to the pleasure she gave him.

One afternoon, gasping as his fists conveyed his frustration at a contract he'd just lost, she had suddenly rolled from beneath him. "Perry," she had said, "you need something special today. Something you've never had. Let me give you special pleasure, darling."

Confused, he had bellowed at her to get back on the bed, but she had been adamant. "Let me help you, Perry," she had pleaded. "Please. If you don't like what I'm about to do, I'll accept any punishment you give me and ask for more."

He had grudgingly agreed, imagining the penalties she would endure later. Calmly, she gestured for him to lie on the bed. Then, reaching into a drawer, she produced three lengths of silken rope.

He rose with a start. "What the hell are you doing?" he yelled, grabbing for her.

She danced beyond his grasp. "Now, Perry, you're going to have to trust me. Lay down. Relax. You're so much bigger than I am. Do you think these little strings can hold you? Besides, you have my promise. If you don't like this, think of the discipline you'll give me."

Reluctantly, he had lain down once again. Quickly, deftly, before he could react, Marianne had tied each of his wrists to a bedpost. Now straddling his chest with her back to him, she had shown surprising strength in tying his feet together at the ankles with the third piece of rope. "You're really going to like this," she had breathed.

Intermittently frustrating and exciting him, she slowly brought him through what seemed like an eternity of increasing, maddening pleasure. Finally, she mounted him, riding him to the most intense orgasm he had ever experienced. As he spent himself, she had untied his bonds. Weak as a kitten, he had wept in her arms.

After that, Marianne had ceased to be just a thing to be used for his pleasure. In Perry's mind they had become both lovers and coconspirators, sharing the secret of his special needs. He thought of her constantly, even debating divorce. He did everything in his power to advance her career and had made sure that she came before the apprenticeship boards as quickly as possible. Since Marianne had no college degree, this was her only avenue to professional credentials.

She had continued to beguile him and seduce him with her wonderful knowledge of his cravings. He became sure she must love him, as well. Why else would she smile and laugh at his blows, bowing to his every need and rising to his desires?

Then, abruptly, it had ended. He had returned from a business trip to find her clearing out her desk. "Marianne, this can't be!" he had cried, careless of who heard him. "Who did this? I'll fix it. Don't worry."

She had stared at him coolly, continuing to pack. "Perry, stop waving your arms. You're making a fool of yourself. No one's fired me. I quit. I've gotten another job, with Geller Associates, based on the quality of my work. My work, Perry! Not whether or not I put out for a sadist."

He had gibbered in his disbelief and had started around the desk to hold her and to prove to her how he really felt. She had turned and said, her voice harsh and shrill, "Touch me, you bastard, and I'll scream my head off. I've put up with your hands on me long enough." Then, softening, she added, "Did you really think I cared, Perry? Yes, I guess you did. My God, I had to do something. You were beating me to death. I did what I had to, for my child and for my life. I'm grateful for the help you gave me. For the way you've used me, I despise you. Now leave me alone. I don't have to put up with you, not anymore."

He had grabbed her arm roughly and pulled her to him. "It's not that easy, Marianne," he had threatened. "Do you think your friends at Geller will be so anxious for you once they know you've been my whore for a year?"

Pulling herself free, she had laughed. "Are you going to tell them, Perry? Don't bother. It's old news. They hired me in spite of you. Because my work is good. Learn a lesson. Stick to people who can't make it from now on. Now go away, and never bother me again. If it comes to telling stories, I'll bet mine would be much more interesting than yours."

She had walked out of his life, and he had been powerless to stop her. For weeks, he had imagined that the people he passed in the halls were smirking behind his back. He had tried calling Geller himself, but the man had laughed at him, out loud. Finally, after weeks of humiliation, he had managed to bring in a fairly large contract, one he'd been working on for almost a year. Soon after that, he had found a new mistress—a secretary who'd been caught in some petty theft. She hadn't lasted long, but oh, how she paid for the suffering he'd had to endure.

He told Karl everything. When his memory failed him, a searing jolt of electric agony revived him. He frantically searched his memory for every detail, afraid of the pain that he knew he could not bear much longer.

Karl became bored. The man needed no more incentive. In fact, more shocks would only interfere with his confession. The words he sobbed into the recorder made Karl sick. Haldron was demented, in his own way as warped as Karl himself. A noise from the bed caught his attention. Marcie was calling to him.

"Mister?" she called softly. "Mister, what are you doing?"

He walked to her side. Perry didn't notice, engrossed as he was in completing his narrative. Karl bent over her and caressed her gently. "Why, Marcie. You can call me Karl. What am I doing? I'm making your boyfriend pay for what he did to my wife. I'm afraid he's going to suffer a great deal."

Marcie was beyond reason. Perry's brutal treatment and her own fear, compounded by what she had just witnessed, had finally propelled her into the cottony edges of insanity. But she had a desire. "I want to help," she said breathlessly.

Karl was puzzled. "Help? What do you mean?"

"I want to help you, Karl. I want to help you hurt him."

A thought occurred to Karl, an opportunity he hadn't expected. "You know I can't let you go," he said softly.

"I know," she answered dully. She had expected to die here anyway. She had been sure that Perry was going to beat her to death. "You can let me loose. I won't run. Just promise not to hurt me."

"I promise," Karl said, loosening Marcie's bonds. He untied her hands and legs but left her torso tied to the heavy bed. She wouldn't move from the room in a hurry.

He guided her to the edge of the bed. Her movements were jerky and uncoordinated. Carefully, he put the transformer in her hands. "He's almost done now, Marcie," Karl explained. "But don't start yet. Let me tell him what's going to happen first. He should know who is going to hurt him."

Perry was still talking, still remembering, when Karl walked to his side and silenced him with a sharp slap to his ear. Perry began to weep again. "Please don't hurt me anymore," he begged. "I've done what you asked. Please …"

Karl mopped Perry's brow with the damp cloth, speaking softly. "There now," he said, "our time is almost over. You've done what I asked. Look over on the bed. Your friend wants to talk to you now."

Perry looked up and noticed Marcie for the first time, staring at the awful black box she held in her hands. "Marcie!" he wailed. "Oh God, no! God, no! God, no no no no …" His words dissolved into a meaningless shriek as his most recent victim turned the switch. After a few timeless seconds, Karl gently removed the box from her nerveless hands and turned off the power. Perry convulsed for several seconds more before he collapsed into semiconsciousness, his thickened tongue protruding from between his lips.

Putting the switch box back in Marcie's hands, Karl whispered to her. "I'm going to finish Perry now. You can help. When I tell you to, turn the switch." She nodded dumbly, unable to speak. Her mind had twisted far into the numbness of lunacy.

Leaving the bed, Karl walked to Perry's side, where he doused his victim with another glass of water. "Perry," he called softly, shaking the bound man by the shoulders, "are you awake? Wake up, man. What I'm going to tell you is important."

Perry jerked to attention and tried to speak but could only moan. His eyes searched Karl's—eyes that held the same bottomless fear Karl had seen in Marcie earlier. They were the eyes of a beaten animal, the eyes of prey.

Karl took the alligator clips from Perry's ruined genitals and reattached them to his nipples. Perry moaned and whimpered, moving weakly in his chair.

Karl knelt before his victim, making sure to make eye contact. "Listen to me now, Perry," he said in a low voice. "This is the last thing, the most important thing, you will ever know. My friends, the Vietnamese, have a belief. It has become mine as well." He reached into his gym bag, bringing forth the large kitchen knife. "They believe that the way you die is the way you go to the afterworld. That's why they used to cut us up when they caught us—one reason, anyway. Think of

84

it, Perry. Not just a moment of pain, an eternity of horror! My final gift to you. Marcie, turn the switch!"

Marcie did as she was told. As Perry opened his mouth in a silent scream, Karl calmly castrated him with the knife and stuffed his scrotal sack down his throat, blocking his airway. At the same time, he held his victim's nose closed.

Perry bucked mightily, breaking the chair that held him to splinters with his convulsions. His face quickly turned from deep red to a cyanotic blue. Soon the combination of suffocation and enormous pain defeated him. Within minutes his movement had ceased; his chest no longer tried to rise. Karl walked to Marcie's side and turned the hideous switch off for the last time. "Shocking," he said brightly.

Marcie sat on the edge of the bed, unmoving. The man who had driven her to insanity lay dead before her, murdered by an even greater monster. She tried to think, to know what to do, but thinking hurt her. She winced at the pain. A man stood before her with his hands on his hips, just the way Perry used to stand.

She knew what she must do. She reached up and unbuckled his belt. Pulling his clothes aside, she caressed his bare buttocks and drew him to her waiting mouth.

Karl looked down, momentarily surprised. Then he remembered. When they'd cleared out a village, it wasn't unusual for the women to lie down, waiting to be raped. They wouldn't fight, they didn't cry, and they often had the same broken look that this one had. He'd wondered if he could be with a woman again. This was the time to find out.

\* \* \*

# November 4

Karl waited until just before dawn to return to his car. He had taken a leisurely shower, thoroughly washing away the reek of his recent work. His gym bag held a change of clothes, which he now donned. As he walked from the room, carefully checking for any items he might have forgotten to pack earlier, he looked sadly at the still figure on the bed. Marcie had coaxed him to levels of excitement he hadn't felt for years. It was a shame she'd had to die. He had been gentle, just as he had promised. With an overdose of morphine, she had not died in pain.

As he swung behind the wheel of his car, starting his daylong trip back to Maslo, a symphony erupted in his mind. Woodwinds shrieked as trumpets blared, with drums defining a pulsing rhythm. He hummed along, totally immersed in the music behind his eyes.

# CHAPTER 10
# Tucson, Arizona—December 5

Some crimes pass unnoticed—a few lines in the newspaper, a change to a statistic. Others demand attention. The Haldron murder was big news, and that meant big pressure. Chris felt it, along with the rest of his division. The initial explanation had seemed simple enough: evidence pointed to the man's torture and eventual murder by his mistress, who had then committed suicide with an overdose of drugs. Too many loose ends made that theory unlikely. The woman was not a known drug user. And where had she gotten the morphine? Why the torture? Why that kind of torture? How had she managed to overpower the man in the first place? Where was the knife she had used to mutilate him? So on and so on. The knife and the morphine suggested a link to the Grissom murder, and the media caught on to it right away. "Gambling Mecca Maniac?" and its variations ran as headlines in tabloids from Denver to LA.

Chris had suspected a link as well. As for motive, a two-week investigation had turned up plenty, from Haldron's own family to some of the women he'd preyed upon during the last decade. The man had been a brutal sadist. Marcie Sherman's bruises and abrasions were from his hands. So here was the puzzle: two men had been murdered along with the women they had brought with them to different resorts. Both men had been tortured beforehand, probably for hours. What did they have in common? What bond had condemned them?

Television misrepresents police work. It has to, in order to fit a complicated story into less than an hour's time. Most investigations take weeks, and many stretch into months. Meanwhile, more work piles up and must be attended to as well. Evidence builds in fits and starts, seldom in a single thrust of effort. Blind alleys and wrong guesses can cause a case to remain unsolved for years and get consigned to a file cabinet or overtaken by more recent events. Much of the time, only a squealing criminal eager to trade information for a deal against another crime brings it to some kind of completion. The seldom-stated truth is that a noticeable fraction of all murders are never solved at all.

Chris pushed himself through endless interviews with frightened, bitter women and self-important J & D executives. His investigation centered on two questions: Who had Marcie Sherman and Perry Haldron known, and what link did they have to Harry Grissom? The Sherman woman hadn't been in Grissom's little black book. According to her neighbors and her coworkers, she was a devoted parent who seldom, if ever, dated. Haldron hadn't been part of Grissom's clique either. The J & D executive's public life had revolved around charity balls and quiet evenings, while his private passions had been far too dark to share with anyone.

Finally, after almost a month of fruitless work, Chris found a connection. He had been talking to Rae Ann Morrisey, a senior switchboard operator who had been with Janes and Delott for more than twenty years. She had watched Perry Haldron's career from its start. "Yeah, I knew him when he was just a pup, fresh out of U of A," she drawled, drawing deeply on her cigarette. "Hell, in those days, he used to say hello when he saw me." She smiled a wide, tobacco-stained grin. Chris didn't interrupt. It was better to let people talk, he had found, than to break their train of thought.

Right now Rae Ann was remembering Haldron vividly. She might have a fact in her memory she wasn't even aware was there. "He was nice as pie in those days," the older woman continued, "but he just couldn't stand to lose. Once, at the company picnic, he and his wife lost the three-legged race. It was a small thing. No one else noticed, but I saw his face. It was black with rage. Two days later, his wife came in to pick up his paycheck—he was out of town on business, you see—and she had a bruise on her face that all the makeup in the world couldn't hide. I knew it then. I knew he was a mean one, and things only got worse."

"What do you mean?" Chris asked.

"Well, Perry did real well. I think lots of people were afraid of him. He was big, you know, and he could push a lot of folks out of his way. After he got his office, after he made partner, he stopped hitting his wife, I think. I think he got tired of hurting her."

"You mean he got better?"

"Lord, no," Rae Ann whooped, pausing to light another cigarette. "If anything, he got worse." She leaned forward in her chair. "He started picking up girls who worked here," she whispered heavily, looking around the cafeteria where they sat. "You know, the ones afraid for their jobs, who'd done something wrong or couldn't cut it. He was real cagey, but word gets out about things like that. Hell, Sergeant Carpenter, this place is like a small town."

"What do you know about it?" Chris asked casually. He hadn't realized Haldron's activities were common knowledge.

"Just what I heard, but I heard plenty. You didn't have to be a mind reader, you know. You just had to look at those gals to know he was hurting them. He'd use one until he got tired of her or until she ran away. My God, he must have gone through twenty or more that I know about."

Chris reached into his pocket and handed her a list of typed names on a sheet of paper. "We know about these. Can you add any names to this list? Any more women he might have been with?"

Rae Ann scowled and reached into her purse for a pair of sequined glasses. Putting them on, she examined the list intently and then looked up. "You sure got most of them, Sergeant. Good work. Only one I can remember that you missed." She looked back at the paper, almost talking to herself. "Hell, she must have been the only one to beat him at his own game."

Inwardly, Chris groaned. Another Haldron victim to interview! He had come to detest the murdered executive from talking with the misused women he had cast aside. "What's her name?" he asked. "Do you remember?"

"I sure do," Rae Ann said proudly, slapping the small table with the flat of her hand. "I'll never forget that lady, lord no! Marianne Thibault, Sergeant. Only one I knew who played Haldron for a fool. I can even tell you where she's at now, if it's important."

"That's all right, ma'am," Chris said over his shoulder as he rushed from the cafeteria. "I think I know where I can find her."

\* \* \*

# December 6

As his flight settled into its final approach to Tucson, Tom Waters looked again at the sagebrush and cactus rushing by. The total lack of green continued to surprise him. *The place does have a beauty all its own*, he decided. *You just have to get used to it.*

His thoughts turned again to the message he'd gotten from Chris Carpenter, the Tucson cop he'd met his last time here. Just six words: "You were right. Karl came home." But that had been enough. He had been flying most of the day. Getting to Tucson was not the easiest thing in the world, especially on short notice.

Chris was at the gate to meet him, his eyes bright with excitement. He waved Waters to a row of empty seats, unable to wait any longer to tell him what he had found. As they shook hands, Waters looked at the younger man intently. "I know you're too good a cop to waste my time," he said. "What made you change your mind?"

In answer, Chris handed him a local newspaper, dated three weeks earlier. "Have you seen this?" he asked.

Sitting down, Waters examined the paper. The front page was dominated by the lurid account of a murder at a Lake Tahoe resort involving people from Tucson. After scanning the page, he looked back at Chris, now sitting beside him. "No, I missed this. I've been busy. We've tied at least seven more murders to Karl, you know. He's killing people all over the country."

"I think you can make it an even dozen, then," Chris said. "I found a link between the murdered men, between the Vegas killing and this one in Tahoe. It's Marianne Thibault, the wife. Both men knew her; both men slept with her. Both men were tortured and murdered, and I think Karl did them both."

"You're sure?"

"Yeah. We can cover the details later at the station, but there's no doubt. The question is, What do we do about it? How long do we have before something else happens?"

"You know my feeling," Waters replied. "It starts and ends with the wife, with Marianne. You've just confirmed it. We have to find out how much she knows, how deeply she's involved."

"Do you think she could be helping Karl find these men? You think she knows where he is, that she's talking to him? I don't know. I've met her. I don't think so."

Waters smiled. "I know she's pretty, but think a minute. Someone had to tell Karl who these men were. If not her, then who?"

Chris looked at the agent sadly. This wasn't the first time he'd been disappointed by people. He shrugged. "Okay. Let's say you're right. What do we do?"

"Three things right away. First, get full surveillance reinstated on the Thibault house now. I'll get a wiretap as well. Second, I still want to go over the transcripts of Karl's trial. I think there's a clue buried in what he said on the stand, something we can use to help us find him. Finally, after all that, we're going to have to talk to Marianne. Maybe you're right—maybe she's just a bystander to all this. I don't think so. I've been in this business too long to believe in so much coincidence." He arched his eyebrows. "You have too."

Chris rose, turning toward a kiosk of pay phones. "I'll start the paperwork going for the tap."

Waters nodded. The kid was good, just a little too human sometimes. "Okay. I'll meet you in baggage claim. Can you arrange to have the trial transcripts sent to your office? Use my authority, if you have to."

Chris waved his agreement. The men parted, each deep in thought.

* * *

David answered the phone right away, just as he'd been taught to do during the afternoons after school. He was good at taking messages too, using the legal pad his mother always left nearby. He seldom missed a name or got a number wrong.

"Hello?" he asked, trying unsuccessfully to cradle the receiver with his thin neck.

The answering voice made him grab the receiver with both hands. "Hi, Tiger!" his dad growled. The boy's heart raced. Was today the day? Would his dad be coming for him now?

"Oh, Dad," he sighed. "I've been waiting for your call. I've done everything you said. I've studied Brazil, and Portuguese, and South America, and everything! Are you coming? Is it now?"

"Soon, Tiger, real soon now. Listen, you wouldn't want to miss Christmas with your mom, would you? That would make her very sad. Right after that, David. Right after that, I promise."

David sighed again. Dad was right, just as he always had been. Even when he'd been so sick, he'd always been right when he'd talked to David. The kids had teased him and made him cry, but Dad always made him feel better. The kids had left him alone after a while, once they found out that his small fists were quick and accurate. "Okay," he said slowly. "I guess you're right."

"You know I am, Tiger. Now listen, two things. They're very important. You're going to have to take notes."

David grabbed his pencil and bent to the pad near the phone. "Go ahead, Dad," he said seriously. "I'm ready."

"Okay, son. First, I won't be able to call you here anymore because of the mission I'm on, son. I don't want to put you and your mom in any danger." Karl wasn't lying. He assumed that Marianne's house would be watched and her phone tapped now that the Haldron murder had been front-page news. In any case, he couldn't take the chance that it wasn't.

David gasped. "But Dad, how will I hear from you? How will I know when—"

His father chuckled. "Calm down, David. Calm down. I'm going to give you a number. You can call me! Not too often, now. Only from a public phone. Do you have one at school?"

"Yes, Dad, we do. It's right by the principal's office in the hall. I can use it during lunchtime. I'm a hall monitor. I have to stand right by it."

"Fine, son, that's fine. Now, do you know how to make a collect call?"

"Sure, Dad!" David was proud of his knowledge, his grownup skill. "I do it when I have to call Mom at work. Just dial '0' before the number, right?"

Karl was genuinely pleased. His son was so bright, so perfect. He loved the boy so! "Now, copy this number down, and put it in a safe place. It's 555-702-7255. Got it? 555-702-7255."

The boy wrote quickly but carefully, his numbers covering almost a third of the yellow sheet he used. "Got it, Dad," he chirped in a few seconds.

"Now listen, son. I may not be there when you call. If I'm not, call back the same time on the next day. Okay?"

"Okay, Dad. I'll do it." David's spirits soared. This was just like secret agent stuff! "Now, what's the second thing?"

Karl smiled. The boy was so sharp. What a life they would have once they escaped. "The second thing is this: have you heard any more about that policeman who came to see your mom?"

"No, Dad, I haven't. Nothing at all."

"Okay. Keep alert. Remember to write down anything you hear. Anything, okay? Call me at the number I gave the very next day."

"I'll do it," the boy agreed. "Only, Dad?"

"Yes, son?"

"I don't think he'll be back. It's been a long time since he was here."

"Maybe not, son. Just in case, you'll do as I ask. Right?"

"I will, Dad. I'll do it for you. I love you, Dad."

"I love you too, son. With all my heart. I have to go now. Remember what I said."

"Yes, Dad." The boy wished his father didn't have to go. He was so lonely most of the time.

"Remember, son. The number I gave you is a secret, a big secret. Don't tell anyone about it, not even your mom."

"Don't worry, Dad, I won't tell anybody. Don't worry about Mom.

She told me a long time ago that she never wants to talk about you. So I don't."

Though David couldn't hear Karl grimace, he did hear the sharp sigh. His father's voice remained warm and soft, though. "Fine, son. That's fine. It will be just our secret, then. Just for us. Now, give me kisses. I have to go."

The airy sound that had thrilled him during his years of captivity came to his ear again. As he hung up the phone, he heard the small voice pipe, "I love you, Dad!"

# CHAPTER 11

# Tucson, Arizona—December 7

The late afternoon sun shone low through the windows of the big room, casting grotesque shadows across the wall. Today's sunset would be spectacular, but as Chris worked with Tom Waters, neither man would notice. Both were fully engrossed in the thousands of pages that made up the transcript of Karl Thibault's trial. Half a dozen paper cups littered the table they shared, and the room reeked with the stale odor of the fast food they'd ordered. They'd been studying Karl's testimony for more than ten hours, without the slightest notice of the time they'd spent. When one or the other came up with an idea, it was immediately scrawled on a blackboard that ran along one wall of the room. By now, the blackboard was almost covered with semilegible script.

The phone at the end of the table rang. Waters looked up from the sheets he'd been studying and reached to answer it. Chris looked up as well, quizzically searching his friend's mumbled replies for meaning. In less than a minute, the agent hung up with a tight grin on his face.

"The tap's in place, and surveillance starts today," he said. Stretching and rising from his chair, he reached for a new pack of cigarettes from the jacket he had carelessly hung by the door. He had cut down to less than a pack a day just a few months ago. He sighed. Thibault would end up killing him too—with cancer.

Chris nodded, hardly looking up. "How things can move when the Big Uncle's behind them," he muttered. Then he rose as well, stretching and shaking the fatigue from his upper body. "Let's stop for a minute,

Tom. We've damn near filled up that board with ideas. Why not go through what we think we've found? Maybe we can make some sense out of this mess."

"Good idea," Waters agreed. "After that, let's take a break. I could use some dinner and a drink. You could too. I'll buy. Tonight, Sergeant Carpenter, you're a guest of the bureau."

Chris laughed. "Thank God," he sighed, rolling his eyes and holding his midsection. "If I have another one of those cardboard burgers you ordered, I'll have permanent stomach damage." He turned to the blackboard. "Okay. Karl Thibault. What have we got? Who is he?"

Waters walked to one of the notes he had written. "First off, he's a vet. Five years in the army, three of them in Southeast Asia. Went in as nothing, came out a captain. Silver star, bronze star, air medal, army commendation medals, Vietnamese Cross of Gallantry. A hero."

Chris shrugged. "You'll have to help me through this, Tom. The military is a mystery to me. He was supposed to be signal corps, but all of his assignments are something else. All this alphabet soup: ARVN, CCN, MAF, PRU. What do they mean?"

"What they mean is that he wasn't anymore signal corps than you or me. Thibault was intelligence. ARVN, that's easy. Stands for 'Army of the Republic of Vietnam,' the guys we fought with. CCN, well, you'll almost never hear about that one unless you were in it yourself: 'Command and Control North'—the guys who fought the covert war in the northern provinces, in Laos and Cambodia. Some say they went into North Vietnam itself." He paused, thinking.

"MAF, that would be 'Three MAF,' 'Third Marine Amphibious Force.' When the marines were a big part of the war, before 1970, that was the outfit that ran them. After '70, the army took over most of their AO—oh, excuse me, their area of operations."

"But Karl was army, wasn't he?"

"Karl was intelligence. I'll bet he wore a lot of uniforms when he needed to. What's the other one?"

"PRU."

"Oh, yeah. Stands for 'Provincial Reconnaissance Unit.' Murkiest of them all. It was a CIA program designed to assassinate local politicians who supported the bad guys, just like they killed the ones who supported our side."

Chris asked, "So what's the bottom line?"

Waters paused to light another cigarette. "The bottom line, Chris, is that this man was a real warrior—one of the elite. He fought with all the units that really did major damage to the enemy, and he won a chest full of medals doing it. From what I can see, he had a great career going. The army doesn't like to lose men who've had his experience."

"But he quit, right? He got out. In '72."

"Yeah, and he had to fight to do it. Why? I wonder. Looks like he had found his place in life."

Chris pointed to the board. "He talked about that. His testimony, at his trial, page 1023. Here, let me find it." Striding back to the table, he quickly leafed through page after page of typed manuscript. "Here it is," he said, looking up after a few minutes. "Listen, Karl was asked specifically why he left the army. He says, 'Because I had reached the point where I could no longer obey a direct order without question. Any soldier who can't is a danger to himself and the men he commands. A second's hesitation can mean loss of life. You've never been there; you can't know what I mean.' Sounds like he'd given it a lot of thought."

Waters nodded. "He's right, you know. The trouble with the service is there's too many who don't feel that way. I have to wonder. Karl was such a good soldier. There has to be more to it. What got him to the place where he questioned orders?"

"There's not much more about it. A few pages further along, he talks about a mission, the one that got him his Silver Star. Apparently it was a botched deal. Someone who didn't know what he was doing thought it up. Karl and his unit were sent in and got pretty badly shot up. He lost some men."

"I read more about that one, back in Virginia. Karl was running a recon detachment. Their 'official' job was to bring communication lines to remote areas. Unofficially, they were dropped into enemy-held areas to plant sensors and to vector in the B-52 strikes, what we used to call the 'Arclight' missions. The mission we're talking about, the one that cost him his men, required him to go back into an area he'd already covered once. He knew the North Vietnamese would be waiting for him."

"So why'd he go?"

Waters sighed. "Orders. He argued all he could, and then he did what he was told, just like you or me. According to the debriefing documents, he had to be thrown into the chopper that finally rescued him. He didn't want to leave without those men who didn't make it back. He couldn't believe they were dead."

"And then he got out of the army."

"Yeah." Waters paused to light another cigarette. "Got out. Went back to school. Came out two years later with a degree in civil engineering. Out of Virginia Tech. Good school. He linked up with a small computer company that got big, then small, and then big again with oil exploration. Ended up traveling around the world for them. Met Marianne. Married, had a kid. Settled down. Got a job with a contractor working with the army at Fort Huachuca. It's the big army security base in southern Arizona. Moved to Tucson. That would have been seven years ago. Two years later, he murdered his wife's boyfriend with a kitchen knife."

Chris frowned. "Except for that last sentence, everything seems okay. What happened?"

Waters turned to his own stack of transcripts. "Apparently quite a bit, at least according to Marianne. She testified that he became moodier and more withdrawn as the years went by. He began having bad dreams, recurrent nightmares, started smoking and drinking heavily. The drinking began to make him very sick."

"What was Marianne's part in the trial?" Chris asked, pausing as he leafed through his own notes.

Waters grinned. "Oh, she was the prosecution's star witness. The divorce was over long before the trial began. You guys do it quick out West. From her testimony, it's obvious she had no love left for her ex. She wanted him put away for a long time or executed, either one. That's what puzzles me. If she's in cahoots with him, she's had a real change of heart. It doesn't make sense."

Chris shook his head and then rose and stretched. "Hell, if solving these things was easy, we'd both be out of a job. It's all pieces to a puzzle, but it's a puzzle we've got to solve, quickly. I don't want any more murders."

Waters nodded in agreement. "I know how you feel," he said flatly. "Look, we're getting stale. How about taking me up on that steak? We'll think better after a few hours away from this place."

Both men rose to leave. As he paused to turn out the room's lights, Waters turned to Chris. "You know, I can't help thinking that all this goes back to something that happened to Karl, probably in Vietnam. Something that changed him. It lay inside him, getting bigger all the time, until Marianne triggered it. That's my theory. I just can't figure what it could have been."

## INTERIM: KARL AT THE WALL

# Washington, DC—November 15, 1986

After his "raid" in South Carolina, Karl's escape route took him through the nation's capital. Between flights, on a whim, he decided to take a cab to the Vietnam Veterans Memorial. He had read about it while he was in Benniston. An overcast sky promised rain in the future, but not just yet. It was a cloudy, blustery day—not quite overcoat weather, but cool enough to make walking outdoors without a jacket uncomfortable.

His cab hurried through hectic daytime traffic, circled the Lincoln Memorial, and left Karl on a grassy stand near his destination. There, he joined a crowd approaching the wall. Vendors from several veteran-connected organizations walked in front of him, each wearing some fraction of a uniform and patches or placards of various kinds. They obscured his view of the monument and seemed sloppy, garish, and out of place. He forgot them and all else when the wall came into full view.

It seemed less a construction than a parting of the earth itself. As he came closer, the wall took on dimension—as though there was space behind the inscribed names incised into the basalt slabs. Its sheer size was breathtaking, stark evidence of his nation's determination to endure a conflict that was never understood. Though many who approached it were middle-aged men like himself, people of all ages—from children to the very old—were represented. Some left flowers, medals, or other pieces of life behind when they departed. Many looked grim or sad. No one smiled.

He found his unit quickly enough—there were Easton, and Henley, and the others. Morris too. Karl hadn't known he had died. Karl touched the first name, and as he did a near-electric shock pulsed through his arm. He sensed movement within the stone, as though the men themselves were there, somewhere within the monument itself, reaching out to him. He could almost see them—or was it just the reflection of the sun against the clouds? He felt tears welling in his eyes. He missed these men so much. He longed to tell them how sorry he was, how he would gladly trade his life for any of theirs. There was no sound save the breeze tumbling through the surrounding glade.

He looked further and saw Truly's name as well. Anger rose within him at the idea that such a man could be memorialized near heroes. Then he realized that their fate was bound together. All of them, himself included, were beyond judgment or redemption.

Slowly, Karl pulled his hand from the unyielding black stone, stood, and walked away, refusing to look back. He hailed another cab and was returned to the airport in minutes. As he sat waiting for his flight to Las Vegas, he knew he had experienced something beyond narrow reality. He wondered if, somehow, his name would appear on the wall when his work was finally done.

# CHAPTER 12

## Maslo, Nevada—December 10

The place was generally neat, so there was little cleaning up to be done. Still, the linens did need changing and dust was always a problem here in the desert. Judy Carnover hummed as she cleaned Ken Talley's apartment. It was good to have a man in her life again.

She hadn't been sure that things would work out. Ken was often remote beyond shyness, and though he could talk a lot once he got going, it seemed hard for him to say what was on his mind or in his heart. After their dinner date in Caliente almost two months earlier, she had wondered whether or not he really wanted her as a woman. He had been so distant, as though there was something he wanted to talk about but couldn't bring up. Since then he had warmed to her, gradually. Finally, last week, they had become lovers.

He had come over, as he usually did when he was in town, to help her close the restaurant. Archie and the waitress had already left. They were alone. She had sensed the change in him at once. He was nervous and jittery, as though he was waiting for something to happen. Finally, as she locked the front door, he had gone to the jukebox and, after a few moments of intense study, had inserted a quarter to play a song. She had recognized the music at once. It was an old song, "Cherish" by The Association. He had walked to her side as the music began. "Let's dance," he had said softly.

He had guided her between the tables, as if the diner were a ballroom floor. Though his step was a little rusty, his obvious emotion was not. He had held her closely and told her how he'd missed her during his last trip. "I've needed you," he had whispered.

Judy had responded to his touch and his words, swept away and bewildered by his sudden change in attitude and her own feelings. As the music stopped, she had taken his hand. She had quickly extinguished the lights and locked the remaining doors to the diner. Then, pulling him behind her, she had hurried them to her apartment upstairs.

Once inside, he had looked at her, confused, as though he was unsure of what to do next. Quickly, Judy had put her arms around his neck and kissed him hungrily. From that moment, his movements had become sure and precise. His tongue had found hers as his hands caressed her breasts and then her thighs and buttocks. She had responded eagerly, moving her hands quickly from his chest to his crotch. After an age of silent touching and exploration, she had led him to her bedroom.

She had turned from him and removed her blouse. As he kissed the back of her neck, his hands quickly found and unhooked the clasps of her bra. He had caressed both of her breasts at once as he continued to kiss her, rolling each nipple separately between his thumbs and forefingers. She had sighed and raised her head, glorying in the sensual attention she had not felt for so long. She had not realized till then how much she missed it.

Rising quickly from his embrace, she stepped from her skirt. Almost at once, Karl had pulled her panties from her waist and lowered her to her bed. Kneeling on the floor beside her, he had caressed her thighs, his lips and tongue quickly following his hands from her knees to her vagina. He had licked and sucked and kissed her for timeless minutes as she panted and gasped in ecstasy. Finally, after an unexpected wave of orgasm had passed through her, she had leaned forward, her eyes bright with desire, to bring him into her.

He had been awkward and tentative, so sensitive to the possibility of somehow hurting her. She smiled as he entered her for it brought back such memories. This was so good!

They had made love slowly at first, then more and more quickly as his passion consumed him. Finally, with a sound that was more a cry of anguish than a sigh, he had relaxed and, lying in her arms, had buried his head in her breasts and stroked her hair. "Thank you," he had said softly. "You've made me whole again."

They had spent the rest of the night together, exploring and expanding their knowledge of each other's needs and desires. He entered her twice more, and each time lasted longer and was more pleasurable than the last. They had finally parted after coffee in the morning—he to change and pack for another business trip, she to hurriedly open the diner. He had been gone for three days now, but he called her every night. She waited anxiously for his calls. They said very little to each other, just traded banalities really, but she could sense the strength of emotion behind every word he spoke. It was good to be in love with somebody again.

\* \* \*

# Kent (Akron), Ohio—December 12

The bar at the Holloway Lodge was half empty. Every third seat held a salesman staring into space over his beer or his drink, while two couples huddled over their low tables at the large room's corners. The small dance floor remained unused, although a steady stream of music rose from the jukebox that stood along the room's center wall. The lights remained low. A lone waitress made desultory conversation with the bartender, her eyes darting to the occupied tables from time to time. All in all, the place was like a dozen bars Karl had seen in the last six months, just as the motel that housed it was a carbon copy of several others he'd visited and killed in. He walked slowly toward the bar, letting his eyes adjust to the gloom. One of the five men he saw outlined by the room's indirect lighting would be his victim tonight. He was sure of that.

His job now was to choose his prey. He slid onto a stool and casually ordered a beer, although his pulse was pounding through his skull. *Control!* He willed himself to be calm. The strength of his conviction pervaded his limbs and his body like the spray of a cold shower. He became aware of every muscle, every movement, and felt his pulse and respiration slow. This was the waiting time, the choosing time, the stalking time.

His gaze finally fell on a short, balding man sitting four stools to his right who had just ordered his third drink of the evening. The man wore a dark suit, white shirt, and striped tie, now loosened in his button-down collar. Karl decided this one would be an easy victory. He was wrong. The object of his concentration, Bert Pardoe, was an FBI agent.

Pardoe was celebrating, in a low-key, lonely way. He and his partner had been part of a Tom Waters plan to catch Karl in the midst of one of his murderous sprees. Waters had identified several areas within two hundred miles of major hub airports, like Cleveland, where Karl might strike and had covered the larger motels in the area with roving teams of agents. Since it was night duty, it didn't detract at all from the normal daily chores of these men and women. It simply did away with their home lives for a while.

Pardoe and his partner, Jack Devine, had completed a five-night swing that had taken them from Lorrain through Akron. As they had driven to work in Cleveland that morning, Devine had complained. "Bert, I should spend some time at home tonight," he said. "It's the school play, and my kid's the lead. Nothing's going on here anyway. That looney is probably in Texas or Montana." Pardoe had agreed. This duty stank. The chances of being in the right place at the right time were astronomically slight. The reprieve came later that day. Thibault had been spotted in southern Florida. Everyone was released to normal duty.

The motel reservations ran for one more night, and Bert Pardoe had an idea. He decided to enjoy himself tonight—kind of a small vacation. No more ginger ale! Tonight there was real bourbon in his glass. As he stared into his third drink, a darkly humorous thought ran through his mind. He had always had bad luck, had always been the one on the spot when something wacky went down. What if . . . what if tonight was the night? What if the reports out of Florida were wrong? What if that psycho had picked Cleveland to operate from instead of the score of other cities he could have chosen? What if he was right here?

Pardoe looked slowly around the bar. Hell, half of these guys could be Thibault: fortyish, dark brown hair, light complexion, mustache, medium build. Still, he was satisfied. None of them was the man he was looking for. Finishing his drink with a hard swallow, he motioned for the bartender as he reached for his wallet. Settling up, he swung from his stool. Unlike his partner, he had no marriage to worry about anymore. A motel room was just as comfortable as the littered efficiency where he normally slept. He left the bar and walked slowly to his room, humming to himself. If the bureau wanted to pay his bill, he'd do this for a year or two—no sweat!

Karl waited less than a minute before following his victim from the bar. He grinned with satisfaction as he noted that the man was heading for a ground-floor room. So much easier to escape! He assumed his attack stance—slightly crouched, moving forward on the balls of his feet, arms outstretched in front of him. As soon as the prey put his key in the door, Karl launched himself at the man's back, swinging his right forearm around to deliver a disabling, larynx-crushing choke hold.

Perhaps it was some sixth sense that made Pardoe turn as Karl leaped for his neck. Or maybe he heard a small noise or felt the displacement of air. In any event, he was able to block his assailant's lunge. Even with his drink-slowed reflexes, he used Karl's own momentum to send him slamming into the next room's door.

Automatically, the agent knelt to draw his revolver. Karl lay in front of the door, stunned by the impact of his fall. No prey had ever fought back like this! He shook his head to clear his thoughts, noting with alarm that his intended victim seemed to be reaching for a weapon—probably a gun. Just then, the door behind him opened.

As Pardoe's gun went off, the irate occupant of room fifteen stepped directly over and in front of Karl, just in time to receive two well aimed rounds in his midsection (Pardoe had been aiming for Karl's head). The man fell forward, masking Karl as he jumped through the room's open door.

Pardoe's mind raced. If he'd had a partner, one of them could have watched the room while the other ran for backup. Unfortunately, he was alone. If he left, Karl would be gone before he could return. His only option was to follow the killer into the dark motel room. Holding his gun in front of him, Pardoe advanced through the empty door, reaching as he did so for the room's light switch.

As Pardoe groped for the switch, Karl swept the gun from his hand with the base of a table lamp he had just picked up. Now unarmed, Pardoe launched himself at his assailant, grabbing him by the lapels of his coat and attempting to drag his opponent's nose into his vicious knee lift. Karl broke the agent's hold with an explosive wrist chop and ripped his open hand across the man's eyes, momentarily blinding him. Reaching again for the shattered table lamp, he fractured Pardoe's skull with a single blow.

Catching the agent as he slumped to the floor, Karl quickly dragged him to the back of the room and then strangled him with the lamp's cord. Was he dead? There was no breathing, no pulse—and there was no time to lose. Karl pushed the body under a bed and ran out the door.

The man who'd been shot, who'd saved Karl's life, lay on the walk moaning weakly as he bled heavily from his stomach wound. Picking him up by his armpits, Karl dragged him back to his room and lay him on one of the twin beds. Maybe this trip could be salvaged yet.

Karl went to the door once again to listen for the noise of pursuit. The motel hadn't been crowded. Maybe no one had heard the shots. Maybe he still had time to get away. He closed the room's door and turned to his bleeding, semiconscious captive. Advancing to his side, he slapped the man's face savagely with his open hand. "I don't have time to be friendly," Karl growled. "Do you want to live?"

"Yes, yes ..." came the weak reply. "I ... I'm hurt. Get doctor. Help me ... please."

Karl had the man's wallet in his hands—credit cards, two hundred in cash, aha! A bank card. Leaning forward, he viciously pressed his hand against the man's open wound. The man screamed.

Releasing the pressure, Karl whispered in his victim's ear. "I'll keep pressing, giving you pain, until you tell me your bank card's PIN number. What is it?" He pressed the wound again.

After a few minutes, having heard and memorized the four-digit code, Karl smothered the man to death with a pillow. Going to the door once more, he marveled at his luck. No one had heard the scuffle or the shots. He still had time for a clean escape.

Escape from whom? That was the question. Who was the victim who had almost killed him? He pulled Pardoe's body from beneath the bed and rifled through his clothing until he found the FBI identification. Now at least he knew who was hunting him, and it was worse than he had thought. Pardoe's notes included his full description and a recent photo from Benniston. So they knew who he was and what he was doing, and they had guessed where he might strike next.

This was trouble. He wouldn't have his normal two day's grace. He had to leave tonight. He was trapped, just as he had been back in Laos, and the bad guys were closing in. He stuffed his victims beneath the twin beds and searched for car keys. Luckily, his last victim's car keys identified a vehicle—in this case, a white Buick with Indiana plates.

Taking care to lock the door, Karl left the room warily, tense with sensitivity to any noise of pursuit. He heard nothing, just the normal night sounds of suburban Ohio. He walked quickly to his car—the one he'd taken at the Cleveland airport yesterday—and removed his small suitcase from its trunk. He soon found the white Buick parked within twenty feet of the unfortunate traveler's motel room. Throwing his bag in the back seat, he drove from the motel and turned onto Kent Street. He was careful to obey all speed limits. His adrenaline would keep him alert for the two-hour drive to the airport.

As he drove along Route 71, his thoughts kept returning to the luck of his escape. The FBI agent shouldn't have been alone and normally wouldn't have missed. Without astounding luck, he would be dead.

He pulled off the road twice, once in Ghent and again in Richfield, to make withdrawals from his victim's bank account. The numbers worked, and he was able to collect $400 more—a disappointment considering that this would be his last raid. It was obvious that he wouldn't be able to venture from Maslo to attack salesmen again.

As he neared the airport exit in Middleburg Heights two hours later, other thoughts were heavy on his mind. His tickets back to Chicago should still be good, but the airport might be watched. Perhaps

Pardoe had a partner, after all. There was no way to be sure. Perhaps the alarm was already out. He would have to be very careful.

He parked the Buick in the short-term lot—after all, he didn't have to worry about the fee—and walked quickly into the terminal. The next flight to Chicago was a 12:30 a.m. red-eye out of Columbus that still hadn't landed. He had some time. He checked through security and walked to the gate, intent on exchanging his ticket for a seat on the Columbus flight. Caution made him loiter by a convenient water fountain, watching the attendants for signs of unusual activity, extra people, or anything that looked out of the ordinary. There was nothing. He was safe.

He walked confidently to the check-in counter and presented his ticket for conversion. "There will be a fifty-dollar charge, Mr. Bramerton," the counterperson informed him. (That must have been the name on the credit card he had used. It was so hard to remember all of the names!). He paid it in cash. As he had suspected, there were plenty of seats available on this midnight flight. The plane was on time, arriving at the gate fifteen minutes later. In less than an hour, he was airborne for Chicago.

The flight was short, barely long enough for the stews to serve drinks and collect the plastic cups. By early morning, Karl was walking the maze that is O'Hare International Airport. He settled down in a waiting area to take a short nap.

\* \* \*

# Indianapolis, Indiana—1:30 a.m.

The phone still hadn't rung. Anna Giovanni looked at it forlornly from her bed, as though her will alone could make the call come through. Something was very wrong. Al always called. Always. For more than fifteen years.

He had been offered promotions—promotions he should have taken. "What would I do, Anna?" he would ask, shrugging those big shoulders with a wide smile on his face. "If they put me inside, took me off the road, I'd die of boredom. I swear it! It's the road that keeps me young!" Then he'd grab her in his long, strong arms and give her the crushing hug she loved so much.

Well, it wasn't as though he had to cover the country, just most of Ohio. He was home every Friday, without fail. He always called, no matter what, every night.

Anna made up her mind. She knew where he was staying. He had used the same Holloway Lodge for the last decade. She would call. Something had to be wrong. Rummaging through the nightstand, she found the list of motels and numbers that Al had left her "just in case." She dialed quickly, too quickly, and had to redial twice. She felt nervous, as if she was doing something she shouldn't. It didn't matter. She had made up her mind.

A groggy night clerk answered on the sixth ring, "Holloway Lodge, Kent."

"I need to speak to my husband, Al Giovanni. It's important." Anna's own voice surprised her. It sounded so harsh and shrill. It was silly, getting this upset. Still …

"Know the room number?" replied the sleepy clerk.

"No, but I know he's checked in. He stays with you all the time."

"Just a minute please." The long silence twisted her tension to new levels.

*My God*, she thought, *what if he isn't there?*

He was. "Just a second, lady. He's in room fifteen. I'll put you through."

The phone rang for an eternity. She knew he had to be here. Maybe he was sick. She hung up and dialed the night clerk again. "Please," she pleaded, "I must speak to my husband. It's very important. He's not answering his phone. Could you go and check? Please, it's urgent!"

"Look, lady, maybe he's asleep. Or maybe he went out. Hold on, I'll try the room again."

It was no use. As he came back on the line, her pleas began anew. "If you won't help me, I … I'll call the manager. I'll call the police! Please. Go check his room. I know something is wrong."

Joe Tannenbaum, the night clerk, had had enough by now. This wasn't the first call he'd gotten from an outraged wife in the six months he'd been with Holloway Lodge. Usually the guy was too drunk to wake up or shacked up with some broad. They didn't pay him enough for this aggravation.

There was no way out of this for him either. If he got rude or hung up, she'd have management on his neck for sure. If he checked the room out, the guy would get mad and never stay here again. Any way things fell, he was the loser. "Look," he said, "I'll go knock on the door. If he's up, I'll have him call you back. Okay?" It was okay. Joe hung up, put on his parka, and shambled out into the sharp, cold Ohio night.

Five minutes later, he found that room fifteen had a badly dented door. Two minutes after that, upon entering the room, he noticed a hand sticking out from under one of the beds. Within ten minutes, a shaken Joe Tannenbaum had called the state police. It would be the longest night of his life.

* * *

## Chicago O'Hare Airport, 3:00 a.m.

Karl looked up from an uneasy nap as the airport security forces rushed around him. Something was up! He couldn't guess how, but his intuition was that the bodies in the Ohio motel had been discovered. Maybe that FBI agent had a partner, after all.

Whatever the reason, he was trapped. His tickets would be no good, the gates would be watched, and his credit cards would be identified. He had to get out. Now.

He lay, unmoving, in the darkened waiting area, one sleeping holdover among dozens, while his mind searched for an answer to this new dilemma. He could buy a ticket with the money he had, but they would be waiting for that, with his description in hand. He could run to Chicago and lose himself in the enormousness of that city, but he'd be out of his element there. He would make a mistake or be noticed. No, his only chance was to leave this place entirely—to get back to Nevada.

Karl rose from his seat. Clutching his small suitcase, he walked slowly toward the baggage claim area. Maybe something would occur to him. At any rate, he wanted to get out of the airport security area as quickly as possible. There were still people moving about, as there always are at O'Hare. He wasn't noticed.

As he descended to the baggage claim area, a sign caught his eye: the bright red and blue logo of the Access Rent-A-Car booth. "We're closed," the neatly printed card on the counter read. "For service, use this phone to call for the bus to our rental center. Thanks for choosing Access!" The germ of a plan formed in Karl's mind. He picked up the phone.

\* \* \*

## Tucson, Arizona—3:15 a.m.

Thomas Waters picked up the phone on its second ring, though he had been fast asleep. He had felt that something was going to break soon, even as he had settled down for the night in his motel room. Still, the news was better than he could have hoped. They had Thibault trapped, bottled up in O'Hare. Even better, Karl probably wasn't aware that he was trapped. According to all signs, he was probably asleep in some gate area, waiting for a morning flight.

There was no way Waters could get to Chicago in time to take part in the fugitive's capture. Everything would be over before he could get there from Tucson, even on the earliest possible flight. He wasn't worried. The Chicago bureau office was damn good, and they were already at work, as were the Chicago police. Karl wouldn't get out of the airport. Within an hour, the cordon around him would be unassailable.

\* \* \*

## Elk Grove Village, Illinois—4:10 a.m.

The bright blue and red minivan pulled up to the Access rental center. To Karl's surprise, he hadn't been the only passenger. Three other people had gotten on from other stops around the giant airport.

As he climbed from the van, Karl could see the two sleepy attendants huddled over their computer terminals through the floor-to-ceiling windows of the reservation center. He had no intention of entering the building. Instead, he moved quickly to the maintenance area, some fifty yards away. There, silhouetted by the dim light of a service bay, a tall African-American man in a red and blue jacket and cap leaned against the maintenance building, clipboard in hand as he smoked a cigarette. He looked up as Karl approached.

"Help you, sir?" he said casually.

Karl answered with exuberance he didn't feel. "You sure can," he said. "It's a damn good thing I found you. Do you have the keys to these cars?" He pointed to the line of cars left by renters, waiting for service.

"Some still have the keys in 'em," the attendant answered. "What seems to be the trouble?"

"Well, I left a package in that Camaro over there, something I bought for the wife. I'd hate to go back without it. Can you help me get to it?" Smiling, Karl reached in his pocket and flashed a twenty-dollar bill.

The attendant grinned broadly and snatched the bill quickly from Karl's outstretched hand. "I shouldn't do this, ya know," he said, still smiling and shaking his head. "But since you came all the way back, let's see what we can find." He turned and walked toward the red sports coupe. Karl followed.

When they reached the car, the attendant turned. "Now, where'd you say this package was?"

"In the trunk, way in the back," Karl answered helpfully.

The man opened the Camaro's trunk and looked in. "Man, I don't see nothing."

"You've got to look way back, on the left side. It's a small bag, kind of hard to see."

By now the helpful attendant was fully halfway in the car's trunk, groping fitfully. "I still can't find—"

Karl slammed the trunk lid down with all the force he could bring to bear and heard the man's pelvis crack. The attendant started to scream. Karl opened the trunk and pulled his victim out by his jacket, turning him as he did. More bones scraped and popped. Holding the screaming man's head erect, he killed him quickly with a brutal series of upward chops that broke his victim's nose as they sent the cartilage slivers straight into his brain.

Quickly stuffing the body back into the car, Karl donned the dead man's jacket and cap, picked up the discarded clipboard, and slammed the Camaro's trunk closed. Now, if no one had heard him, he had only to wait.

Ten minutes later, a car drove through the gate and parked at the end of the line. A man and a woman jumped out. Karl advanced to meet them. "In a hurry, sir?" he asked politely, shutting the door for the woman. "Charging this to your credit card?" The man nodded.

Karl smiled. "Here, sir," he said, offering his hand, "give me your contract. I'll check you in right here. Leave the keys in the ignition. Just go to the building behind me and to the left. The bus will pick you up there and take you to your terminal."

"Thanks," the man said absently as he and the woman pulled bags from the car's trunk. He paused to hand Karl the contract.

"Thank you, sir," said Karl to the couple's back. "And thanks for choosing Access. Have a nice flight!"

Karl waited until the retreating couple had boarded the minivan. Then, throwing his borrowed jacket and cap into the back seat of the car just vacated, he ran to the corner of the building where he had concealed his small suitcase. Retrieving it, he returned to the car. Karl placed his bag in the back seat, started the engine, and backed the car around. Then he headed for the lot's exit. The security guard at the gate asked for his contract, as Karl had known he would. "Got to go back," he said with a shy smile. "Left a suitcase at the hotel."

The guard nodded absently, handed back the contract, and waved his hand. Karl rolled up his window and began the long drive to Nevada. As the dark swallowed him, heading south on Interstate 55, strident music from the orchestra of his mind boiled through him, dissipating the heat of the tension he had contained for the last several hours.

# CHAPTER 13

# Tucson, Arizona—December 13

There was very little conversation during the drive to Marianne Thibault's town house. What was there to say? The cordon around O'Hare had finally been lifted yesterday, after every possible hiding place had been searched and searched again. The murder of an attendant at the Access rental car facility could have been Karl, but no one was sure. If Karl had killed the attendant, he'd gotten away clean and had almost two days to get wherever he was going. He might be hiding in Chicago. Or maybe he made it through O'Hare before the cordon descended. Ifs and maybes. Waters had known Bert Pardoe. They had worked together on a case five years earlier. Chris shared with him the frustration all good cops feel when a criminal evades capture. So the trip was made largely in silence.

Marianne had not wanted to see them. "There's nothing I can add to what you already know," she'd said when Chris had telephoned her two days before. "Karl went out of my life five years ago. I haven't seen him or talked to him since. I can't help you. Isn't that clear?" She hung up the phone. An hour later, Waters called her back, gently suggesting that an evening meeting at her home might be preferable to a daytime conference at the police department. Marianne had agreed.

The house looked exactly the same, pocketed in its narrow lane as though nothing had changed since the last time Chris had visited. The same cop was on surveillance duty: Juan Escobar, still catching up on his reading. Yet so much was different. If Waters was right—and all the evidence indicated that he was—Karl had committed more than a dozen murders since Chris had last talked to Marianne. A single question loomed above all the others in this increasingly complex investigation, which now spanned ten states and involved scores of FBI, state, and local police: Who had directed Karl to his ex-wife's lovers? Who, if not Marianne herself?

The two men walked to the gate, and Chris pressed the doorbell. Marianne came to the door almost at once, as though she had been waiting by the door for their arrival. Chris's greeting smile was cut short by her scowl. She offered Thomas Waters a perfunctory hello, nothing more.

She closed the door after them and glided to a green, overstuffed chair, where she sat silently, waiting for either of the men to speak. Chris thought her lovely as ever, dressed casually in a pair of jeans and a light sweater. Silhouetted against the flickering fireplace, her pale skin seemed to glow.

Waters spoke first. "Mrs. Thibault, we haven't met, but I've talked to you on the phone. I'm Thomas Waters, FBI." He showed her his badge and identification, but she looked past it, saying nothing and barely nodding her head. "You've met my partner, Chris Carpenter," he continued, gesturing to the younger man.

She nodded again and then spoke in a soft, low voice, almost a whisper. "Yes, I know you both. I know why you're here, but you're wrong. I know nothing about Karl. Nothing. I can't help you. Please believe me."

Chris spoke up. "We'd like to believe you, Marianne. Things just don't add up. That's why we're here tonight. Maybe you can help us put some of the pieces of the puzzle together. Before we go any further, I have to read you your rights. Anything you say to us can and may be used against you in a court of law. You have the right to remain silent, or to request the presence of an attorney. If necessary ..."

Marianne rose from her chair. "What are you talking about? Rights? Are you accusing me of something?"

Waters stood as well. "No ma'am, we're not. Certainly not at this time. There are a lot of unanswered questions concerning your ex-husband, and many of them seem to concern you. We have to tell you about your rights. It's the law. That way, if we find evidence that implicates you later, what you tell us now can be used in building our case. If you've done nothing wrong, you've got nothing to worry about."

Marianne turned to face the fireplace, arms folded tightly across her chest. "Nothing to worry about? Then why am I so worried? Why are you reading me my Miranda rights? Oh, go ahead, Sergeant Carpenter—finish them up. Then maybe you can tell me what I could possibly have to do with Karl's escape."

Marianne's mind whirled. She turned from the two men who faced her without compassion or understanding. It was always the same. As a child, the accusers had been her brothers, both older and stronger than her, including one who had forcibly and systematically abused her from the time she was ten. Her father, a widower turned abruptly old and bitter by the death of his wife and the sudden weight of a family to raise on his shoulders alone, hadn't paid attention. Or, if he was aware, he hadn't cared.

Her older brother had used her to educate himself about every aspect of sex, forcing the young girl to duplicate acts he found luridly illustrated in magazines that came in the mail. By the time she was thirteen, Marianne was also being shared with the boy's friends.

Her sexual education was exhaustive but allowed little time for social development. Besides, her father expected her to "help out" around the house. In practice, this meant that most of the housekeeping chores were left to her. After she reached fourteen, she began working outside her home as well, usually as a restaurant kitchen helper or a sales clerk, to help increase the meager family income.

In school Marianne became an excellent student with few friends. The private torment she suffered at home distanced her from others. She showed a talent for art and drafting that would later give her a career, but there was never any thought of college. She looked forward to graduation and a future of stifling clerical jobs.

She had been unexpectedly swept from the daily brutality of her adolescence by a young marine who met her at the gift shop where she worked. Although she wouldn't find out until much later, Johnny Pound had been told about Marianne by one of her brother's friends. "If you want to get laid in a hurry, she's the one," Johnny was told. "She'll do anything you want. Anything!"

Johnny had gone to the gift shop expecting to find a homely slattern. He was surprised to see instead a shy, pretty, well-proportioned girl with a lucent complexion and a bell-like voice. He wondered if he had been conned, whether this was some sort of prank. He asked her to a movie, not knowing what to expect, but planning to try and score anyway. What the hell? He was on leave and wouldn't be back for a long time. To his astonishment, Marianne had reacted to his every touch and had led him to pleasure he had never expected. She infatuated him. He tried his best to spend every minute of his waning leave with her. By the time he had to return to duty, his addiction to her was complete. Six months later, three days after her high school graduation, Marianne and Johnny were married by a justice of the peace in Maryland.

To Marianne, life with Johnny was in many ways a continuation of her life at home. True, Johnny was more considerate than her monstrous brother and his brutish friends had ever been. She was finally able to enjoy herself sexually, as she never had before. Still, the grinding poverty, the menial work, and the absence of hope remained. By the time her husband left the Marine Corps and returned to his native Connecticut, Marianne had had enough.

She used her knowledge of Johnny's needs to subtly coax him toward a good job at a hobby shop, a job with more future than the production-line work he had embraced immediately after leaving the service. She worked with him to help his success until he became part-owner of the shop. Then, surprising everyone but herself, she left Johnny and quickly divorced him. The settlement put her through drafting courses at a local junior college.

Her ex-husband and his friends, even her own family, condemned her for what she had done. She ignored them and distanced herself from their complaints. They didn't matter. She had to think of her own survival. No one had ever helped her without extracting a price, without using her. She accepted their terms and saw no reason why she couldn't reciprocate in kind. To Marianne, the accusations that followed were always hollow, without basis.

She had seen real promise in Karl. He had been so lonely. She had been so sure of her future with him that she had compromised her deepest instincts and had allowed herself to bear his child. How could she have known about the devils that eventually tore his world apart? Now, through no fault of her own, she stood accused again, suspected of helping the maniac her last husband had become. It was unfair but not unexpected. Smiling grimly, she turned to face the two men, determined as always not to be defeated.

Chris recited her rights to her again. "Do you understand these rights?" he asked formally. Marianne nodded her head. "Do you wish to have an attorney present?"

"No. Just get on with this. I have a busy day in front of me tomorrow." She returned to the green chair and sat down.

"Marianne, have you seen your ex-husband since his escape?" Waters asked softly.

"No," came the choked reply.

"Have you talked to him on the phone?"

"No."

"Has he written to you or contacted you through a third party?"

"No."

"Do you have any knowledge of where he is?"

"No, I don't."

Waters shook his head. This was going nowhere. "How many times have you talked to Karl during the last five years, during his imprisonment?"

Marianne thought for a moment, looking again at the fire, now burning low. "I don't know, maybe twice a year, whenever he'd call David. We only spoke for a few seconds and never to share any kind of information. Just a hello and goodbye kind of thing."

"That's all?"

"Yes, dammit, that's all. What are you getting at?"

"Just this, Marianne," the FBI agent said slowly. "If you didn't tell him, how did Karl find out about your two boyfriends? Who told him about Harry Grissom and Perry Haldron? You're aware that the only thing these men had in common was that both were romantically involved with you. Now they're both dead. We believe Karl killed them and the people who were with them. Now, can you think of anyone else who could have told Karl about your lovers?"

Marianne sat unmoving, her eyes cast down. "No one," she said with a deep sigh. "There's no one I can think of. Karl had no friends that I can remember, no one he really liked or who liked him. We were all he had, just David and me. And even if he'd had a friend, very few people know about my personal life." She smiled bleakly. "Oh, Harry probably told a thousand people he'd had me, but nobody paid much attention to him. Perry kept our relationship very private, for obvious reasons. No one would have known about them both."

Waters nodded. "I'm glad you appreciate our predicament, Marianne. We can't find anyone who could have told him either. From all we can gather, it looks like Karl's hiding out somewhere in this area. He came back here as soon as he escaped. Who else would he have come to see, if not you and the boy?"

Marianne slowly shook her head. "He may have had nowhere else to go, you know. With nothing else to attract him, we'd be the only reason he'd come back here. Maybe he wants to see David. I don't know. You must believe me—I haven't helped him or guided him or even spoken to him. Tap my phone if you'd like." She smiled wildly. "At least maybe I'll get some calls that way. Since Karl's trial I haven't had much of a social life. The men haven't exactly been lining up at my door."

Chris and Waters looked at each other. The older man nodded. "I'm afraid we have already been monitoring your calls," Chris admitted. "For almost a month now. The fact that Karl hasn't tried to call you is one reason we're having this conversation here and not down at the precinct. There are other ways to contact people, though—letters, calls from pay phones, messages relayed through third parties. Karl was in military intelligence. He'd know all the tricks. Until we find some other link to him, you're all we've got."

Waters rose from his chair and faced her directly. "Marianne, you must understand how serious this is. Karl is a maniac. Aside from your two ex-boyfriends, we think he has killed almost twenty other people, robbing them to raise money. He has to be caught quickly. We're not after you, but if you know where he is, if you're implicated in this in any way, you must tell us. Now."

Marianne buried her head in her hands. She moaned. "Please believe me, I don't know," she whispered hoarsely. "I knew Karl was sick, but what you're telling me is beyond my worst nightmare. I wouldn't hide him. Give me a lie detector test if you want. I'll cooperate. Anything to prove that I'm telling you the truth."

Waters rose from his seat and came to her side. "We'll do that, with your permission. I'll schedule the test in the morning." He patted the back of her shoulder gently. "I have another thought, a way that may allow you to help us after all, even if Karl hasn't contacted you."

Marianne looked up, startled. "What is it? How could I possibly help?"

"It's a theory of mine that you've helped confirm," said the FBI agent as he turned to pace the room in front of her. "Let's assume that there is a third person, someone who watches you and somehow tells Karl what you're doing. Let's assume that he or she is the one who told Karl about Grissom and Haldron."

"How would he have found out?" Marianne asked. "Oh, I guess Harry would have been easy enough, but Perry Haldron was very discreet."

"He might be a neighbor, might have seen a car pull up and had the plates identified later. He might work in a motel or at a restaurant where the two of you went. Let's not worry about that for a minute. Just hear me out."

"Okay, I'm listening."

"If we assume this person exists and that he still has contact of some kind with Karl, then he is still watching you. So he'll report to Karl any new boyfriend you start to go out with. If that's true, then we can trap him."

"How?"

"If Karl follows the pattern he's used in the murders of your other friends, he'll try to lure your new lover to a resort town, probably through some fake promotion, to a place where he can torture and kill him. Then we'll have him!"

"So all I have to do is find a new lover. Is that it?"

Waters nodded his head. "I think we can even take care of that, for outside appearances at least. Marianne, meet your new beau—my young friend, Sergeant Carpenter."

They both began talking at once.

Marianne said, "Now, just a minute, is this some kind of—"

And Chris interjected, "Marianne, I had nothing to do with this. Tom, I think you're way out of line!"

The older man quieted them both. "Simmer down, both of you! You'll wake the young boy. Think it over. We have to plant a cop to make it work. We can't endanger anyone else's life. Who better than the man who's been on this case from the beginning? We can't afford mistakes now. This may be our only chance to catch this maniac."

Marianne looked at Chris coolly. "You didn't come up with this just to have an excuse to see me, did you?" she asked.

"Honestly, Marianne, I had no idea Tom was thinking this way. Believe me."

"He's right," Waters confirmed.

She smiled. "Okay, let's say for the minute that I agree to this charade. Believe me, Sergeant Carpenter, that's all it will ever be. What happens next? How do we make this work?"

"It's simple," Waters said, facing them both. "Starting tomorrow, you and Chris will start dating—two, three times a week. Call each other on the phone, be seen together at the malls, all the stuff people do when they're smitten. Then, we wait. If our theory's right, Chris should win a contest or something similar. When that happens, we'll create our net around the trap that Karl plans. We'll have him right where we want him."

Marianne was dubious. "I don't know. How long does this have to go on?"

"Let's try it for six weeks and see what happens," Waters said. "If nothing occurs by then, we'll have to think of something else."

"Meanwhile, I'm still a suspect?"

"Ask me that in six weeks."

\* \* \*

# December 14, 12:05 p.m.

David Thibault stood in the hall by the principal's office, his white hall monitor's belt contrasting his sweater and jeans. His job was to make sure that kids passing by didn't run, but no children played here. Why would they, with a beautiful Tucson winter day outside? There was a bright, cloudless sky and a temperature in the high sixties.

David didn't mind being alone. He liked playing with the other kids well enough, now that they had stopped teasing him about his dad, but he was just as content to be by himself.

Especially today! Today he had decided to call his dad, just as he had been told, to give him important information about the men who had visited his mother the night before. He hadn't been able to hear a lot of what went on, though. After all, he was supposed to be in bed asleep, with the door closed. He had three things to tell his dad. First, Mom would be seeing someone new. He had heard the man called Sergeant Carpenter tell her he would see her tomorrow as he had left. Second, the other man, whom David had not met, talked about finding a man and needing Mom's help to do it. David hadn't heard the name of the man they were looking for. Third, one of the men (David couldn't remember which one) had said that he knew that Dad was around here somewhere.

David's heart beat quickly. Maybe Dad would be so happy to hear from him that he would come to get him right now! Anyway, it would be good to hear his deep, strong voice and to know that he had done something to help. If anyone said anything, he would just say he was calling home. That's what the phone was for, wasn't it?

He reached in his wallet, pulling forth the scrap of paper with the important, secret phone number—the number his dad had entrusted to him! Then, he punched the numbers slowly and carefully: 0 - 7 - 0 - 2 - 5 - 5 - 5 - 7 - 2 - 5 - 5. He got it right the very first time. A recorded voice said, "Welcome to US West's automated call service. For collect calls, dial 0 now."

David punched the "0" button.

The recorded voice said, "At the sound of the tone, state your name."

At the musical tone, the child piped, "David!"

"Please remain on the line. Our automated system will verify acceptance of your call as soon as contact has been made," said the voice. Then, the line went blank. David wondered if he had somehow done something wrong.

After what seemed like hours, a voice came on the line. It wasn't his dad's voice, and it wasn't another recording. Instead, a female voice said, "Hello? Who is this?"

* * *

## Maslo, Nevada—12:07 p.m.

The phone rang just as Judy Carnover was leaving her new lover's apartment. She had stopped by, ostensibly to bring fresh towels but really to see if he had gotten back. She was beginning to worry. He had never been gone more than four or five days at a time, but this morning marked the eighth day of his latest trip. If only he'd told her his route. She hadn't wanted to pry. New relationships are so sensitive, so volatile.

He had called her every night for the first few days he'd been gone, but now he hadn't called for three nights running. Was something wrong? Or had she disturbed him in some way? She chided herself for her anxiety as she put the new towels in Ken's linen closet. She was acting like a schoolgirl! *Leave the poor man alone!* He had probably just gotten tied up with some business deal.

When the phone rang, she picked it up without really thinking, hoping to hear Ken's voice. Instead, a recording said, "Collect call from … David (in a little boy's voice). Do you accept? If you accept, press 1 now."

Judy pressed the "1" key. "Hello? Who is this?" she asked.

Immediately, a small boy's voice filled the phone. "Hello," came the reply. "This is David. I want to speak to my father, please."

A wave of confusion swept through Judy's mind. Ken had never mentioned children. But this must be his son. Why else would have the number? "Your father's not here right now, David. I'm a friend of his. My name is Judy. I'll have him call you as soon as he gets back. Do you have a message you want to leave?"

On the other end of the line, David's heart sank. Dad wasn't there! What could he do? He couldn't leave a message. He would have to call back. "No ma'am," he piped. "Just tell Dad I'll call him tomorrow. Thank you. Well, goodbye." The line went dead.

As she hung up the phone, Judy frowned. There were more sides to Ken than she had realized. A son meant a wife, somewhere. Had there been a divorce? She had never seen him wear a wedding ring, and there were no pictures of family on his walls or by his bed. In fact, there were no pictures at all in Ken's apartment. Aside from the state maps he had tacked up near the phone, the place was still empty.

She felt uneasy, disoriented, as though she had just found out a nasty secret. Maybe he would call today and everything would be all right. Surely he would have an explanation for this call.

For Judy, to be alone again after having had such hopes would be bitter—too bitter to stand. She turned to go, and as she did she tripped over the small chair by the desk that held the phone. As she stumbled against the chair, flailing her arms to avoid falling heavily against the wall, she upset a small box on the desk. It flew to the floor, emptying its contents as it fell.

Shocked by her clumsiness, she bent to pick up the contents of the small box, which now lay all over the floor. They seemed to be credit cards, more than twenty of them, but no three had the same name. *What could Ken be doing with these?* She packed them back into the box as best she could. She and Ken would have a lot to talk about when he finally did get back.

* * *

# Salina, Utah—4:30 p.m.

Karl parked the blue Chevy in a K-Mart plaza, about two blocks from the supermarket lot where he had left his own car over a week earlier. Time seemed to have opened like a chasm and swallowed him. It felt like a year since he had climbed on the bus for Salt Lake City— the beginning of the trip that ended so disastrously in Akron.

He had been very cautious during his drive. He had carefully scraped all of the Access decals from the car with a razor blade and had changed the license plates three times, stealing the replacements along the way. He had scrupulously obeyed every highway regulation, from speed to distance from other vehicles.

He had chosen back roads whenever possible. On his second day out from Chicago, he had stopped at a radio shop in rural Kansas and bought a police scanner radio, which he mounted unobtrusively under his dash. He listened intently for any alerts for blue Chevys but heard none. Now, after three endless days, it was finally over. All he had to do was walk to his own car and drive back to Maslo. He had made sure the Chevy was wiped clean of prints. There was nothing to connect him to the car. He had escaped—again.

An unwelcome surprise awaited him at the supermarket parking lot. His car was gone. The big Ford was nowhere to be seen. He walked the lot twice under the assumption that he might have forgotten where he had parked to no avail. He considered checking with the store manager but decided against it. He was on foot now with no quick way to escape. The car had been the property of a salesman he had killed months ago. It seemed like centuries!

Maybe the car had been identified somehow. Maybe it had been towed away at the store's request. Perhaps it had been vandalized or even stolen. It didn't matter. Despondently, he walked the two endless blocks back to the blue Chevrolet. Getting in, he drove to a motel on the outskirts of the small town and checked in, making sure he got a unit as far from the road as possible.

He entered his room and considered his options. He couldn't drive this car any closer to Maslo. Once it was discovered, it would lead the police to him. He might try to get to Vegas and get a bus from there, but that would take days he couldn't risk. He needed to get back to the safety of Maslo as soon as possible.

He could feel the pressure of the trained eyes and skilled minds seeking him. He knew they would track him down if he remained in one place too long. He had already altered his appearance by shaving off his mustache and coloring the gray from his hair. As a result, he looked years younger. He hoped Judy would like the "new" Ken because he knew now what he must do. Tonight he must call her and ask her to come and get him from this place.

\* \* \*

## Maslo, Nevada—9:10 p.m.

The diner was closed and the chores were done. Judy was mixing herself a tall vodka and tonic when the phone rang. "Must be my day for calls," she muttered as she reached to answer it. Aside from the puzzling call from what must have been Ken's son, she had gotten calls from her daughter (concerning when she'd be home for Christmas break) and from a sister in Minnesota. Nothing from Ken though. Well, she refused to let herself dwell on that.

Still, her heart skipped a beat when she heard his warm, deep voice. "Judy," he began, "I'm sorry I haven't called. I've been very busy."

She swallowed her frustration. No need to argue now. "Oh, I figured you were tied up somehow," she said, trying to keep her voice light. "You've been gone so much longer than usual. Where are you now, Ken?"

He gave a short laugh. "I'm in a little town in central Utah called Salinas. Do you know it?"

Judy thought a moment. "Yeah, I've been through it once or twice. My goodness, what are you doing there?"

"Well, I left my car here on the way out. It broke down. Now it looks like they can't fix it. Transmission and differential went, all at once."

"So you're without a car? How will you get home?"

"I was hoping you could help, Judy. I know it's asking a lot, but could you come get me? I don't want to buy a car here, and I don't want to be away from you anymore. I've really missed you."

Judy's decision was immediate. This would be the perfect time to talk things out with Ken, to get all of these confusing matters out in the open, where they belonged. "Okay. You know I'll do it. You'll have to wait till I can set up someone to mind the diner. I'll try to get out of here right after lunch tomorrow. If you help out with the driving, we can be back by lunch the next day."

"Thanks, Judy. I don't know who else I could have turned to."

"Just remember who loves you," Judy said with forced levity. "This will give us a chance to do some talking, Ken. I think we need to discuss some things."

"Oh? Like what?"

"Oh, lots of things. You know, we hardly know anything about each other."

Karl had to agree. "Yeah," he sighed. "I guess you're right. Look, let me tell you how to get to the motel." The instructions didn't take long. Salinas is not a big town. As they talked, Judy felt the warmth of their new relationship growing inside her again.

Surely, everything would be all right. She was certain of it. "Oh, I almost forgot," she said quickly as their conversation ended. "You had a call today. I was in your place changing towels, so I picked it up."

Karl was genuinely puzzled. "A call?" he asked. "From who?"

"From your son. From David."

# CHAPTER 14

## Tucson, Arizona—December 18

Christmastime in Tucson is an easy, happy occasion, with little of the frenzy that seems to mark the season in other parts of the nation. Oh, the crowds at the mall are larger than usual and the stores stay open a little later, but on the whole the brilliantly clear weather imparts a looser, calmer pace to the season. While the mountains above the city are often crowned with snow, Tucson itself still basks in the mild sixties and seventies. It is a good time to be alive and a good time for lovers to share. There are red chili pepper strings instead of pine wreaths and shoppers in shorts instead of overcoats. It is a season duplicated in few other places.

Always practical, Marianne had decided to begin her sham courtship with a trip to one of the malls to do some Christmas shopping for David. So, promptly at five, Chris had picked her up from her office for several hours of hard exercise. He had never realized the mall was so large! Once she had found the gifts she was seeking, Chris was able to convince Marianne to join him for a late dinner at one of the restaurants that adjoined the mall's parking lot. By then, his stomach's complaints were threatening to become public. They were quickly seated in a comfortable booth and drinks and dinner ordered. There was nothing to do but talk.

"I hope David likes his gifts," Marianne mused as she sipped her daiquiri. She had thoroughly enjoyed herself shopping, and she had to admit that it wasn't bad to have a tall, strong man along to carry the packages. "Now all I've got to do is find a place to hide them. There aren't that many closets in our little town house, you know."

Chris laughed. "If it helps, I'll keep them at my place and then bring them over on Christmas Eve when the boy's asleep."

"I'll take you up on that. Thanks. It'll make David's Christmas a lot brighter if he doesn't stumble over his gifts before they're under the tree."

"You mean if he doesn't go hunting them. I always did when I was a kid. I sure hated it when I really found them."

"David is a very disciplined boy, Chris. He very rarely disobeys me. He hasn't had a happy life for the last few years, you know."

Chris was puzzled. "How so?"

Marianne leaned forward, her voice low. "When Karl was arrested and the news hit the media, David was only five. We were ostracized. My God, it was as though we were on trial instead of him. Suddenly, mothers didn't want David playing with their sons. The kids at school teased him mercilessly. I thought it would end once the trial was over, but it went on for a long time after that, for over a year."

"Kids can be mean," Chris said. He remembered his own childhood. There had usually been one child singled out by the group for special attention, one child none of the others would play with or sit next to at lunch.

"David has learned to stand up for himself," Marianne continued, "and to get along without friends, for the most part. The kids leave him alone now, but he still stays by himself most of the time. I often wonder what that's done to his social development. You know, how it will affect him when he's our age."

"He does seem disciplined for a ten-year-old."

"Believe me, he can be very warm, very loving."

"I'd really like to get to know him better, Marianne."

"Just remember that what we're doing is mostly for show, Chris. David wasn't the only one Karl hurt. I've learned to get along by myself as well. The last thing I need right now is another man in my life." She seemed to be about to say more when their conversation was interrupted by the waiter bringing their food. They ate in silence.

After dinner, Chris drove Marianne back to her car. As she opened the door to leave, he finally said what was on his mind. "I'd like to follow you back to your place and talk to you for a while longer," he said.

She hesitated, frowning. "I don't think that would be a good idea, Chris. Not tonight. I still have to get David to bed, and I've got a full day ahead of me tomorrow. Can we make it another time?"

"We can, but think about this. Whoever may be watching you could be a neighbor, so it's important that I'm seen around your house. More than that, I really have some questions I need you to answer, questions that might help us understand Karl better. It could be important. Believe me, Marianne, I'm not trying to make a pass. As far as I'm concerned, I'm still at work."

She nodded briskly. "Okay. You can follow me back."

By the time they reached Marianne's town house, it was after eight. David had already fed himself, done his homework, taken his bath, and gotten ready for bed. The house was as neat as a pin. Chris considered his own cluttered bachelor pad as he sat in one of the overstuffed chairs waiting for Marianne to finish putting her son to bed. It was so easy to make excuses to yourself when living alone, to let things slide just a little every day until the cumulative result was a mess that required hours of hard work to correct. And Marianne worked hard, he thought. She had to be tired when she got home. Both mother and child showed exceptional discipline.

She came back to the living room, having changed into jeans and a shirt. "Can I fix you a drink?" she asked. "I feel like a dark and stormy, myself."

"Sounds good," he muttered without looking up. He heard the cupboard doors open, then the refrigerator, and then the splashing tinkle of drinks being mixed. In a minute she was sitting on the sofa across from him, handing him a large glass.

"Drink up," she said, raising her own glass in a toast. "Have you ever had one of these before?"

Chris smiled and shook his head. "I'm mostly a beer or bourbon man, I'm afraid. This tastes pretty good."

"It's the ginger. Brings out the flavor of the rum. Now, what was it you had to ask me about?"

Chris thought for a moment before he answered. It was important to phrase this right. "So much of what we're doing involves guessing what Karl will do when he's confronted with a given situation. It's important that we know him as well as we can. We've studied his military record, the transcripts of his trial—everything we can get our hands on. I guess I want to know your perspective, Marianne. I want you to tell me about Karl, about the two of you. Maybe you'll remember something, some fact, some incidental detail, that will help us catch this man. Believe me, it might be vital."

Marianne sighed. "Okay, I understand. Gee, where should I start? I met Karl at a Dale Carnegie course we both attended. He's a gifted public speaker, you know. I was going to try to improve my communications skills and, well, frankly, to meet someone like Karl. Or at least the person I thought he was. He seemed so strong, so sure of himself. He was also good looking, with those gray-blue eyes of his. You could tell that he was lonely, that he didn't have anybody. I decided he was my ticket out."

"Out from what?"

"From drafting jobs that would take me nowhere, from the crush of middle-class poverty in suburban Connecticut, from a career I never thought I'd realize, from a pointless, trivial life." She smiled. "I had big hopes in those days."

"So what happened?"

Marianne threw her head back, as though viewing the past above her. She frowned. "It went pretty well, at first. Karl was considerate, and even if he wasn't the world's greatest lover, he had his moments. I knew he loved me. He was always bringing me little gifts, you know, cards, flowers, whatever." She hesitated.

"What are you thinking?" Chris was beginning to feel uncomfortable. So far, he had learned more about Marianne than he had about Karl.

She shook her head and ran her fingers through her short hair. "Well ... I really don't know how to put this. Karl was always a pessimist. Always. You know the old story about the glass being half empty or half full? Karl's was always half empty. It got worse than that as time went by. Little by little. He began brooding over things, worrying about every real or imagined slight, every mistake, everything that hadn't gone absolutely, perfectly right."

Chris thought he knew what she meant. "You mean, he became a perfectionist, right?"

Marianne nodded. "That, and more. After a while, he became sure that he was somehow being punished for things he had done, especially things that happened during the war. He was sure that one day he would lose control of himself and turn into some kind of monster. He told me about it one night after a party when he'd had a little too much to drink. It was as if he was sharing some dark family secret with me. I can still remember what he whispered: 'I have to be so careful,' he said. 'I can never let the beast get out again.' At the time, I thought the whole idea was silly. Karl wouldn't hurt a fly. I'd never seen a man control himself better."

Chris felt the hair on the back of his neck rise. This was interesting. "Did he tell you how any of this happened?" he asked.

"He said he'd killed a man, one of our own troops, in Vietnam. He said he'd released the beast within him then and that now it wanted to get out again."

"We've been all though his service records. There's no hint of anything like that. Karl was a decorated hero."

Marianne agreed. "Yeah, I know. I told him he was wrong, that the whole thing was a delusion. By then our marriage was in trouble. We were having problems—in bed, if you must know. He kept claiming it was the beast he had to constantly control. I was tired of the whole thing. He was unable to get along with anyone at work, we had no friends, we never did anything. He'd sit around the house all day on the weekends, reading, watching TV, and brooding. Sometimes he wouldn't talk for hours on end. I wanted more. I wanted to have a life, to get out, to have fun. I realized I would never have that with Karl. So I went looking elsewhere."

"Were you surprised at what finally happened?"

"By the time the murder took place I had already decided to divorce

Karl. I knew he would never leave me unless I made the situation at home unbearable, so that's what I did. I made him see that there was no way he could satisfy me sexually or emotionally, and I made it plain that there were others who could. I thought he would finally smarten up and leave. In the meantime, I couldn't wait."

"What do you mean?"

Marianne got up from the sofa and began pacing the room. "Look, I've already had all of the bad publicity. Tucson's still a pretty straight-laced town, you know, underneath it all. It was my affair that triggered Karl to commit murder. That's what the court decided. That's why he went to Benniston instead of death row—that and his war record. I don't know. What was I supposed to do—stay married to him, as sick as he was? Wait until he decided one day to finally do the right thing and leave? Life's too short, Chris."

She sat down again, her eyes looking levelly at his. "I grew up in a family that had no time for anything but work and responsibility. From the time my mother died, I pitched in. I've been working since I was ten, one way or another. Five years ago, I decided to finally do something for myself."

Chris nodded, trying to remain aloof and impartial. He wondered, as he looked at her, how he would have felt in Karl's position. Marianne was beautiful, and now he knew she could also be cruel—as attractive people often are. Was her promiscuity the final push that shoved Karl into insanity? It was a provocative theory. He looked at her intently. "Do you think what you did pushed Karl over the edge?" he asked quietly.

Marianne stared at him, moving back in her chair as though she'd been slapped. She was silent for a long time. "I don't know," she finally answered. "The jury must have thought so, but I honestly don't know. Karl was moving toward what he became the night he killed my lover, without any help from me. I know that. I try not to think about the rest of it." She shook her head and stood. "It's late and I'm tired. Time to call it a night."

Chris stood and stammered a perfunctory good night. He walked to his car under a brilliant starlit sky, his mind ablaze with the implications of what he'd just heard. In a way, Karl had been as much a victim as the man he'd murdered, a victim of mounting mental instability that no one had tried to correct. Could he have been helped? The desert night held no answers.

\* \* \*

# Southwestern Utah

The aging Jeep Wagoneer lunged down the empty highway like a train alone on its track, chasing the setting sun. Karl settled back in his seat, relaxed to be finally free and untraceable, far from the trap that the small Utah town had become. He turned and watched Judy drive. After a while he reached to lightly caress her arm. "Have I said thanks?" he asked softly. "I really appreciate what you're doing for me, Judy."

She smiled broadly but kept her eyes riveted to the road ahead, squinting through the red haze of a spectacular southwestern dusk. "You're pushing all my buttons, Ken," she purred. And then, less lightly, "You have from the first. One of the main reasons I came to get you, instead of telling you to take the bus like I should have, is so we can have a talk."

Her passenger slid up in his seat. "A talk? About what?"

"About lots of things, honey. Before I start, understand that I do love you, that you've gotten to me in a way I didn't think a man could anymore. Got that? I'm your friend, Ken. Probably the best one you've got. So listen to what I have to say, and answer my questions, okay?"

Karl smiled a shallow, half-hearted grin. "Okay, Judy, whatever you say." He began to worry. What could have happened? What could she know?

"First off, Ken, is that your real name? I don't think it is, honey. Am I right?"

"What kind of a question is that?"

"A really good one, I think. Look, you've got no bank account, you always pay in cash, and sitting on your desk is a little box with about thirty credit cards in it. None of them say Ken Talley. Now which one of them are you?"

Karl's thoughts careened through his mind, small animals looking frantically for escape. How could he have been so stupid? He would have to tell her some of the truth. How much would be enough? How much could she know before she would turn from him and force him to kill her?

"Would you believe me if I told you that they all were me at one time or another and that Ken Talley is who I am right now?"

It was Judy's turn to be silent for a while. "Okay," she finally said, "then what does that mean? Are you going to tell me you're some kind of secret agent? You know, I could almost believe it, the way you act sometimes. Look at you now, your mustache shaved off and the gray gone from your hair! Hell, I had to look twice to see it was you. So go on, tell me about it."

Karl forced himself into silence for precious seconds. He would have to tell her most of the truth, applying only a thin veneer of falsehood. The mission he was on and his hopes for escape with David stood in the balance. Without Judy and his safe haven in Maslo, he would not be able to continue. "First, you should know that I love you," he began—and he realized as he said it that he probably did. She had brought emotions out of him that he had not felt for years, since Marianne had begun chiding him into impotence. He had looked forward to returning to Maslo to be with her. His emotions for her did run deep. He reached out again to touch her arm. She seemed to shudder slightly at his touch.

Judy took her right hand from the steering wheel to touch his. "I want to believe you," she said simply. "Just tell me the truth."

"I'm an ex-army officer," Karl continued. "Lots of medals, not much direction. One of this country's security agencies—it doesn't matter which one—decided they needed a special job done, and they picked me to do it. I've been all over the country for the last several months, from the time I came to Maslo until now. Every place I've gone I've had a new identity. In the end, I've always come back to you."

"There's something else, something more you must tell me."

Karl was confused. What could she mean? "No, there's nothing else."

"Then who's the boy who calls you and asks for his dad? Tell me the truth, Ken. Are you married?"

Relief washed over him. It was that simple. It was only the call from David. He wondered what the boy had wanted to tell him. "You're right," he answered truthfully. "There was a marriage, but it's been over for more than five years. I guess I was weak to give my boy the number, but I love him so much. So now you know my secret. I'd have told you anyway."

Judy could sense the truth in the man's words. The talk about the secret agent stuff she didn't understand, but it explained what he'd been doing for the last six months. The money he'd lived on had to come from somewhere. She decided to accept his words, at least for now. Her ache for him grew even as she formed her thoughts. How could she reject the man who showed her the love he had showed? As the old Jeep drilled through the sunset, she made up her mind. She was his, no matter what the price.

\* \* \*

## Tucson

Chris heard the steps behind him as he climbed out of his car. He turned and saw Ginny hurrying toward him.

"Chris," she said breathlessly as she rushed to his side, "I've been looking for you all over town. Have you taken monk's vows or something?"

Chris grinned. Ginny had always known how to make him smile. "Or something," he said. "I've been working pretty hard lately, Ginny. Not much time for social life. I'm okay though. Thanks for checking."

"I missed you, Chris," Ginny said. "I feel like we ought to see each other some more. We know each other. We're comfortable."

Chris was confused. He hadn't planned on this discussion or even thought about his friend and former lover for weeks.

"Ginny," he began, "I—"

"Look, Chris," Ginny said. "I was at the mall today. I saw the gal you were with. She's not for you. Believe me. Give me a chance."

"Ginny, you don't understand," Chris said. "The woman I was with, that's police business. Now look, I'm too tired to invite you up. I'll call you tomorrow. Okay?" He turned to go.

Ginny sighed. Her shoulders slumped. "Chris, you can't just leave it at that. I know police business, and I know the look I saw on your face."

Chris felt himself tense. "You're out of line, Ginny," he said. "Let's not have an argument out here in the parking lot. Not over this."

Ginny grabbed his arm. "Chris, don't you know who that woman is? She drove her husband insane till he killed her boyfriend. She's a man-eater, and you're no match for her. Leave her alone, Chris. You deserve better."

"And that's you, Ginny?"

"Yes, dammit, it is!" Ginny said, backing away from him with her eyes glittering. "Okay, you're not listening. I'm sorry I decided to come. Just remember, I did. Someday you're going to need me. I may not be there." She turned and walked quickly away.

# CHAPTER 15

## Tucson, Arizona—December 20

It was almost noon. David looked furtively around the town house's pool area before entering the fenced and walled enclosure. The pool served fifty units and was moderately crowded during this time of day in the warmer months. Tucson had felt the coming of winter, and no one in David's neighborhood had decided to swim on this cool, blustery December day. David would not have been here either except that the pool area held the only pay telephone within his walking distance. He was out of school today as his teachers prepared to issue grades. He was home alone. The babysitter wouldn't be over to watch him until the afternoon. He knew he had to call his dad.

Earlier this morning, he had looked in his mother's address book, waiting until a full hour had passed from the time she left for work. Sure enough, there was a new entry: an address and phone number for Chris Carpenter. The policeman had been at the house three times this week. Dad would want to know. There were the other things to tell him too, about the other man who had come and their conversation with Mom. And what about Brazil? David was afraid that he couldn't hold the secret much longer. He hoped that his dad would be coming for him soon.

David carefully copied the address and phone number to a piece of paper and then put the address book back in its place on the nightstand by the telephone. Then he made himself wait another hour before walking to the pool.

The whole area seemed deserted and silent. Each town house stood behind its own high wall, and the development itself was ringed by another wall, locking out the sounds of the neighboring community and giving the place a Middle Eastern look. As David walked down the narrow lane from his home to the pool, the only movement he noticed was the trees bending in the stiff breeze off the Santa Catalina Mountains, which reared not five miles to the north and took up a large portion of the sky. The sky itself was a cloudless vault of crystal blue, marred from time to time only by the paths of jets high in the atmosphere as they flew toward the West Coast or circled for a landing at the airport south of the city. It was a beautiful day.

David reached the pool enclosure in a matter of minutes and put his key in the locked gate. By the rules, he wasn't supposed to be there without a chaperone, but since he wasn't going in the pool and since no one else was around, he didn't think it would matter. If anyone asked him, he would tell the truth. He would tell them he had come to use the phone. He opened the gate and walked quickly to the cabana at the back of the pool. The phone hung on a back wall near the shower stalls. He carefully dialed the number his father had given to him, feeling again a wave of pride at having been entrusted with something so important, and listened to the litany of electronic voices that responded to it. He had tried to call three times last week but had never gotten through— except for that one time when some lady answered.

David wondered if Dad was with somebody else, now that he and Mom were apart. He supposed that was possible. After all, Mom had gone out with Mr. Grissom and then with Mr. Haldron, and now with Chris. Somehow he couldn't picture Dad with somebody else. No, Dad would be with Mom, or he would be by himself.

His thoughts were interrupted by the deep, strong sound of his father's voice. "Hello?"

As always, David's emotions at the sound of that voice carried him away. "Oh, Dad," he cried. "It's me! It's David! I'm calling, just like you said I should!"

There was silence for a few seconds, followed by a warm chuckle.

"David," Karl answered. "I've been waiting for your call. I was told you tried to call me last week."

"I did, Dad, but some lady answered. I guess you weren't home."

"That's right, David. I was on a business trip. Now, son, I know you must have lots of things to tell me, but first, how are you? You know I miss you."

The boy's heart melted. "Oh, Dad, I miss you too, so much. I'm fine. School's out today so the teachers can do the report cards. I'm going to get all A's, I'm pretty sure."

Karl listened, genuinely moved by his son's words. His son! A boy any man would be proud to call his own. Karl missed him so. He made up his mind as he listened—he would leave with David as soon as possible with the money he had. He would worry about the future once they were safe in Brazil. "David, I have some great news for you. I'm glad you called. Now, tell me what you called about."

"Dad, some men came to see Mom, just like you said they would. One of them was Chris Carpenter, the policeman I told you about before. Remember? I told you how he showed me his badge."

"I remember. Go on."

"Well, they had a long talk. Some of it was about you. They wanted to know where you are, but Mom couldn't tell them."

"And you mustn't either, David. It has to be our secret."

The boy went on. "Oh, I know, Dad. Don't worry. Anyway, I don't think anyone is going to ask me. The other thing they talked about was some kind of plan, like Mom was going to help them find someone. Someone else, I guess. I couldn't hear it all, through the doors."

Karl nodded to himself. It was time to go. They were going to use Marianne to try to trap him. "Go on, son. Was there anything else?"

David reached for the piece of paper with the address and phone number he had copied. "Just this, Dad. Mom has a new friend. And guess what—it's Sergeant Carpenter! He's kind of neat, but nothing like you, Dad. I got his address, just like the other times. Do you want me to read it to you?"

Karl paused, his plans now thrown to chaos. Marianne with someone new? No. It had to be some kind of trap. It couldn't be real.

"David, listen to me carefully. Are you sure this man Carpenter is really your mom's friend? How can you be sure?"

The boy's answer was matter-of-fact. "Well, I mean, he comes to the house almost every day now, and he always takes Mom places. Last Saturday he brought her flowers, and he went to church with us on Sunday. And Dad?"

"Yes, son?"

"I saw them kissing. Twice."

Karl bit his hand to avoid voicing the howl of rage that welled up from his throat. There was silence on the line for endless seconds. "David," he finally gasped, "give me that address."

Once he'd copied down the address and phone number, Karl decided to end the conversation. Even though he could have talked to his son for hours, he suddenly had many things to do, much to prepare. "I've got to go now," he said, "but I have good news, son. My work is almost done." He grinned wildly to himself. "Almost. I have only one more thing to take care of, and then we'll leave. What do you think of that?"

"Oh, Dad, that's great! When can I tell Mom?"

"Leave that to me. It still has to be our secret for just a little while more. Okay?"

"Okay, Dad. I understand. Can I call you on Christmas Eve?"

"Of course, David. That would be the best Christmas present I could have. Goodbye son, I love you."

The line went dead. David replaced the receiver carefully and then walked back to his home. Dad had sounded so strange at the end of their conversation, like he'd been hurt. David knew that Dad didn't like Mom going out with other men, but he also knew that his mom didn't want to see Dad anymore. She had told him that. Still, he didn't like to hurt his dad's feelings, even if he was only doing what he had been told to do. He decided he would fix himself a sandwich and then play a video game. His mind made up, he entered the house and shut out the beautiful day.

\* \* \*

# Richfield, Utah

Two men walked down a long, dusty line of cars in the large fenced field. It was a warm day for winter in the midst of the Fishlake National Forest, and a strong breeze sang through the big pines.

The Utah state patrolman turned to Thomas Waters. "Wouldn't think we'd pick up this many cars out here, would you?" he said.

The FBI agent nodded in agreement, staring at the hundreds of cars in the lot. "Well," the patrolman continued, "lots of them are abandoned during storms. Their owners never return to pick them up. Some are driven by felons we catch trying to reach Mexico from the north or the west. Drug smugglers make up the rest. We have an auction every couple of months. Helped us build the new station over in Sevier. Here's the one you're interested in."

They had stopped next to a white Ford. "Supermarket in Salina complained it had been left unattended for several days. We towed it in last week and ran the usual checks. Plates had been stolen, but the VIN shows a Herbert Mossbach, salesman murdered in Missouri last June."

Waters nodded absently, looking intently at the dusty car. "Yeah, I know," he muttered.

"Hell, I guess you do. Hadn't been more than an hour we'd tickled that file when you called us. This must be part of some investigation the bureau is running, huh?"

"A very important part. Corporal, I need this car dusted for prints immediately. Do you have the people to do it here?"

"Have to send for a team from Provo. Take about a day."

"I can have my men here quicker. Do you mind?"

The patrolman shook his head. "Don't bother me. Glad to oblige," he said with a grin.

"Okay. I'll need to use your phone when we get back to the office. Now, can you take me to where the car was found? I'll want to talk to the store manager who reported it."

"Sure. Salina is right up the road. I'll call ahead to make sure the man is there for you to talk to."

Waters smiled. "Great," he said. "I really appreciate your

cooperation." He looked at the car again with great satisfaction. This had to be the car Karl used to get back to his hideout. He was somewhere close. The search area had just been narrowed by more than half. He turned and followed the patrolman back to the police car.

\* \* \*

# Tucson, Arizona—December 23, 11:30 a.m.

The dusty Wagoneer stood parked in the lot of the Triple Hill Hotel, a Tucson landmark. It had been hard to find a parking space since tourist season was getting into full swing. Karl had been forced to park behind the convenience store at the edge of the hotel grounds. He had stayed at the Triple Hill for three days, using hard-won cash, but it had been worth it. This would be the site of his trap for the policeman, Chris Carpenter. It would end his mission. After this, he would escape to Brazil with his son.

He knew that they would be expecting him this time and that they would try to trap him. He would trap them instead and exact his vengeance. The thought of what he would do sent a chill of excitement through him. *Control!* He willed himself to remain calm, to suppress the jagged rock and roll thoughts that were beginning to course through his mind. *Not yet, but soon.*

He had his plan. Now he could go back to Maslo and spend a quiet Christmas with Judy and her vapid daughter. Then, in January, he would strike. As he drove from the lot of the hotel, he allowed himself a riff from the music in his mind—the muted wail of a saxophone, the thrum of a bass guitar. He smiled with the confidence he always felt as the beat flowed through him.

\* \* \*

# 10:20 p.m.

Chris parked his Plymouth expertly next to the wall surrounding the courtyard of the Thibault town house. He knew that the surveillance car in the lot behind him had noted his presence. He hoped they attributed it to his work. He left the car and moved around it to open Marianne's door, but as usual she had already opened it herself and was walking toward her gate. "Thanks for a nice time, Chris," she said over her shoulder. "Want to come in for a cup of coffee?"

"Sure," Chris answered, smiling as he walked to her side. "And thanks back. I had a great time myself. I really do enjoy being with you, Marianne."

Marianne glanced up at him as she opened the gate and returned his smile warmly. "You dance pretty good for a big guy, and the food was good. Have you been to that place often?"

"Once or twice," Chris admitted, "but never with anyone so pretty."

Marianne's blush was apparent, even in the moonlight. "I'd swear you were Irish, with all that blarney," she said softly, opening the town house's front door. "Sit down and make yourself comfortable. I'll check on David, then I'll be out to put some coffee on."

Chris nodded. "Okay, I will. Say, do you mind if I put on some music?

Her answer floated down the hallway. "Help yourself. Keep it soft. I don't want to disturb David. Okay?"

Chris walked to the stereo cabinet near the bookcase to pick out a tape. He chose a personal favorite, a collection of ballads, and slid it into the tape deck. Marianne still had not returned. He moved to a chair, sat down, and closed his eyes, allowing the music to flow over and through him to wash conflicting thoughts from his mind.

He knew he was in love with Marianne, beyond doubt. She was everything he had imagined her to be the first time they had met and more. He felt that she was warming to him, as well. When they danced the slow ones, she molded herself to him, resting her face against his chest and breathing softly against him as they swayed slightly to the music.

They had kissed several times in front of her house. It had been agreed that this would occur in case Karl's informant was watching. Lately, the kisses and caresses had become more than perfunctory, had lasted longer, and had ended with more feeling each time. He was spinning into something beyond his control, but he welcomed it.

Marianne brought him back from his thoughts, stroking the side of his face lightly. "I was beginning to think you were snoozing," she said, smiling. "Well, David's fast asleep, and I've removed enough of the junk around his bed so he'll be able to get up tomorrow." She turned and walked toward the small kitchen. "Now, how about it? Do you want coffee or another drink?"

Chris sat up in his chair. Marianne had done more than tuck her son into bed. She had gotten out of her clothes and changed into a satin negligee and matching peignoir. "A drink, I think," he finally said.

Noting his attention, Marianne smiled. "I hope you don't mind. I've been in those clothes all day, and I like to get comfortable when I'm home."

He rose and followed her to the kitchen. She stood at the counter, reaching for the bottles to fix their drinks. He put his arms around her and kissed the back of her neck. "Mind?" he said. "You're driving me crazy, but I don't mind. You're beautiful, Marianne. Turn around."

She turned in his embrace and put her arms around his neck, opening herself to him. He kissed her deeply, his mind spinning. All thought of the investigation, of everything but her was gone from his mind. "I want you," he murmured in her ear as his hands roamed her breasts.

She pushed him away. They were both panting. "And I you," she answered, her words slurred by the passion behind them. "Not here. Come with me." Holding his hand, she led him from the house, through the garage, and to the attached guest cottage. Opening the door, she led him inside. "This was Karl's office at home," she explained. "The bed is for guests. I guess you qualify." She quickly turned down the covers of the large brass bed in the corner of the room. Removing her robe, she lay down and reached out for him. "I've waited for this—for you, Chris. I need a man like you to protect me. Come to me, now."

As she spoke, Chris was already removing his clothes. His erection was a throbbing, living thing with a life of his own. He was consumed by his desire. He climbed on top of Marianne, crushing her in his arms. She responded, her hands quickly finding and stroking his penis. "Wait," she whispered. "You must wait, lover. I'm not ready for you yet."

In answer, he lifted her to his mouth, and as she lowered herself to him, he licked and kissed her with a passion that soon had her moaning with anticipation as she reached for him. "Now lover," she cooed, "you've done all the work. Let me do some work for a while." With that she mounted him, lowering herself and impaling herself on his manhood. He grabbed her hips as she moved up and down on his shaft, both of them beyond words.

Finally, he whispered, half crying, "I'm close."

"Then come for me, darling," she answered, the flush of orgasm already coloring her breasts. "Come for me, right now," she sighed as she increased the strength and the speed of her strokes.

In breathless seconds, Chris's world exploded. Afterward, as she lay in his arms, his hands explored the wonder of her. She had given him all he had imagined she could and more. "I guess that's the end of proper police procedure," he murmured with a sigh.

"Oh, I don't know, Sergeant," Marianne answered with a grin. "I'd say there's lots more to investigate. And we've got hours till you've got to go." In the dark, she reached for him again and he for her.

# CHAPTER 16

## Tucson, Arizona—
## December 26, 12:15 p.m.

The time between Christmas and New Year's is a hollow, empty time in most offices around the country. Many people have contrived to take the whole week off, and those who must work often have their minds on other matters. The Christmas festivities are over; the New Year's Eve parties are on the horizon. Not very much gets done.

On the other hand, police and hospital staffs find this a crazy time, when people's emotions seem to run amok. Suicides and attempted suicides are up, as well as murders, car accidents, fires, assaults, and other crimes that involve passion or a lack of common sense.

Chris had spent an enjoyable Christmas Day, first with his own family and later with Marianne and David. His time with her had been one of continuing passion. When they touched, it was almost like an electric shock for both of them, and neither could keep hands off the other. They made love as often as possible. Chris could not remember ever having been so drawn to a woman. He had always thought of himself as a calm, low-key lover, but his desire for Marianne was acute and continuous. A heady admixture of love and lust consumed him.

Today he was too busy to think about anything but his job. He had just gotten back from handling a domestic dispute—his third that morning—when he found the note on his desk; Waters needed to see him right away. He checked out, walked back to his car, and drove to the federal building, where the FBI agent had set up his office.

"Happy day after, Tom," he said, smiling as he entered the outer office and removed his coat. The agent's secretary was nowhere to be seen. "Where's Ruth?" Chris asked.

Waters rose from his desk and walked into the larger, outer room. He wasn't smiling. "I told her to take a long lunch, Chris. I needed to talk to you, and I didn't want anyone else around. Sit down." He motioned Chris to a chair at a small conference table.

Chris frowned. "What's the matter, Tom? Has there been more trouble? Some more deaths?" He sat down at the conference table, puzzled at his older friend's sternness.

"No, it's not Karl. Not this time. As far as we can tell, he hasn't stirred from his hiding place since we almost caught him in Chicago. We even found the car he stole from the Access lot there, hidden in a gully a couple of miles from Salina—the town where he left his first car. He's nearby, Chris. Somewhere in Utah, Nevada, or Arizona. I'm sure of it. We just need him to make another move."

"Maybe this thing with Marianne will work," Chris offered. "It seems like she's our only hope. I've been seeing her almost every night, just like we planned."

The agent looked at him intently. "Yeah, I know. That's what I called you here to talk about. Chris, I've made an appointment to see your lieutenant tomorrow. I'm going to ask him to take you off this case. I wanted to tell you first, though, one on one."

Chris stood, his face reddening. "What the hell are you talking about, Tom? What's going on?"

Waters looked at his young friend calmly, almost sadly. He slowly drew and lit a cigarette. "Sit down, Sergeant," he said. "Yelling won't do either one of us any good. You know what I'm talking about as well as I do. You know the Thibault house is under constant surveillance. How long did you think it would take for word to get to me about what you and the woman have been doing?"

Chris felt his face redden even further. He couldn't look Waters in the eyes. "Jesus, Tom," he managed to say, "the whole point was to get close to her, to make it look like we were lovers ..."

Waters nodded his head, a grim smile on his face. "You said it, partner. The idea was to make it *look* like you were lovers, not to get close to her for real. You've fallen for her. Don't bother trying to deny it. You've lost whatever objectivity you had. You're a liability now, Chris, whether you're willing to admit it or not."

Chris forced himself to speak slowly and calmly, his eyes still cast down. "Marianne and I are lovers, Tom. I'm not going to lie about it. What does that really change?"

"For God's sake, Chris, think a minute! What if she's still involved with Karl?"

"I know she's not."

"Show me your evidence."

"I can't. You know I can't, but I believe her. She's not the link to Karl we're after. It has to be somebody else."

"Even if you're right, Chris—and I don't know that you are—I've still got to take you off this case. You're no good to me now. You're too close to things, no objectivity. I'm sorry. You know I'm right."

Chris sighed, then shook his head. "I guess you are, Tom. I wish I knew how this happened. I've never met a woman like Marianne before. I think I'm really in love."

"She's awful pretty, Chris. I guess she was looking for someone herself. She's also a prime suspect. Hell, you read her the Miranda rights yourself, remember? I hate to do this, but there's no other way."

Chris got up from the table and extended his hand to the FBI agent. He tried to smile, with partial success. "Well, it was a pleasure to work with you, Tom. You taught me a lot. If this is the way it's got to end, let's not stop being friends. Do what you have to do." He turned and walked from the office.

* * *

# 3:15 p.m.

If the day had been less busy, Chris would have taken some time off. High call volume prevented that, so he forced himself to work through his anguish. He still had tonight to look forward to, tonight and Marianne. Just the thought of her made him sexually tense. He shook his head to clear his mind and rose from his desk to go for yet another cup of coffee. His phone rang, jarring his thoughts fully back to the here and now. He retreated to his desk and picked up the receiver.

"Detective Sergeant Carpenter. Can I help you?"

There was a long silence on the line. Chris began to think the other party had hung up. Finally, a gravelly, muffled voice said, "Friend of mine wants to meet you."

Chris tried to think. Which case could this relate to? He knew of four where informants were being sought. This must be one of them. "What's your friend's name?" he asked mildly.

"I'll tell you later. He'd be mad if he knew I was talking to you. He doesn't like you much."

"What's your name?"

There was another silence on the line. Finally, "Morrison. Gilley Morrison."

"Okay, Mr. Morrison."

"Call me Gilley. Everybody calls me Gilley." The voice really sounded muffled, as though cloth was being used to disguise its true sound.

Chris tried again. "Okay, Gilley. You're going to have to give me some more information if you want this conversation to continue. Things are pretty busy here today, and I've got lots of work to do."

"This has to do with a case you've been on, one that you're really involved in," the man who called himself Gilley continued. "Word is, this is a case you're really enjoying, Detective Carpenter."

"Who are you?"

"A friend. A friend of a guy who got a raw deal five years ago. His name is Karl. You know who I mean?"

Chris gasped. This was the break they'd been waiting for! "We've got to meet," he said hurriedly.

The man on the other end of the line chuckled. "Not likely. Not likely I'll stay on the line much longer either. You might trace my call.

I'll call you back in an hour. I've got more to tell you. Stay by the phone." The line went dead.

Chris immediately put in a call to Tom Waters. He could hardly wait for the agent to come to the phone. "Tom," he blurted. "We just got a call from a friend of Karl's. Calls himself Morrison. Gilley Morrison. He's going to call back in an hour. Can you get over here? I'm going to try to arrange a meeting."

The answer was immediate. "Yeah, Chris, I'll be there. I guess the fat's in the fire. Too late to pull you out now. Say, you ever know any ranchers?"

"No, I really haven't."

"Well, sometimes, to catch a wolf or a puma, a rancher will stake out a cow just to draw the critter in. Sometimes, the varmint gets killed before he gets to the cow, sometimes not."

Chris was puzzled. "What's that got to do with me?"

"Just this. I meant what I said today. You've lost your objectivity. As a cop, you're no good on this case anymore. Right now, all you are is a staked cow. I hope we get the bastard before he gets to you."

\* \* \*

## Maslo, Nevada—4:30 p.m.

Karl hung up the phone, unwrapping his handkerchief from the receiver as he set it down. Things had gone just the way he had hoped. The policeman, Carpenter, had agreed to meet Gilley Morrison at the Triple Hill Hotel in three days at two in the afternoon. Naturally, the police would be there early. So would Karl. The meeting would never take place, at least not the way Marianne's newest lover envisioned it. By the end of the day, Carpenter would be dead and Karl would be free. He planned to leave for Brazil before the end of February, as soon as he could get the necessary passports and visas for himself and David. He felt charged with an energy he could not release. He walked around his apartment, humming a nameless tune. There was much to be done, more planning—and a shopping trip to Las Vegas tomorrow. He had a lot to prepare.

A knock on his door interrupted his thoughts. He answered it to find Judy waiting on the landing, a frown furrowing her deeply tanned face. "Ken, we have to talk," she said shortly. "Can I come in?"

"Sure, come on in, honey, I'm glad to see ..." His words died in his throat as she brushed by him to sit in the living room. Puzzled, he followed her to sit on the couch. He couldn't imagine what could be on her mind. Since they had returned from Utah, she had spent more time in his bed than in her own. Their lovemaking had passed from the stage of discovery to the easy dispensing of mutual pleasure. They were learning to truly enjoy each other, physically and emotionally. As he looked at her, sitting stiffly by herself, he knew that something had to be seriously wrong. Her attitude toward him had changed completely.

He had chosen his seat deliberately, positioning himself so that the sun through the window in back of him made his face hard to see, silhouetting his head against its brightness. "Judy," he asked earnestly, "what's the matter?"

"It looks like you've been lying to me—that's what's the matter. Lying. Now I don't know how much of you is real and how much is just an act. You're going to tell me what's real. Today. Right now."

"What do you mean, honey? You know I can't tell you everything about what I'm doing. That's just for your own good."

"Bullshit, Ken. The facts say you're nothing but a murderer."

Karl fell back in his seat as though he'd been hit. How could she know? He found it impossible to frame a response of any kind although his mind labored to find one. He was speechless with shock and surprise.

Judy nodded, a grim smile appearing on her face. "Yeah, I thought that would get to you. That TV show—*Those Most Wanted*—says you're the Gambling Mecca Maniac they've been talking about and that you've killed people all over this state, all over the country! They showed a picture too. The guy could be your brother."

Karl blanched. His mind reeled. Would he have to kill her too, this woman who had finally awakened him to love again? He stared at her, still unable to think of anything to say.

"Ken, I came here to find out the truth. Talk to me. If you're the psycho they say you are, then kill me and get it over with. Because if you are, I don't want to live. I love you, no matter what you've done. Talk to me, honey. Tell me the truth about who you are." Tears formed in her eyes.

Karl finally spoke. "What are you talking about?" he whispered.

"It was Nori. She's been following the whole thing. It's part of a course she's taking, abnormal psychology. She was showing me her term paper—she's so proud of it—when I noticed the dates. The murders in Nevada occurred at times when you were gone. Not on business trips either. Just gone for the weekend. Then I remembered one of the names on the credit cards in that little box. You know, the one you've thrown away now. It was Grissom, the name of one of the first people killed. I'm sure of it."

Karl forced himself to think clearly. Judy was so much sharper than he had thought. "Judy," he finally said, "you're behaving like judge and jury. At least give me a chance to defend myself. Because I'll tell you right now, you're wrong."

Judy's scowl deepened. "Okay, Ken. Convince me. Nothing would make me happier than to know that I'm wrong, that I'm just a silly woman chasing fantasies."

"You're far from that, Judy. After all, I'm in love with you, and I couldn't fall for just anybody. Sure, I was gone those weekends, just like I'm going to be gone tomorrow, if you'll lend me the car. I was shopping for clothes in Vegas. New identities need different duds, you know. As for the credit card, I like to pick names of people I recognize. Gus Grissom was a famous astronaut. I still remember him. Don't you? The fact that a man with the same last name was murdered is pure coincidence, nothing more. Now, I want you to stop this third degree. I won't tell you everything I'm doing for your own good. I will tell you this: my work is almost done. Soon, when I'm finished, I'm going to pick up my son and the three of us are going to have a wonderful, quiet life together. What do you think about that?"

She rose from her chair and walked toward him, tears streaming down her face. "Ken," she sighed, "I hope to God what you're saying is true. I don't think I could stand to lose you. Not now. No matter what you are, I'm yours."

Karl rose as well and opened his arms to her. Holding her close, he gently wiped the tears from her eyes. "There," he whispered, rocking her gently as he held her. "That's better. I'm just who I say, and not that glamorous either. Just a man about to finish a dirty job. Now, Judy, when I go to Tucson on the twenty-ninth, I'm going to need your help, darling."

# CHAPTER 17

## Tucson, Arizona—
## December 29, 11:30 a.m.

Chris and Tom walked from the room they had set up as their field headquarters to the balcony overlooking the lobby of the Triple Hill Hotel. Chris explained the security arrangements that had been put in place. "We have teams of men at all exits and a roving patrol in the parking lot. We have four squad cars ready to block off Alvernon Way, two blocks north and two blocks south, if that becomes necessary. We have a chopper ready to start orbiting the area, beginning two hours from now, half an hour before the meeting is supposed to start. This Morrison can get in, but he won't get out unless we let him."

The FBI agent nodded. "We have some of our people here as well. Where are you running your comm from?"

"From the room. That's where you should spend most of your time. Officer Sheldon has set up a comm link with all teams. We have descriptions of Morrison and of Karl, of course, just in case he shows up too. They've been issued to everybody involved."

Waters smiled. "So this Morrison fella really exists, huh? What did you find out about him?"

Chris shrugged. He was clearly excited about the prospect of getting past the stalemate they had all endured on this case. "Morrison was the editor of the local business paper, the one that folded a few years back. Karl used to write for him from time to time. Apparently, they got to be friends. No one's seen the man for a couple of years. Last anybody heard, he was selling diet cookies in Tennessee."

"Uh-huh. What does he look like?"

"Little guy, about as wide as he is tall. Brown hair, graying. Bright red moustache, though. Quite a character, from his description. Hard to miss in a crowd."

"Any priors?"

"Got into some trouble as a kid and had a few complaints when he ran the paper, but nothing that got him in front of a judge. He did have some tax trouble before the paper went under. That's about it."

"Well, he's in trouble now, big time—that is, if it's him you're dealing with."

Chris was puzzled. "What do you mean?" he asked.

Waters smiled. "I don't think you're dealing with this Morrison character at all, Chris. Hell, nobody's seen him here in years. No, I think we're going to see Karl today—the man himself."

He leaned over the balcony, looking at the lobby below. "I wish we could have cordoned this place off entirely, kept all the citizens out."

Chris nodded in agreement. "We asked. Couldn't do it, not in the middle of the season. It seems the Kiwanis are coming in today."

He joined the older man at the balcony. "It won't matter. Look at Karl's MO. He never carries a gun. There are enough of us. We'll make him if he shows up. Once he's in here, he's ours. There's no way he can escape."

* * *

# 12:15 p.m.

Judy drove past the Dew Drop Inn, a small bar on Grant Avenue just off Alvernon. "Pull over now," Karl directed her. "I'll get out here."

Judy frowned. "Are you sure?" But even as she spoke, she turned the car into the next parking spot available.

"Yes, let me off right here. I have a tight schedule to keep."

He smiled. No reason to spook her now. "Remember what I told you," he reminded her as he pulled his heavy knapsack from the back seat and climbed from the car. "Be at the drive-in on Alvernon for the eight o'clock movie. Try to put your car somewhere in the middle of the parking area for movie number three. I'll find you, and then we'll leave. Do you have any questions, baby?"

Judy shook her head. This was all kind of exciting, in a dreamy sort of way. Ken was leaving her to do God knew what, but he was her man and she trusted him. She wondered if she would read about what he did today in the papers.

Her thoughts were interrupted by the brush of his lips against hers, the stroke of his hand against her neck. Then he was gone from the car and moving away as she turned back into the traffic of one of Tucson's major streets. She looked back to wave goodbye to him, but he had vanished from view as if he had never been there.

Karl scanned the inn as he walked toward it, keeping well within the sharply defined midday shadows of the buildings around him. Good, the man hadn't shown up yet. Just then, the dark green van from Roberts Exterminating (the logo was a golden revolver shooting the words "Say Goodbye to Bugs & Varmints") pulled up in back of the building, parking in a secluded spot impossible to see from the road. The driver got out and went into the bar to drink his lunch, just as he had the week before when Karl had followed him from his company's yard. The man wouldn't be long, no more than half an hour. Karl hoped he would enjoy his lunch. It would be his last.

* * *

## 12:45 p.m.

Vince Barnabali was a man of firm habit. He had stopped at the Dew Drop for lunch every workday for the past seven years, almost since the first day he had been given the job at the Triple Hill by his company. It was an easy assignment, requiring only that he get in before one and out before three so as not to disturb the guests leaving or coming in.

He did his utmost to comply. Since spraying the rooms for bugs was dull work, Vince liked to dull himself a little before attempting it. Two stiff drinks at the inn usually did the trick. They certainly had today. He stumbled from the darkness within the bar, squinting and scowling at the intense sunlight of midday. He was a big, long-armed man with a mop of steel-gray hair atop a lean, lined face that refused to tan. Tucson was the end of a long trip for him that had begun with a hitch in the army and ended with two failed marriages back east.

As he walked stiffly toward the dark green van, his thoughts were of his second wife, Blanche, and her continual nagging. How glad he was to be done with her! As he put his key into the van's door, firm pressure on his back made all other thoughts flee. A calm voice said, "Go around to the back of the van and open the rear doors. Hesitate and I'll shoot you."

Vince started to raise his hands. "I've got no money. Take the van, go ahead."

"Shut up!" commanded the voice. "And don't turn around. I don't want to shoot you, but I will. Now, just do as I say. Walk to the back and open the doors."

Vince did as he was told, as he had always done. It was his final act of obedience. As he opened the van's doors, Karl crushed his skull with a crowbar, killing him instantly.

Quickly, Karl deposited the body in the back of the van and then stripped it of the dark green Roberts coveralls. Pulling the coveralls on over his own clothes, Karl climbed into the van, dragging the body farther inside and covering it with a tarp to keep it out of sight. Finally, he transferred three thermos-sized containers from his knapsack to the dead man's utility cart.

Reaching into the knapsack again, Karl removed a small electronic control device and put it in his pocket. He was ready to go. Walking back to the front of the van, he climbed in and started the motor. He was light with anticipation and tension. His final mission was about to begin.

* * *

## 1:05 p.m.

It was hot on the landing by the hotel's service bay and getting hotter. Jan Severson tried to make the best of it, smoking cigarette after cigarette and carrying on a perfunctory conversation with the other cops and the assistant hotel manager who had been assigned to help them. It was rapidly getting too hot to talk. "I'd sure like to lock the door and just keep everybody out," he said idly.

"I wish you could," said Ryley, the manager from the hotel. "I don't like it out here anymore than you do, but we can't shut the hotel down. There are deliveries due through here all afternoon." He rolled his eyes.

Just then, a dark green van moved into view, rolling to the end of the bay and parking. A man in olive coveralls got out of the truck and began to walk toward the vehicle's rear doors.

"Who's this?" Severson asked.

Ryley consulted his clipboard. "Let's see ... should be the guy from Roberts Exterminating. Comes here every day but Sunday to spray the vacant rooms."

"Let's go meet him," Severson said. The quartet moved toward the van.

* * *

## 1:07 p.m.

Karl was careful to pull into the same bay he had watched the Roberts truck use last week. He assumed that he was being watched, even now, by the police. Sure enough, four men came down the ramp from the hotel to meet him as he climbed from the van. Two were obviously not from the hotel, and one stopped to speak into a small radio transceiver as they approached him. Karl grinned and waved. "Hi," he said nonchalantly, as he opened the rear doors to remove the exterminator's service cart.

The men surrounded him. "You here to spray the rooms?" the man from the hotel asked.

Karl continued to smile. "Yes, sir, that's me. That's us, rather. Roberts Exterminating. I don't usually rate a welcoming committee, though. Look, do you want me to come back later? What's going on?"

One of the two men—who Karl realized must be police—spoke. "Just a routine check, sir. There's a dignitary coming to the hotel this afternoon. I'm afraid we're going to have to search you."

Karl forced himself to laugh. He would be okay as long as they didn't look in the truck. Deliberately, he slid his cart from the van and closed the rear doors. "Oh, I see. You want me to 'assume the position'? Just like on TV? Okay, whatever you say, officer. Please, give me a break. I've got to be out of here by three. Can't interfere with the guests, you know." Then, complying, he leaned against the van with his hands spread above his head. One of the officers gave him a thorough patting while the other picked through the cart. The small control in his pocket was quickly found, as was his wallet.

"What's this?" Karl was asked.

Still smiling, Karl shook his head. "My hobby. Model planes. It's a remote control unit. I'd had it in for repair and picked it up on my way over here. I'm afraid you caught me cheating on the job, officer. I'd appreciate it if you wouldn't report it. I'm new with Roberts, and good jobs in Tucson aren't that easy to come by."

The cop's partner, who had been looking through the equipment on the cart, held up one of Karl's three thermos-like containers. "And what are these?" he asked.

"Just some special insecticide for corners and hard-to-reach areas. Here, hand one to me. I'll open it and show you."

Karl opened the container, showing its interior for all to see and then passing it around so everybody could smell the strong, kerosene-like odor. Then, regaining it, he replaced the container's cap and put it back on the cart.

The cop who had searched him spoke again. "Okay, thanks for your help. Now, show us some ID and we'll be done. Driver's license will do."

He held out his hand.

Karl passed the cop his wallet, relieved that he hadn't forgotten about this detail of the mission in his planning. During his recon last week, he had picked the pockets of several people at a mall. The man described in this wallet bore the closest physical description to his own. His interrogator examined the license closely. "Says here you live on Columbus, Mr. Lucien. That right?"

Karl nodded, holding out his hand for the wallet. "That's me, officer. Right off Fort Lowell." The policeman moved away from him, speaking into the small radio transceiver in his hand.

After a minute, he returned. "Okay, Mr. Lucien. You're clean. Thank you for your cooperation."

"See the household office for the list of the rooms you're to spray," said the man with the clipboard, who wore a hotel blazer. Karl smiled and vigorously nodded his agreement.

The four men turned abruptly and walked up the ramp and into the hotel. Karl followed, pulling his utility cart after him. He was in!

* * *

## 1:30 p.m.

Tom Waters sat on a sofa in the room Chris had set up as a command post, distractedly watching a football game on TV while he listened to the monotonous drone of communications as the various surveillance teams in the hotel continued to check in.

He'd left the door to the room open so that he'd immediately hear any commotion from the lobby. His spirits were beginning to sink. Maybe Karl wasn't going to show up after all. Maybe his training had alerted him to the trap he'd be walking into and had scared him away.

There was no doubt that the man was clever, the way he'd wormed his way through authority's cordons before. "He'd have to be a fool to come in here," Waters muttered to himself, reaching for another cigarette.

A figure appeared in the doorway, a man in dark green overalls with a canister in one hand and pulling a utility cart behind him. "Excuse me, sir, is this room occupied?" the man asked.

"Just for the moment. Why? What do you want?" Waters asked, hardly looking up from the football game.

"I'm spraying the empty rooms. I'll come back later if you want."

"No, go right ahead. We'll be out of here in an hour or so. Might as well get your work done now."

"Thanks." The man moved along the walls, spraying from corner to corner with his handheld nozzle and pumping the canister from time to time to maintain pressure. Soon, he entered the suite's bedroom, where Officer Sheldon had set up the comm links. Finally, smiling and nodding, he left the room. Waters reached for the remote to change the channel. Maybe there was a movie on that he could get into.

\* \* \*

## 1:32 p.m.

Karl opened the empty room with his passkey. He had found them! Just as he had suspected, the police had surrounded the hotel, and the center of their activity was the suite he had just been in. Pulling the utility cart, he entered the room and carefully closed the door behind him. In the inner room next door, the bedroom, a policewoman with several radio receivers and a clipboard was keeping regular communications open with what must have been a dozen teams of police. In the outer room, a single man sat watching the TV.

Could it be Chris? David had not described the man. But who else could it be? He couldn't wait. Every minute he spent here made the danger greater. He must attack now and leave as soon as possible—before the others became aware that something was wrong.

As he was spraying the police room, he had unobtrusively opened the door between the two rooms on one side. Now, if he opened the connecting door on his side, he could walk through, into the bedroom where the policewoman worked. She would not be expecting him.

\* \* \*

## 1:34 p.m.

Waters heard a thud, as though something heavy had been dropped on the floor of the suite's bedroom. Could Sheldon have dropped one of the radios? Unlikely. He decided to investigate. "Officer Sheldon," he called. "Are you all right?"

He entered the bedroom. The policewoman was nowhere in sight. His last memory before unconsciousness was of a whistling sound behind him, before Karl hit him behind his left ear with the butt of the dead woman's service revolver.

* * *

## 1:40 p.m.

The man started coming to as Karl finished tying him to the bed frame using the electrical cord he had brought along. He moaned. Karl, pressed for time, ran to the bathroom, got a glass of cold water, and threw it in the man's face to hurry his return to consciousness.

The man tried to reach for his head but struggled with his bonds. He looked up. "You'd be Karl," he said simply.

"You must be Chris," Karl returned. The man hesitated, as though puzzled, and then nodded slowly.

"I'm afraid I don't have a lot of time to spend with you," Karl continued. "If we were alone, there'd be lots of time to talk and many things I'd like to tell you. Too bad you've brought so many friends to this party and I don't want to get to know them." He could feel the power building in him, filling him with the delicious energy that always amazed him in its complete, syrupy consumption of his mind and soul. "So I've got just one message for you, one thought to take with you when I send you to hell."

The man frowned. He was old, too old for Marianne, Karl thought. He guessed her choice of men had become eclectic, if the last two lovers were anything to judge by.

"Karl, you can't get away with this," his latest victim finally said.

"You'll be caught. There are dozens of police out there. Let me free. I promise you won't be harmed. I'll protect you."

Karl's eyes grew wide. He pulled a paring knife from his utility belt. "You'll protect *me*," he hissed. "It's you who defiled my Marianne. No one will protect you!"

Turning the helpless man to one side, he stabbed him savagely in his right kidney, twisting the small knife in the wound to produce the maximum amount of pain and damage. As the man began to scream, Karl stuffed a hotel towel into his mouth.

Karl began to hum. He sat on the edge of the bed, looking his victim in the eyes. "Ever wonder why some of us never got over the war, Chris? I used to, during all the dark years I spent in Benniston. Here's what I believe. You take it with you, where I'm sending you. Tell the others about it. I think that everybody feels the same way when they're confronted with something frightening. We all experience a narrowing of perspective. Just like you are, right now. You're not thinking about the next election, or when to clean the refrigerator, or the book you've been reading. You're only thinking about me and this knife."

Karl paused, got up, and moved to the other side of the bed, and then he sat down again. "Yes," he said, chuckling, "your eyes follow me like I'm the only person in the world.

"Well, for most of us—you included, I'm afraid—these frightening situations go away in a short time. Seconds, minutes, maybe hours at most. What if they didn't? What if they went on for days, or weeks, or months? That's what Vietnam was like, Chris. We were always scared, always wondering what was going to happen. Most people snap back to their old selves after they've been frightened. A few of us got frozen, Chris. We couldn't get our perspective back, even when the scary times were over. We're the narrow men."

Even as he spoke, Karl rose from the bed and, turning his victim again, repeated the vicious wound to his left kidney. The man's eyes grew wide with pain and fear and then started to glaze. Karl smiled.

"I'm told the kidney wound is the most painful one there is when it's inflicted as I've just done it," Karl said. "I understand the Borgias used to kill their traitors in a similar way. I wish I could let you die like this, slowly," he continued as he raised a pillow above the dying man's head, "but—"

A pounding on the door interrupted his soliloquy.

\* \* \*

# 1:50 p.m.

Chris first realized something was wrong when Sheldon didn't answer his comm check. He was sitting in the lobby, directly across from the check-in counters in a secluded alcove. He decided the female officer must be using the bathroom, waited a few minutes, and tried again. Still no response.

He signaled one of the roving patrols in the lobby as they passed within ten feet of his seat. "Have you heard from Sheldon lately?" he asked. Both heads shook no. Chris rose from his seat. "Let's take a quick trip to the room to see if everything's all right," he said. "I want some more backup. Contact one of the other teams and have them meet us there."

As he spoke, Chris was sprinting to the staircase. He ran up the steps two and three at a time. Thoroughly winded, he stopped at the head of the stairs. He could see that the door to the room was not open. The four men he'd asked to back him up emerged from the elevator. They all snaked along the hotel wall with guns drawn, following standard police procedure.

Chris signaled them to the side of the room's door. "I'll go in first," he whispered. "I'm going to knock on the door now, act like nothing's happened."

Standing to the side, out of the main line of fire from the room, he pounded on the door. "Officer Sheldon," he called, "are you in there? It's Detective Carpenter. Let me in."

There was no answer. Chris gently tried to turn the door knob, but like all hotel doors it was locked tight. He turned to his companions. "Stay back," he said. "I'm going to break it down."

Standing squarely in front of the door, he raised his right leg and kicked it near the handle with all of his might. The door began to crack. He kicked it again. The door split in two and then collapsed off of its hinges in a shower of splinters. The five men rushed into the empty front room. An old movie was playing on the TV. Chris could hear muffled moans from the bedroom.

"Sheldon!" Chris called. "Are you in there?" A weak cough was his only answer. Without waiting for the others, Chris rushed into the bedroom.

Tom Waters lay bound where Karl had left him, awash in his own blood from two ghastly wounds. "My God!" Chris cried. "Get a doctor up here! Right away!" He bent to the bed, began untying his friend's arms, and pulled the hotel towel from his mouth. Waters was gray from loss of blood. Chris could see that the FBI agent was dying.

He was trying to speak. Chris had to bend close, his ear almost touching the agent's lips, to hear what Waters was trying to say. "Chris ..." he whispered, "thought I ... was you. Exter ... exterminator. Gr ... green overalls. I ... hurt ... so bad. Didn't tell ... him."

"It's okay, Tom. We'll get him now. He can't get out. You'll be okay."

"Liar. I'm ... dead man. Glad ... he ... missed ... you." Waters choked and coughed, spitting up blood. His newly freed hand gripped Chris's arm with surprising force. He tried to raise himself up from the bed. "Chris ..." he murmured with his last breath, "is she ... worth it?" He died.

Chris pulled his gun, his mind focused on avenging his friend's death. Where could the bastard be? They'd come in the only exit from the room. He noticed a closet and opened it to find Officer Sheldon's body carefully laid among some towels. His rage grew. Another killing!

He noticed the connecting door, now closed and locked. Karl must have left that way. Shouting to the men with him for assistance, he moved toward the door.

* * *

# 1:55 p.m.

In the adjoining room, Karl quickly climbed out of the green overalls. They had served their purpose. He dressed casually, in a shirt, slacks, and a tweed sport coat. The small control he had brought with him went into his coat pocket. He decided to keep the revolver he had taken from the dead policewoman. Although he hated to use guns—and was, in fact, a poor shot with a hand gun—he knew he might need the momentary advantage that showing a weapon could give him.

Now he needed all the advantage he could get. The men in the next room would begin hunting him relentlessly. There were probably scores of additional police officer all over the hotel. He knew getting out would not be easy.

As he had sprayed each room along this hall earlier, he had opened all of the connecting doors between the suites. Now, he passed through each of the rooms he had prepared, careful to lock the doors behind him. He figured the police would cluster around the room where he had killed Chris. His objective was to emerge into the hall as far from that room as possible.

Five rooms away, Karl opened a connecting door to find a man and a woman sitting at the edge of a bed in their underwear. The woman leaped from the bed with a tiny shriek, while the man stared at him, wide eyed. "Sorry," Karl said lamely. "Wrong room." He quickly shut the door and then ran to the hall. Looking to his right, Karl noted the grim men leaving Chris's suite. He decided to walk the other way to the nearest elevator. His plan was to get to the service area in the hotel's basement and to hide there until after dark.

As he turned the corner to the elevators, Karl noted what had to be plain-clothes police on station, blocking his escape. He turned quickly. He would have to use the stairs. Walking back the way he had come, he almost walked into the man he had surprised just minutes earlier, now dressed in a shirt and slacks.

The man grabbed Karl's shoulders and turned to yell, "Here he is! I found him!" A man in a hotel blazer was advancing toward them. Karl pushed himself away from the man, out of his grasp. The man scowled and reached for him again. "Oh, no," he cried. "You're not getting away that easy!"

Time seemed to slow down for Karl. He watched the man reach for him in slow motion. He knew he could not afford to be delayed by this situation. He had to escape right now, before the police organized a plan to hunt him down. He certainly had to get off of this floor and back to the lobby, where he had the chance to lose himself in the crowd. Reaching forward with one hand, he grabbed his assailant by the shirt collar. "Shut up, you fool!" he hissed. "I'm a police officer!" He pulled the gun he carried from under his coat, showing it to the man and the advancing hotel employee, to prove his point.

The man's eyes grew round with fright. "Sorry, officer," he said in a small voice, stepping back several feet very quickly. The man in the hotel blazer hurried away as well.

Karl nodded without answering, replaced the gun, and turned to walk down the hall. As he did, he stumbled into a group of five men moving in the opposite direction. One of them, a tall blonde man who seemed to be in charge, looked at him strangely as their eyes met. Karl pushed himself away, muttering an apology. The men continued past him.

Karl walked quickly to the stairwell. Closing the door behind him, he stopped on the landing to catch his breath and gather his thoughts. He decided that his best chance was still the basement. So after a minute's hesitation, he started down the steps. He heard a shuffle below him as he reached the first landing. Someone was coming toward him, up the steps. He peered over the railing, trying to get a look at who might be coming without exposing himself to view at the same time.

Two men, one in a police uniform, had stopped below him. The one in plain clothes pulled a cigarette from his pocket, lit it, and inhaled deeply. "Brass," he said. "Do they really think the asshole would lock himself up in the stairwell? I mean, this is stupid, you know? We should be out in the lobby. The bastard's probably having dinner in the hotel restaurant by now."

His uniformed companion shook his head. "Hell, he's gone by now.

Long gone. Kills two people in a hotel full of cops and gets away with nobody seeing him. The guy must be a ghost."

They continued to talk, their words careening up the walls toward Karl like carelessly aimed tracer rounds. What had they meant about a locked stairwell? Carefully, silently, he climbed back to the door he had just closed behind him and tried to turn the handle. It didn't move. He was trapped.

\* \* \*

## 2:10 p.m.

The lieutenant showed up to take charge of the operation. Chris was relieved. His grief over losing his friend and the savage rage he felt made it hard to concentrate, hard to plan a cordon that would trap the maniac before he could escape. He was sure Karl was still in the hotel. Where was he hiding?

All the exits had been blocked. Chris and his five companions had immediately begun a room-to-room search. The overalls and utility cart were quickly found, as was the murder weapon. Karl's method of entry and his method of escape were obvious. Still, the elevators and the stairs had been under guard from the first few minutes of the hunt. Karl could only be hiding on the floor where the murder took place. He walked down the steps to the hotel's lobby. It was time to report for instructions.

\* \* \*

## 3:00 p.m.

Karl edged up the steps to the next landing. According to the stenciled number on the door, this was the eighth floor. Careful not to make any noise, he tried the door's handle. Still locked. He wanted to scream, to howl in his frustration! How could he have been so stupid? Now he would have no choice. He would have to use his final contingency for escape. He wondered how many people would be hurt by what he was about to do. With a sigh, he pulled the electronic control from his pocket and pushed three buttons, one after the other.

The device had been bought in a hobby shop in Las Vegas. It was designed to allow users to guide the flight of model airplanes by remotely actuating tiny servo motors that controlled pitch, yaw, and acceleration.

Karl's signals had another purpose. Each was directed to one of the three thermos-sized containers he had placed in the hotel's linen closets earlier in the day. The containers all held gasoline thickened with laundry detergent (or "foo gas," as his army instructors had named the mixture). The spark from his signals set them ablaze, spattering globs of burning gel throughout each closet. The fires would be difficult to put out.

Within a few minutes, alarms were going off all over the hotel. The stairwell doors opened. People streamed down the steps to safety, just as the hotel procedures told them to do. Karl went with them out to the street below, anonymous in a crowd of hundreds, safely escaped.

* * *

## 5:00 p.m.

The hotel was ablaze—"fully involved" in fire department jargon. Most of Tucson's fire department was on the scene. Many of the guests milled about outside the fire lines, waiting for the buses that would ferry them to other quarters for the night.

Chris and the other officers on the scene tried their best to continue the search for Karl, but other duties intervened. Crowd control was important now. With tears of frustration in his eyes, Chris watched his hopes for catching the mass murderer he had been chasing for so many weeks go up in smoke with the hotel before him.

He felt a hand on his shoulder. His lieutenant stood beside him. "Go home, Chris," his boss said sadly, shaking his head. "We've done all we can do here. The crowd's been searched twice. Thibault's gone, or maybe he's still in that hotel. I hope so. Anyhow, you're off duty as of now. I'll see you in the morning."

Chris nodded and turned to leave. His anger was fading, replaced by a growing sense of sadness and loss—and the realization that Karl had somehow managed to escape once again.

\* \* \*

## 8:15 p.m.

Judy sat in her car, watching the credits for the first part of a double feature roll before her. She had come to the drive-in early, careful to follow Ken's instructions. A good thing too! There were roadblocks all along the main street because of a major fire at a hotel nearby. She had had to go several blocks out of her way around it as part of a slowly moving traffic jam that still snaked through the surrounding streets. Anyhow, she had made it. Now all she had to do was wait. She wondered idly what her lover had been doing and whether he had been successful.

A persistent tapping on the passenger side window startled her. She looked to see Ken suddenly standing by the door, peering at her through the smudged glass. A wide smile of relief crossed her face. She immediately opened the car to him. "Ken!" she cried as he climbed in, "I'm so glad you're here. I was so worried, with the fire and all. Are you okay? Did you finish what you had to do?"

Her lover's grin stretched from ear to ear. He put his arms around her and kissed her hungrily. "I sure did, baby," he whispered in her ear. "It's all over now. From here on out, it's just you and me." He looked around them, still smiling widely. "You know," he said, holding her to him, "I just had a thought. We've got some time to kill and no place to go but back to Maslo. How about you and me getting in the back seat? That's what drive-ins are for, isn't it?"

Judy laughed. She'd never seen Ken in this good of a mood before. Make love in the back of the old Wagoneer, in the middle of a drive-in? Why not! Giggling, she climbed over the seat, pulling him after her.

# Chapter 18
## Tucson, Arizona–January 15, 1987

The Triple Hill fire made headlines for a long time. Miraculously, only four people lost their lives in the conflagration, not counting Karl's trio of victims. Panic had been averted by the presence of police teams already stationed at the hotel's exits. They kept the evacuation of the building from degenerating to the confusion of a frightened mob. By the time the first fire trucks arrived, the fire lines had been formed and most of the guests were already out of the burning structure.

Burn it did—it was a stubborn, vicious fire, fed by the jelled gasoline that had ignited it and fueled by the gas lines and electrical cables it reached until it became virtually unstoppable. The hotel was completely incinerated, a total loss.

Two of the four who died in the fire were positively identified: a man and his wife from Kansas, trapped in their eighth-floor suite and suffocated to unconsciousness before they could escape. They had probably been taking a nap when the fire began. The remaining two resisted identification. Neither was a hotel guest, and both were found in stairwells among the higher floors during an inspection of the building the day after the fire was extinguished. The intense heat of the fire and the damage to the bodies from the collapse of the structure—one victim's head was completely crushed—made positive identification difficult. One of the dead was suspected to be a hotel thief. The other was thought to be Karl.

Chris thought about all of these facts as he sat before his lieutenant.

The meeting they were having was not a pleasant one for him. "Chris," his boss was saying, "I want you to put the Thibault case on the back burner for a while. We've got a big caseload to take care of right now. I just don't have the time to spend on it. Besides, I think the guy is dead. I think it was his body they found the day after."

Chris pounded the desk with his fist in frustration. He had been concerned that this would happen. "We can't let up now," he said slowly, trying to mask the emotion behind every word. "We've almost got him."

"I know how you feel," the lieutenant continued. "I know how close you were to Waters. That was too bad. Just try to look at the facts—"

"There *are* no facts!"

"There are, if you're willing to see them. First, there's the body: right height, right place, even an arm broken in the same place."

"No solid evidence. No prints. No dental records. Karl was of average height. Come on, half a million people break their arms like that when they're kids. It's a coincidence."

"Looks like a pretty good one to me. We staked out Alvernon, north and south. Checked every car leaving the fire scene for four hours. Nothing. Put out an APB on him, full description, all over the state. Nothing. Checked all of the border crossings in case he tried for Mexico. Nothing. If he wasn't in that fire, where did he go, Chris? The man's not a ghost." The lieutenant smiled, settling back in his seat. "Or, then again, maybe he is, by now."

Chris shook his head, refusing to agree. "He could have walked away from the fire. We'd never have seen him. He's smart; he would have had an escape plan already mapped out. He could have stayed the night at any one of a dozen motels nearby. We'd have missed him. Tom Waters was sure he was operating from somewhere near here. Hell, maybe he's still in town."

The lieutenant continued to smile. "Then he hides pretty good. We've been looking for him hard for two weeks, and nothing has surfaced. It's time to ease up. Look, Chris, it's not just me. The FBI haven't assigned a new agent to the case, have they? They buy the body in the hotel, and so do I. As of now, so do you." He stopped smiling. "Do I have to make it an order?"

Chris rose from his chair, raising his hands in surrender. "No, I understand. Are you closing the case down entirely?"

"Let's just say I'm rearranging your priorities. If the feds get hot again, maybe things will change. How's that?"

"I know how to take orders, but you have to know how I feel."

The lieutenant smiled again. "Then take your feelings with you to the street. We've both got work to do."

* * *

# January 18

The food at the restaurant had been good, a cultural jumble of American and Mexican cuisine that's called Tex-Mex by those who enjoy it. Chris and Marianne had finished their dinners and were savoring coffee and brandy—and each other. Chris seemed distracted all evening, as though something on his mind kept him from thoroughly enjoying himself. "I have some news for you," he said softly, sipping his brandy. "It's about Karl."

Marianne looked up, a frown on her face. "What is it?" she asked. "What has he done now?"

"A lot of things, darling. A lot of things I didn't want to tell you about until now, to make sure they were true. Now, I think you should know. We're going to remove your home from surveillance. It looks like Karl is dead."

She gasped. Her hand flew to her mouth. "What makes you think so?" She finally asked. "What has happened?"

Chris looked at his drink, refusing to meet her gaze. "Karl caused the fire at the Triple Hill on the twenty-ninth. He killed Tom Waters, the FBI agent you met, before the fire got started. We found a body in the remains of the hotel a day later. No one can be absolutely sure, but it looks like it's Karl. He must have been trapped, or maybe he was afraid of being caught by the police teams we had at every door and stayed in the stairwell too long to get out. Anyhow, just about everyone's sure it's him we found."

"Just about everybody?"

"Yeah," Chris growled. "Just about everybody but me! Marianne, I just don't feel right about it. Then again, we've looked everywhere and no luck. I have to agree, the body we found is more likely to be Karl than anyone else."

Marianne sat back in her seat. "I hope what you're telling me is true, Chris. I hope the nightmare is finally over."

"Well, everybody on my end is acting like it is. As I told you, we're removing surveillance and the tap from your home, and the whole case is being put on hold indefinitely. At least until the FBI assigns someone new to honcho things."

"When will that happen?"

"They've shown no sign of putting anybody new on it." Chris shook his head slowly. "Unless something happens that proves he's still alive, I'd say the case is closed. Right now."

Marianne reached across the table to touch his hand. There were tears in her eyes. "Oh, Chris, I hope it's true. You don't know how happy you've made me. Now I can really start my life again—and David's too—without worrying about what he's going to do. I'm finally free of him!" She smiled. "I know you're not too happy about it, darling, but I almost feel like celebrating. Let's go home. I'll bet I can think of a way to make you feel better. A whole lot better."

\* \* \*

# January 19, 12:15 p.m.

Marianne called David from his room. They had each spent a lazy morning: he, watching his normal selection of Saturday morning cartoons; she, catching up on her reading on the patio. Now it was time for lunch and, maybe, a shopping trip to the mall. First some important things had to be said.

David walked toward the kitchen, but his mother redirected him.

"Come sit down," she called. "I have something I must talk with you about."

David turned and walked to the green chair. He sat there, puzzled, looking at his mom. What had he done wrong? His room was a little messy but no more than usual. His grades were good, and there was no trouble at school. Maybe she was going to nag him about finding some more friends again. The truth was that there weren't very many kids his own age around here, and he liked to be by himself anyway, most of the time. He would listen to her, as he always did. Then maybe they could go to the mall. She would probably buy him a book or something once they got there. She usually did, after one of their talks.

"David," she said softly, "I want to talk to you about your father."

"Okay. Is he coming to see us again?" Although he was outwardly calm, David's hopes soared. Maybe Dad had called Mom, just like he had said he was going to when it was time to go to Brazil!

Marianne shook her head. "No, David, he's not. I'm afraid there's been an accident. Your father has been killed." She leaned forward, opening her arms to her son. She was sure he would rush to her.

David stayed in his seat, tears welling in his eyes. Dad couldn't be dead! He couldn't! "Oh, Mom!" he cried. "Are you sure? How did it happen? Where?"

Marianne sat back in her chair. David wasn't reacting at all as she had thought he would. After all, it had been five years since he had seen Karl. Since then, he'd gotten only the occasional phone call and cards at birthdays and Christmas. His attachment to Karl should have diminished past this.

"Now, David," she said evenly, "try to understand. There was a fire. Other people were killed as well. It doesn't matter where it happened."

"He was coming to see me! I know he was! He was going to take me with him!" David's tears fell freely now. His thin body was wracked with sobs as he tried, unsuccessfully, to contain the grief that flowed through him.

His mother came to him and tried to hold him, patting his back. "There," she crooned, "there. It's all right to cry. I know you loved him very much. I'm sure he was coming to see you. I'm sure he wanted to tell you how much he loved you, David, but he is gone now. There's no mistake. Chris told me about it himself. I'm sorry."

David sprang from his chair suddenly and rushed from the house. "Then Chris is wrong! He's not dead! He's not!" he cried over his shoulder, slamming the door as he ran.

Marianne ran after him and watched him run down the narrow lane toward the swimming pool cabana. *Let him go*, she thought. *He'll be back soon.* She resolved that if he was gone for more than half an hour, she would go looking for him. Maybe it would be better to let him work his grief out for himself in the interim.

Meanwhile, Marianne had other things to do. Without Karl to worry about, her need for protection—her need for a man like Chris— was over. She had to think about her future, once again. Hers and, of course, David's. There was a call she had to make. Smiling, she turned to the phone.

* * *

# 1:00 p.m.

David had walked for what seemed to him like hours under the desert sun in the cactus and brush that surrounded the town house development. His tears soon dried. He was sure that his dad wasn't dead.

There was one way to find out for sure. Climbing the wall back to the town house compound, he walked to the pool cabana. To his immense relief, no one was there. He decided to call his dad's number. That way he'd know for certain, one way or the other.

He punched the numbers into the pay phone three times before he got them right, rubbing his stinging eyes. Finally, the line went blank as the robot operator placed the collect call, and then, after an agonizing, timeless wait, he heard the sound of his father's voice!

"Oh, Dad!" he cried, the tears welling in his eyes once again, "I knew you would be there! I knew it! I knew what they said wasn't true!" The little boy began to sob uncontrollably.

"Whoa there, Tiger," came the deep, strong voice from the other end of the line. "What are you talking about? David! Why are you crying? Is everything all right, son?"

Panting and choking, the boy managed to rein in his emotions. "Oh, Dad," he gasped, "Mom told me you were dead. That you'd died in some kind of fire. I knew it wasn't true! I knew it!"

In his apartment in Maslo, Karl realized what had happened. He had read what he could about the hotel fire, but details had been sketchy this far from Tucson. Apparently, he had been lucky—far luckier than he had thought. There must have been someone caught in the fire who had passed for him! Now he was finally free.

"Now David," he said calmly, trying to subdue his son's emotions, "try to think. Who told you I was dead? How did they say it had happened?"

The boy's voice sounded much calmer as he responded. "Mom told me about it, Dad. She said there had been a fire and that other people had died as well. Is it true, Dad? Were you in a fire? Were you hurt?"

His father laughed. "No, son, I'm just fine. There was no fire that I'm aware of. Your mother has me mixed up with someone else. Did she tell you how she learned about all of this?" Karl grinned to himself as he asked the question. Maybe she'd heard it from the FBI or from the police. That would be clear evidence that he was free to escape without the worry of being recognized or traced.

"She said that Chris told her," David answered soberly, his piping voice still quavering with emotion.

Karl's mind rebelled. Something here was very wrong. "David," he gasped, almost losing his composure, "are you sure, son? Are you sure it wasn't someone else?"

"I'm sure. He must have told Mom when he saw her last night. They went out to dinner, and Mom didn't get home till after I went to bed."

Karl almost dropped the phone. Chris? Alive? Then who had it been in the hotel room? He had been so sure. He tried to calm himself, to master his emotions. "David," he said, "are you sure you mean Chris, the man you told me about, and not someone else?"

The boy responded, instantly, much happier now. "Oh, yeah, Dad. I'm sure she said it was Chris. He's a really good guy, you know. He's going to take us to the zoo tomorrow."

"David, listen to me. This is very, very important. You must not tell anybody that I'm still alive. Do you understand? Not anybody! Not even your mother."

"Why, Dad? Aren't you going to come to get me soon? I have to tell her, don't I?"

Karl paused. He realized his fate hinged on the ability of his son to keep the secret of their escape for just a little while more. He had already applied for the passports and visas they needed. The post office in Las Vegas would have them in a matter of days. They were almost free. Now, something else had to happen. He must finish the work he had started. He must punish Chris and take his son. A plan began to form in his mind.

"David," he said carefully, "I want to tell your mom about what we're going to do myself. It's important that she doesn't know about what we're planning until I can talk to her. I want to talk to Chris as well, to show him I'm still alive. Do you understand?"

"Sure, Dad. You want me to keep things a secret some more. How much longer? I don't like keeping secrets from Mom. It makes me feel bad inside."

"I'll tell you what, son. We'll arrange a surprise for your mother and for Chris, okay? You tell them you want to take the tram at Sabino Canyon next Saturday and then hike all the way to the top of the canyon. Just like we used to do!"

"You mean to stop eight?"

"Yes, son. That's the one. I'll be waiting for you there. At ten o'clock in the morning. Then, I'll tell your mom about everything, and we can leave right from there to go to Brazil. What do you think about that?"

"Wow, Dad, that's great! Won't we have to stop by the house first to pick up my stuff?

Karl chuckled. Maybe things would work out, after all. "Sure, Tiger, we'll run by and pick it up. Remember, it's important that you keep everything a secret till then. Otherwise, things may not work out. Do you promise?"

"I promise, Dad," the boy answered solemnly. As he spoke, he heard his mother calling him in the distance. "Dad," he said quickly, "I have to go now. Mom is calling me."

"Okay, son. Remember, keep everything a secret, but just till next Saturday. Can you do that?"

"I can, Dad. I love you." The boy kissed the phone as he always did when he said goodbye to his father. "Well, I have to go. See you next week!" The boy hurriedly hung up the phone and then sprinted through the gate toward his mother's voice.

Marianne saw him leave the cabana. As he approached her, he saw her scowl. "David," she asked, "what were you doing by the pool? You know you're not allowed to go there by yourself."

"Sorry, Mom. I really wasn't by the pool. I just wanted to use the phone to call a friend."

"Well, come inside now. Are you feeling better? Do you want to talk some more?"

He fell into step beside her as she put her hand on his thin shoulder. They walked toward the house. "Yeah, I'd like that. I've been thinking. Could we go to Sabino Canyon next week—you and me and Chris? Remember, Dad used to take me there all the time. What do you think?"

Marianne smiled. The boy really was taking this well. "Well," she said, "we'll have to see. I'll have to ask Chris, but I don't have anything planned. I think it can be arranged."

David beamed, hugging his mother's waist as they walked along. "That's great, Mom," he said.

* * *

## 4:00 p.m.

Chris stepped from the shower just as the phone rang. He had needed to freshen up after a hard game of racquetball at the Y. He toweled himself furiously as he walked to the phone, wondering who was calling. *Probably Marianne*, he thought, calling to find out where they would be going tonight.

His guess had been right, but the voice on the other end of the line sounded strained. It lacked the warmth he had come to expect over the past several weeks.

"Chris," she said, "I can't see you tonight. I've just told David about his father, and he's taking it very badly. I hope you understand."

"Sure, Marianne. I hope the boy is okay. Does he still want to go to the zoo tomorrow?" Chris had been looking forward to the outing. He genuinely liked the boy.

"I don't think so, Chris. Not now. Listen, I have to go. I'll let you know when I'm free again, okay?"

Chris was puzzled. "Wait a minute, sweetheart! It's all right for me to call, isn't it? I miss you already, Marianne."

There was silence on the line, broken by a sigh. "I know you do, Chris. Look, maybe things have been going too fast for both of us. Maybe we need a little time to ourselves, to get things into perspective. I know I do."

"Before I agree to that, we'll have to talk face to face. You mean too much to me now."

"Okay, I agree. Look, David wants to go hiking in Sabino Canyon next Saturday morning. It's something his dad used to do with him. It would be a good time for us to talk things out."

Chris's answer was immediate. "What time do you want me there?"

"About nine. We'll pack a lunch and catch the tram to the top at ten."

"Then it's a date. Will I see you before then?"

Marianne sighed again. "I don't think so, Chris." The phone clicked. She had hung up.

\* \* \*

## Maslo, Nevada—10:00 p.m.

Karl lay by Judy's side in the darkness, fondling her left breast and watching the nipple grow in its miniature erection. They had just made love, but he could feel her continued desire as she stretched and tensed to his touch, humming her consent. He gave her a series of long, lingering kisses, moving from her breasts to her lips to her ears. "Darling," he whispered, "I need another favor."

She turned to him, gently massaging his penis with one hand while she stroked the back of his neck with the other. "What is it, lover?" she sighed dreamily, not really paying attention. "I'm up for it, but not right now. Just keep on doing what you're doing."

He kissed her again, deeply and hungrily. "We need to go to Tucson again," he murmured. "Next Friday night. For the last time. I promise."

Judy smiled broadly, stroking him more vigorously. "Next Friday, huh? Well, okay. That gives us plenty of time to finish what we started." She licked her lips. "Now, stop talking," she purred. "There's other things we can do with our mouths." They both laughed.

# CHAPTER 19

## Tucson, Arizona—
## January 26, 8:45 a.m.

The old Wagoneer pulled into the parking lot. Pushing a tumbleweed before its bumper, it came to a stop at the edge of the tarmac. The lot was deserted. Judy stepped from the car, lit a cigarette, and watched the sun climb the mountains in front of her.

It was just as Ken had said. This place was beautiful. She had dropped her lover off a mile down the road, where the hiking trails began. He had dressed in the Boy Scout leader's uniform he had bought the night before. She had spent an hour sewing the patches on for him in their motel room.

He was meeting someone on one of the trails, he had explained. This would be the final part of his work here. After this meeting, they could go home to Maslo for good. She almost believed him. If it hadn't been for the far-off look in his eyes and the distant manner he'd had all morning, she'd have been sure that everything would be okay. Now, she just didn't know. Nevertheless, she would wait, just as he had asked. If anything out of the ordinary happened—if the police showed up, for instance—he'd shown her where to go to wait for him to return. She would do as he said, hoping with her heart that her mind was wrong.

* * *

## 9:50 a.m.

Karl struggled up the final path above Sabino Canyon, searching for a good ambush position. He'd brought with him the gun he'd taken from the policewoman the month before, but he had no plans to use it. He had decided to simply push his prey from the trail, letting the mountain do his work for him. He knew about where David would lead the man, based on where he'd taken the boy all those years before. He remembered a boulder that should give adequate cover halfway to the top from the tram stop, where the trail began to narrow. He would wait there. Trying to relax for a few minutes before hiding himself, he looked over the spectacular view. It was as beautiful as he recalled it. *Deadly things are often beautiful*, he thought.

\* \* \*

## 10:05 a.m.

Marianne, Chris, and David walked from the ticket booth toward the bright blue tram. It was a brilliant, sunny day, though chilly. Several people were already on board, although the seats were far from filled. Few tourists visited Sabino Canyon this time of year. It was still a little too crisp for good picnics or sightseeing.

Marianne and Chris walked together, though neither spoke. He carried the picnic lunch she'd prepared in a large basket. She carried a thermos of iced tea. David ran before them, grinning happily and almost skipping, his youthful energy pouring from him.

Marianne finally broke the silence. "I haven't seen him so happy in a long time," she said.

"You told me how much he loves this place," Chris responded. "How he and his dad used to come here all the time. Maybe he's reliving some of those memories now." He grinned. "Whatever it is, the kid's sure having fun. Maybe we should bring him here more often." He reached out his hand for hers.

Marianne pulled back and turned to face him. "Chris, we're going to have to talk ... about us. Today is a good day to do it, as long as we don't disturb David's good time. You know I've been giving things a lot of thought."

Chris nodded. "Before you say anything else, understand how I feel. I've never loved anyone the way I love you, Marianne. You're like an addiction to me. I can't get enough of you. I've stayed away from you all week, just like you asked. It's been hard, like a piece of me was missing. I don't want to be without you like that again."

Marianne returned his gaze without blinking. "I wish I felt the same way, Chris. I thought for a little while that I did. Now—"

She was interrupted by her son, who had reached the tram. "Hurry up, guys!" the boy called. "Come on, you're holding everybody up!" He scrambled inside and found a seat near the center of the large car. As soon as Marianne and Chris had joined him, he cried to the conductor, "Come on—let's go! Let's get to the top!" The two adults with him watched his happiness, each with thoughts as far from each other as their bodies were close.

* * *

## 10:40 a.m.

The trio left the tram at stop eight, the highest point on its route. They were the only passengers to have traveled so far. Marianne had wanted to get off on one of the lower stops, but David insisted that they continue. "Dad and I always used to go clear to the end," he stated. "Please, Mom, it's important we go all the way up."

"Okay, okay," Marianne said, laughing. She really hadn't seen her son so happy in a long time. She hoped that Chris's presence had nothing to do with it since that would not continue past today.

There was just no place in her life for him, not any longer. She had made arrangements with a new man, a man with the connections and the future she needed. Randy Erskine was an architect with a future in Tucson—in the whole Southwest, for that matter. His family had come to Arizona long before statehood and was still socially prominent. She was sure he cared for her. She could sense it. They would go out tonight, but she wouldn't rush things. There was plenty of time to convince him that she was the only woman for him. Chris had to be pushed aside.

Chris watched Marianne move in front of him, mildly aroused by the shifting of her buttocks beneath the tight jeans she wore. His thoughts kept wandering to the activities they'd packed into the few short weeks they'd spent as lovers. He still felt the electric charge whenever Marianne was near. He also sensed, as he watched her, that her attitude had changed somehow. He hoped they could work things out. He knew that losing her now would be like losing a part of himself.

They had just passed below a large boulder, at a point where the trail narrowed, when Chris heard the sound of shifting gravel behind him, followed by the impact of a body against his. He fell, grasping wildly for a handhold to keep him from rolling off the trail to the rocks below. Gaining his balance, he heard a loud curse behind him. Turning, still on his hands and knees, he saw Karl Thibault rise before him.

"Freeze. Stay on your knees and put your hands behind your head," Karl said calmly as he pulled a police revolver from his jacket pocket. He was dressed in some kind of uniform, as a scout leader, Chris suddenly realized.

Chris rose to his knees and then did as he was told. Turning his head, he called to Marianne. "Run!" he shouted. "Get the boy up the trail!"

Marianne looked back, saw Karl, and screamed. "My God!" she cried. "Karl!" She grabbed David's arm at the wrist and pulled him up the trail. He struggled against her.

"Mom! It's just Dad!" the boy cried. "He's alive, see? Let me go! Let me go to him! He's going to take me with him!"

Chris turned to face Karl again. "Let them go," he pleaded.

Karl smiled. "Don't beg for them. It's you who is going to die. I'd have had you over the edge without any trouble if I hadn't slipped on that gravel. Now, it's going to have to be the sloppy way." He raised the revolver and shot Chris in the left side. Chris spun to the ground, clutching his wound.

"Damn!" howled Karl. "I never could shoot worth a shit!" He

had been aiming for his victim's heart. He raised his gun to shoot the policeman again. Just then David slipped from his mother's grasp and ran down the trail to his father.

"Dad!" he called. "I'm coming! Don't hurt Chris anymore! It's all right!"

As he ran by, Chris rose and grabbed him by the waist. "Is this who you came for, Karl," he growled, "or was it Marianne?"

Karl was upset. He couldn't chance a shot at Chris without the possibility of hitting the boy. "Son," he cried, "come to me! It's time to go! Come to me now!"

David struggled against a weakening Chris Carpenter, squirming and yelling. As he did, Chris reached for his own revolver. Drawing it from the holster in the small of his back, he shot Karl three times.

Karl dropped his gun as the impact of the rounds drove him from the trail. Too late, he tried to reach for something to keep him from falling past the edge of the cliff. Then he weightlessly tumbled toward the rocks one hundred feet below.

He cried out in his agony and his frustration as he fell. "David!" he cried. "David, I came back for you!" Then he was lost, careening among the rocks and shadows of the canyon.

In the timelessness of his fall, Karl's mind transported him through his dreams once more. First, he was falling again into the slavering mouth of the beast, then he was flailing at the tiny yellow men who dragged him from his perch. Finally, he found himself walking again toward the silent pier under the gray sky. His men waited, as always, but this time they moved to meet him. Though no words were spoken, he knew it was time for them to sail together across that awful lake.

Suddenly, silence pervaded the trail, punctuated finally by the crying of a child and the low moans of the wounded policeman.

From up the trail, Marianne called. "Karl?" she asked. "Is that you? Don't hurt me, Karl!"

Chris called back to her. "Marianne, it's all right. Karl is gone now. Come and help your son." He turned to David, who was weeping by his side.

"He came back for me," the child said as he wept. "He was going to take me with him."

"Some things can't be helped, David," Chris said softly, stroking the boy's head. "Your father loved you. You must always remember that." He tried to climb to his feet but collapsed in dizziness and realized that he could not stand. "Marianne," he called again, "come get your son and go for help. I'm hurt pretty bad."

\* \* \*

# February 4

Days had been lost in a kaleidoscope of pain and light, but they were over. Chris had been wounded far worse than he had realized. Karl's bullet had touched a lung, causing extensive internal bleeding. He had spent several hours on the operating table once the rescue unit had gotten him out of Sabino Canyon.

Now he was recovering and feeling better every day, except for that curious hollowness in his side and the painful stitch he felt whenever he tried to walk for any length of time. He was growing more bored every day with his hospital stay, with the dreary food and the lack of activity. He enjoyed the visitors he got, and he got many. His friends on the force, his family, reporters covering the end of the Gambling Mecca Maniac story, and many others.

Ginny had come to see him every day. They'd talked for hours. He knew that she wanted more than his friendship, and a big part of him wanted to give her more. She was right, he knew. They were comfortable together and shared so many things. Maybe it could happen but only after he'd tied up some loose ends.

Today, Chris was happy to get a visit from his boss. Deciding against waiting for him in bed, Chris got a nurse to push him to the visitor's lounge in a wheelchair. The lieutenant smiled as he saw Chris coming. "First time I've seen you let a gal push you around," he said, laughing.

Chris grinned back. "You're right, boss. You know, I kind of like it!" He held out his hand for the lieutenant to shake.

"I guess you know which one of us was wrong about Thibault," the older man said, shaking his head. "There was no way to predict it though. I'm glad you were the man there when he made his move."

"Hell, it wasn't my police work. He came back just to get me," Chris replied. "We all had it wrong. Who could have guessed it was the boy who was feeding him the names?"

"We've managed to keep that out of the papers, just like you asked."

"Thanks. No reason why the boy or his mother should get any more press. The kid was doing what any boy would do for a dad he loved. They've both suffered enough. Have they found the body?"

The lieutenant scowled. "We've had teams out since the hour after they took you off that hill. Dogs too. No luck. Lots of places to fall down those gullies. He'll probably turn up in the spring. Some tourist will find him."

Chris nodded. "Anybody figure out where he was hiding yet?" he asked.

The lieutenant shrugged. "Nah. Could have been anywhere in this area. There are enough small towns and cheap motels around to hide a thousand like him. We'll never know. Look, I've got to be going. Just wanted to stop by and see how my best detective was doing." He slapped Chris's knee. "You hurry up and mend. We need you back." He rose from his chair and walked quickly to the elevator.

Chris asked the nurse to wheel him back to his room. Everyone he knew had come to visit him during the five days he'd been conscious and able to receive visitors except for the two people he had most wanted to see—everyone but Marianne and David.

\* \* \*

# February 28

The phone rang and rang, far past the five rings it takes most people to hang up. She would have to answer it. "Hello," said Marianne, the bell-like tones of her voice belying her true feelings.

"Marianne." The voice on the line sounded almost surprised to hear her. "I ... I've waited to hear from you. I thought I should call."

She sighed. "Chris," she said, "I wish you hadn't called. You know I've sent back your flowers. I thought I'd made myself clear. Whatever we had is over. For one thing, David could never accept you, not after what happened. Surely you can see—"

Chris laughed. "Oh, hell, I know you're blowing me off, Marianne. I expected it. You know, I've had a lot of time to think about things while I've been laid up. A lot of time. I thought about all the men you've been with for the last ten years—the ones I know about, anyway. They've got something in common, all except me. They're all dead, Marianne. What do you think about that?"

"Surely you're not accusing—"

"No, no. Nothing like that. You got what you needed from every one of those guys, and then you left them for somebody else. Karl was your victim as much as they were his. That's the way I figure it, anyhow. No, I guess I'm lucky—lucky to be free of you and still on my feet. I just wanted you to know that I know. One thing I'm sorry about though."

Curiosity alone kept her from hanging up. "Oh?" she asked sarcastically. "What's that?"

"I feel sorry for the kid. For David. Between you and Karl, he hasn't had much of a life, has he?" The line went dead.

Marianne shook her head, trying to suppress the anger she felt. She had no time for such emotions. Randy was coming by any minute to take her to look at the house he'd just finished building. She was sure it would end up being theirs. No reason to rush. She had time.

# EPILOGUE

# Three Months Later

The sound of a car's horn announced Randy Erskine's arrival. Marianne ran for the door. "David," she called over her shoulder, "there's dinner for you in the fridge. I shouldn't be too late." The door slammed, and she was gone.

David stayed in the den, playing his newest video game with grim intensity. After an hour, he grew bored, turned the game off, and padded to his room. He was reading a book when the phone rang. He talked on the line for a few minutes and then carefully walked to his mother's room, where he quickly scanned the pages of her address book. He still had his work to do, after all.

# Epilogue

## Three Months Later

# ABOUT THE AUTHOR

Since his birth in New York City, Kip Cassino has traveled the world. He has run microtool factories in Israel and Hong Kong, studied art in Munich, and assembled nuclear weapons in South Korea.

His articles have appeared in publications as diverse as the *Crain's Chicago Business, Smithsonian Air & Space, Entrepreneur,* and *Ad Week.* He has most recently been interviewed by *Meet the Press, BBC,* and *Vice.* He has written science fiction for *Analog* and numerous technical industry analyses. He was awarded the Research Award of Merit by the Newspaper Association of America in 2008.

Along with Helen, his wife and companion for far too short a time, Cassino lives and works in Tucson, Arizona. This is his first novel.

Printed in the United States
by Bookmasters

Printed in the United States
By Bookmasters